# Huscarl!

*The saga of a young Viking archer*

*Pressed into service, first with Harald Hardråda*

*Then with*

*Harold Godwinson*

*Two of the most feared men in Europe.*

*Follow Olaf Slagbjørn in his quest to survive*

Book 1   by Graham Dalby

# Dedication

*I would like to dedicate this book to Linda Dalby for her patience, encouragement and the long hours she devoted to proofreading. Her support for this project has been invaluable...thank you.*

# Contents

# *Chapter One:*
# *Midsummer Tragedy*

It was the day before *'Midtsommer Solverve'* (Summer Solstice) in the little mosquito-infested village of Dalby in the Norwegian forests near the fjord and settlement at Lillehammer. The maidens were busy making *'blomsterkransar'* (flower wreaths for their hair), whilst the boys put the finishing touches on a great bål, a huge bonfire filled with herbs to drive away *'völga or heks'* (witches and evil spirits).

Erik Ohlson was easily the largest man in the village and one to steer clear of when he had been drinking. They joked behind his back that he was in fact Erik 'Ølskalle' - pronounced the same way but meaning 'Beerhead'. But no-one would dare say that to his face. On this day, however he had kept a clear head. He had two sturdy sons of whom he was justly proud and a third whom he had named after his father, Olaf. His wife had died giving birth prematurely to a beautiful golden-haired boy but who was painfully small by Viking standards.

To make matters worse, young Olaf was embarrassingly effete. When asked to go hunting elk with his brothers for tomorrow's feast, he replied that he had already promised the girls to help them in making their *'blomsterkrans*ar'. Erik was not impressed, almost to the point of despair, and it was in a sullen mood that he set off into the forest with his two sons, Sweyn and Magnus, in the hope of finding an elk. Usually, the elks moved about at sunset but at this time of year there was no sunset. It was around eight o'clock therefore, armed with spear and shield that they departed. Seventeen-year-old Olaf happily mingled with the girls and maidens in the arranging of the flower crowns.

In the dark, heavy forest, Erik and his two young warriors aged eighteen and nineteen, stalked an unseen prey. The huge Nordic mosquitos created a continuous hum of blood parasites as the three figures moved swiftly and silently through the dense undergrowth. Overhead, the hot sun was all but blocked out, but in his Viking armour and helmet, Erik could feel the sweat trickling down his broad chest under his tunic.

The boys made no complaints but followed his every move. Just ten minutes outside the village boundary, Erik dropped suddenly to his knee and the boys followed instinctively. Gesturing to the boys, they could make out the magnificent silhouette of a fully grown bull elk standing proud at the top of a gorge. Suddenly, the air was rent with a terrifying high-pitched scream which was combined with a low roar, all coming, simultaneously, from the same animal. Erik turned to his sons:

"We may be fortunate; it's the rutting season and he's challenging a rival. If we are careful, we may kill both." The boys nodded and grinned.

Sure enough, within a short time, a second large bull-elk appeared and issued a similar scream and roar as a challenge. The two massive beasts seemed in no hurry to lock horns but circled and eyed each other with menace.

"First one to look away", whispered Sweyn.

As Magnus chuckled, both elks looked across to their position, as if they had heard them speak, which, at that distance, would have been impossible.

"Do they have our scent?" suggested Magnus.

"Not likely, the wind is still, unless one of you young stinkers has farted. I smell something too and it's definitely not us", said Erik. "Something has alarmed them."

A crack of antlers announced that whatever had disturbed the rival elks, it was no longer as important as establishing the order of seniority within the herd. Erik turned to Sweyn:

"Boy, work your way round to the right of the elks to ensure no wounded animal gets away. If we get both, we'll be the toast of the village." Sweyn, nodded and slipped away, spear and shield in one hand. A minute later as Sweyn ran at the lope, the smell became very pungent when, in an eyeblink, there was a rushing of undergrowth and thundering upon the ground. Looking up, the last Sweyn knew of anything was a huge, clawed paw in a lethal, powerful swing that caught him across the side of the neck.

The instant welling up of blood from the artery ensured that he was unable to cry out for help, even had he been conscious, and his terrible end came swiftly. Erik and Magnus, watching the elk battle, had felt the ground tremble but had heard no sound from the direction that Sweyn had taken. Erik gestured and the two set off to check on Sweyn. It wasn't long before he came upon his son's blood-soaked body and the huge tear in his neck. His open, staring eyes still carried the expression of complete surprise and ambush. Magnus let out a howl of despair and Erik fell to his knees. The pungent animal aroma still remained. Erik, regaining his senses, handed his horn to Magnus:

"We need to summon help, boy, give it all you've got."

Back in the village all was festive and the øl was already being passed around. There was chatter and laughing and Olaf was happy at all the attention he was getting from the prettiest girls in the village. The village elders were sat outside enjoying the evening when one stood up suddenly:

"*Stilhett!* (Silence!) Quiet, everybody! Listen!"

"Ears like a bat!" joked one.

There was immediate obedience and soon everyone heard the distant sound of a horn blowing a distress call.  Olaf leapt to his feet, sensing at once it was the hunting party of his father and brothers. Not waiting for any of the other young men, who were collecting their swords and shields, he grabbed his hunting bow and quiver and sprinted into the forest in the direction of the call. The shouts of his fellows behind soon became distant as, with no shield or helmet, he was able to run at speed towards the sound of the horn.

Suddenly the horn stopped, and Olaf redoubled his effort until he came within earshot of shouts and animal roars and the pungent smell of a man-eating bear. Olaf entered the arena to find his brother Sweyn clearly dead, his other brother Magnus semi-conscious, oozing blood and possibly dying, and his father locked in a death struggle with a huge brown bear, roaring and snarling, quite obviously incandescent at the wounds it had suffered from the hand of his father's short axe. Erik's spear lay broken, and his shield had been torn from him.

"*Far!*" shouted Olaf and, instinctively, Erik turned around for a second. It was the second the great bear needed to land a ferocious swipe to Erik's head, sending his helmet flying and rendering him temporarily unconscious. To throw his arm over his right shoulder and nock the arrow onto the string was, with Olaf, the work of a moment. Within two seconds the arrow was streaming with unerring aim to the throat of the great beast. In the motion of going forward to finish the battle-scarred Erik, the bear paused for a split-second to register the sound of an arrow whistling through the air.

It was his last action as the arrow struck home with deadly accuracy and the magnificent creature fell to the ground gasping his last. Olaf stood panting and instinctively drew a second arrow. But it was not needed. The great hulk of fur lay, breathing ever more slowly, next to the bodies of his brothers and his father. Magnus was the first to stir, still clutching the horn with his left arm, but his sword arm, bereft of any weapon hung limply, with blood running from a hideous gash below the shoulder.

He groaned in pain, but Olaf lit up to see Magnus still alive and turned to check on his father. Erik was still out but was breathing heavily and starting to come round. He had sustained a nasty triple wound from three of the bears claws right across his face and a bite to his shoulder that only just penetrated the armour and wasn't serious. Olaf moved swiftly to the motionless bear which had the glinting tip of his arrow protruding from its neck. Quickly, Olaf grabbed the arrowhead and pulled it through, throwing the blood-stained shaft as far as he could into the undergrowth. Erik was regaining consciousness although his vision was very blurred. He could just make out the figure of Olaf kneeling in front of him.

"*Far*, you killed the bear that killed Sweyn!"

"*Ah Satan!*.......eh?" Erik tried to blink away the blood from the gash that went from his eyebrow to his chin.

"You slew the bear that killed our Sweyn!"

Magnus started laughing and crying in shock and relief and tried to cheer but the pain prevented him. Just then a commotion of a group of people running through the forest distracted their attention and the air was filled with shouts from the young warriors of the village, each armed with sword and shield. Soon the clearing was full of these men so that Olaf shouted at them to move back and give the wounded air. They all wanted to see the great bear that the mighty Erik had felled. Olaf had created a myth.

They all knew what to do. Soon, the forest echoed to the sound of axes on stout branches. These were tied to shields to create a stretcher for Magnus and the body of Sweyn. Erik was too large to be carried and a horse was sent for to harness his stretcher, made of four shields and two great branches, to the horse, who was then able to drag his considerable bulk the mile or so back to the village.

The village, decorated and ready for a great feast-day, had all heard about the terrible battle with the bear, the death of young Sweyn and the wounding of Magnus. But all the talk was about how the greatest warrior in the village had slain the huge beast, which was growing in size with every re-telling. Of Olaf, there was no mention, and that was how he wished it to be. As the horse came into view, flanked by sword-waving warriors, the whole village erupted in wild cheers and a maiden rushed out, wearing her *blomsterkrans*, with a drinking horn of øl, gratefully received by Erik, who drained it in one, demanding a refill. The laughter changed to roars and howls of merriment as Erik stood up from his stretcher, unaided and held his drinking horn aloft. Olaf stayed with his brother Magnus and the body of Sweyn which was being seen to by the *Lech*, the healer, and surgeon. He was also responsible for preparing the body of Sweyn for the funeral pyre.

In front of the great *Ölbod* (mead hall) the elderly acting chieftain, Leif, had gathered with the other elders of the village and Magnus and Olaf were sent for. A heavy table was laden with some silver. Leif spoke as of one whose voice had been heard on the field of battle and it rang clear:

"People of Dalby! Today, it is with much sadness that we say farewell to Sweyn Ohlsson, who will soon be feasting in Valhalla, as he died spear in hand. He will receive a Viking warrior's funeral in Lillehammer in the next few days. Our condolences to Erik and his surviving sons. Erik Ohlsson, you are our greatest champion, and you defeated the great bear-god '*Bjørn*' in mortal combat. I therefore bestow upon you and your heirs the name Erik '*Slagbjørn*' *(*smiter of bears*)*, and gift to you this great silver drinking horn which tonight we will fill with mead and drink till dawn. Magnus, you fought bravely at your father's side, and you are gifted this smaller, but beautifully crafted, silver goblet and you too will drink mead in the hall tonight - but first you must see Ålfgerd the *Lech* and have your wounds tended. Let us light the great bonfire and feast till dawn."

Loud cheers from everyone as the great *bål* was lit. But of Olaf, there was no mention.

# *Chapter Two:*
# *Love and Loss*

Despite the death of Sweyn, *Midtsommar* was celebrated in the Viking way with both Erik and the wounded Magnus drinking in the *ölbod* until five in the morning. One cannot say dawn as at midnight the sunset bounces off the horizon for about sixty seconds and then starts its sunrise. Olaf did attend the Bacchanalian rout for a while but slipped away unnoticed with one of the exceptionally pretty girls with whom he had been making flower wreaths. With everyone engaged in the hall, theirs was a night of uninterrupted passion and pleasure, observed with indifference, only by the horse who had dragged the weighty body of Erik to the village.

The girl, Freya, named after the Goddess of love, lust and fertility, was herself quite a beauty and was regarded by the young warrior boys as aloof and obdurate and impossible to get to know. She was always with her father Ålfgerd the *Lech*, mixing remedies and combining herbs and sealing the wounds with boiled-down cow's urine to fight infection. She was a skilled *laeknir* (healer) and could set a bone or heal a stomach stab wound. Like most of the girls, she had plaited golden hair and limpid blue eyes. Olaf had barely spoken to her before, but he watched her at work in silence as she skilfully assisted the *Lech* in laying on the herbs before bandaging the terrible gash in Magnus' shoulder. The doctor spoke softly to Olaf:

"If it doesn't get infected, he may well not lose the arm although unless he learns to fight with his left arm, he will never be a warrior".

Olaf knew at once that a one-armed warrior was of no use in a shield wall as they needed to be locked together, right to left with the other hand holding a spear, sword, or axe.

"Alright, Magnus, you may go to the ölbod as it may dampen the pain but take it steady and mind that wound. Olaf, you take Freya and keep an eye on him. If that stitching breaks he could bleed to death".

Magnus went on ahead after thanking the *Lech* and Freya, the *laekni*r. He was clutching his silver goblet and eager to fill it with mead. Olaf and Freya walked behind when suddenly, Olaf froze. Beside him, Freya had slipped her long pale fingers through his and he could feel his pulse racing as he turned to her. She looked at him with an expression that could only mean: "I choose you!". Her soft fingers were a contrast to his rough two fingers, hardened by pulling the bow string in his years of practice.

She closed them around his and pulled him forward to catch up with Magnus who was diving into the mêlée that was the ölbod. Inside was the smell of sweat, roasting pig and the sweet aroma of fermented honey and herbs that constituted the *mjørd* (mead). Magnus was greeted with a loud cheer and disappeared into the throng. There was no such cheer for Olaf.

Taking the lead, Freya pulled Olaf out of the ölbod and ran across the yard and into a stable.

"How old are you Olaf?" she asked as they fell onto the straw.

"I think I was born seventeen summers back when your father was not able to save my mother's life.

"Seventeen?" Freya's eyes widened and her brow furrowed in doubt. She was herself nineteen and had learnt all her healing skills from her father but had never before found boys interesting. She had, however, warmed to the effete gentleness of Olaf, so different from the other loud, bragging lads. She too had had a mother who was lost in childbirth and in that coincidence, she felt a bond of misfortune.

"My mother died nearly twenty summers back. Do you know what to do?"

Olaf shook his head, mistaking her meaning for medical learning.

"Well, neither do I" she said, smiling. "Let's learn together."

The night passed with much kissing and fumbling but they soon discovered what went where and what was pleasant or pleasing. By five o'clock they lay in the warm hay replete and asleep as the last of the mead hall revellers also fell into an alcoholic stupor and the village finally fell silent, but for the lowing of some un-milked cows and the crackling embers of the *bål*.

Their sleep was rudely awakened by an unmusical cackle posing as a laugh. Standing over them, wooden bucket in hand, was a woman from the village, *melkepike* (milkmaid), with a prominent black tooth who they both recognised by her large hips and pungent breath as Hertha Blåtand (Bluetooth). As they scrambled for their clothes, she chivvied them telling them she needed the stable to milk the cows and added that her father was asking where she was as he needed her urgently. They rushed, heedless of the straw in their hair, to the long-house of Ålfgerd. One look at them and there was no need for further questions, so he held back the 'where the *Faen* (devil) have you been' and changed it to:

"You were both supposed to be looking out for Magnus! He is now seriously injured having fallen from a table onto a shield with his wounded shoulder! The bone is broken and splintered, and we will have to remove the arm and cauterise it if he is to live. Olaf, build up that fire and heat up this knife as hot as possible, Freya come with me and hold him. Fortunately, he is still very drunk."

The surgeon and his daughter went through a curtain to a back room where there was a strong smell of alcohol. Ålfgerd inserted a piece of wood between Magnus' strong, white teeth and began carefully stripping back the bandages and torn clothes. The bone had fragmented just above the elbow as there was little muscle to protect it given the wound the bear had inflicted. The whole arm below the bicep would have to come off. He looked at the boy's white face as he picked up his bone-saw.

"Sorry boy. Olaf is that blade red hot yet?"

Magnus' eyes opened wide in agonised astonishment as the doctor quickly and skilfully went to work. Olaf handed Ålfgerd the knife using tongs and there was a terrible hiss and stench of burning flesh and blood as the wound and the bleeding were cauterised. His scream was muffled by the stick and his movement restrained by Freya holding his shoulders.

Magnus lay motionless as the trauma to his nervous system had caused him to pass out and the alcohol-dulled agony had allowed for unconscious sleep. The doctor tied leather straps around his shoulders and ankles and under the bed to prevent his turning.

"Olaf, I think you had better go and find your father who needs to know what has happened, Freya, go with him."

Entering the *ølbod*, it appeared there had been a massacre not seen since the time of Beowulf. The wooden boards were sticky with *mjørd* and *öl* with bodies strewn around randomly, and the sound of snoring shook the room till the shields rattled. The sun streaked in through the rafters and hit upon a gleaming object near the top table at the far end of the hall. It was attached to a hand of such a size that Olaf knew there could only be one owner. He ran to the gleaming silver horn and kicked at the body slumped on the floor.

"*Far! Far*! Wake up now, Magnus is in terrible trouble and is in danger of losing his life!"

"Eh?" The bearded face of Erik 'Slagbjørn' turned and blinked in the bright sunlight, revealing the fresh, terrible scars the great bear had inflicted. Freya stepped back a pace from the appalling breath of the huge man with the terrifying face.

"Erik Ohlsson! Sober up quickly. Your son has lost his arm and may well not survive. Drink some water and wake up if you want to see him."

Erik was astonished at being so ordered by a female voice and his eyes tried to blink away the blur and focus on what appeared to be a very attractive young girl in the company of Olaf.

"And who in Odin's name is this?" roared Eric, speaking across her to his son.

"Freya Ålfgerdsdotter, she is a *laeknir*. She and Ålfgerd have amputated and cauterised Magnus' broken arm and he now lies at the good doctor's long-house. He may survive, he may not".

"What?" the roar echoed around the Mead Hall and there were groans from the bodies and noises of men turning over to try to get comfortable while sleeping on an axe or a scabbard.

"Take me to him!" Erik pulled himself up with the help of a table, thrusting the silver horn into his belt, he set off in the wake of Olaf and Freya who were careful to step over the strewn bodies of sleeping Vikings. Erik observed no such niceties and the journey out of the hall was punctuated with yells and oaths as he either kicked their heads or trod on their stomachs and legs or, sometimes, more painful parts.

At the doctor's long-house, Ålfgerd was draping a wet cloth over Magnus' forehead. His body, stripped to the waist, was sweating profusely, and had attracted the interest of a large number of flies and midges. Magnus' sunburnt face was now ashen-grey. The doorway was darkened by the vast bulk of Erik 'Slagbjørn' who entered by throwing back the door and yelling:

"What have you done to my son you bedevilled sawbones?"

Ålfgerd looked up but did not stand.

"Was he with you when he fell off the table?"

Eric hesitated: "Of course, we were feasting together and drinking mead. It was a small fall and nothing to concern anyone." His voice sounded defensive now.

"Yet two of his friends brought his profusely bleeding body to me - a body that I had stitched up not five hours earlier. His arm was shattered, the stitches all broken, and the loss of blood has been considerable. He would be dead already but for their action. The triple-trauma of the bear's claw, the break and the amputation with cauterisation may well prove to be too much. He may well die, but we will know in the next twelve hours if he pulls through."

Erik looked down on the pale face and heaving torso of his son and said nothing. He turned to leave with a mumbled thanks and said that, after bathing, he would return. Olaf followed his father, leaving Freya behind.

During the day as the villagers began the clear-up of the festival, a wagon came into the village bearing the body of the great bear. For a Viking community such a beast meant valuable meat and fur, claws and teeth for jewellery and bone for carving. The wolves had had a few bites from the legs but generally it was all there. The butchers and the furriers set about removing the fur to dry and the meat to be salted and hung.

Ålfgerd came out of his hut for some air and watched the bear with all the interest of one who knows a bit about anatomy. He observed the wolf bites in the legs and the axe wounds to the bear's arms and chest. Nothing however that could be described as a mortal wound. The heart was untouched, and the head was intact. Closer inspection showed a great deal of blood in the mouth and throat of the bear and then, after moving the thick matted hair from under the bear's jaw, there was the killing wound. An arrow entry in the throat and an exit wound. It must have gone clean through. But there was only one archer in the village who could have made that shot, and he was seen making flower wreaths. Could it be that young Olaf had in fact saved the life of his father and brother and had said nothing about it?

Returning to his hut, with pots of herbs boiling, he looked in on Magnus to see Freya leaning over him with damp cloths. Olaf was seated next him clutching his remaining hand and arm. Magnus was shaking, his face ashen with sweat seeping from his body.

"*Far*", she said turning, "he's much worse."

Ålfgerd could see at once that Magnus' whole system had gone into shock with his immune system producing a high fever. The cauterisation process was brutal, and many did not survive.

"Quickly, run to Erik and tell him to come at once."

Freya left the hut immediately and shortly found Erik in a deep alcoholic depression. He refused to go with her.

"Leave me, I want to remember my son as he was before your butcher of a father hacked off his sword arm. How will he be greeted into Valhalla? He is already dead, go!"

In this assumption Erik was, in fact, correct. Shortly after Freya left, Magnus' body went into a spasm of twisted contortion for a few seconds as he suffered a huge and fatal heart-attack. Holding his arm Olaf looked in despair at the lifeless body and fought back the tears. Two bothers lost in twenty-four hours; it did not seem possible.

# *Chapter Three:*
# *Viking Funeral – A huscarl in the village*

Leif, the village Ålderman, declared a time of mourning and preparations were made to give the two brave boys as close to a Viking funeral as possible using an old, leaky longboat in dry dock, a few miles away at Lillehammer. The longboat was not a fighting boat, but one used for trade. Ålfgerd, Olaf and Freya prepared the bodies of the two boys in new clothes, complete with their swords, shields and small axes. On their bare arms they bore the 'Oath Bracelets' they had been given at the age of twelve when they were taken by boat by Erik to Nidaros (Trondheim) in 1042 and 1044 to swear loyalty to the young Magnus the Good, the son of King Olaf II of Norway. The whole village dressed up and painted their faces in grotesque styles to ward off any evil spirits who may try to prevent Sweyn and Magnus from entering Valhalla. They formed a long torchlit procession with Erik leading the horse pulling the cart carrying the bodies. Leif and the other village elders led the way down to the fjørd. After a short journey, the torches of the Lillehammer people became visible, standing on the West bank of the fjørd where the boat was raised on wooden rollers. People from both villages had been busy decorating the boat and had built a high pyre of wood, covered with blankets to lay the bodies on. Sweyn and Magnus were carried onto the pyre where their shields and other weapons were laid on either side. Between their heads was placed the head of the great bear, jaws open, and at Magnus' feet was placed his hunting horn with his silver goblet laid across his chest.

The tattered sail and the wooden pyre were soaked with a pig-fat based flammable liquid. Twelve strong men, including Erik, took either side of the stern and pushed the boat out into the fjørd. After reaching about fifty metres from the shore, Olaf produced a fire-arrow which a villager lit and, with great accuracy, he let it loose into the mast where the sail immediately caught, in turn dropping pieces of burning cloth onto the pyre. At this, the villagers all loosed their fire-arrows into the boat and soon the fjørd was lit up in the waters' reflection. There was much cheering and drinking as the two boys sailed off to Valhalla in an ancient ceremony and honour usually reserved for chieftains.

After half an hour, when the boat had slipped under the water, Eric and Olaf left their vigil on the shore and went and joined the wake, which was already getting a bit rowdy. Ålfgerd and Freya approached Erik:

"I am sorry Erik Ohlsson that I was unable to save your son, my daughter and I did all we could."

Erik grunted: "it was his time," and walked to get his drinking horn filled. Olaf remained behind, giving Ålfgerd the opportunity to ask the question that had been troubling him:

"Olaf, when you reached your father and your bothers, was the bear already dead?"

"Yes, Erik had killed him with his axe, that's why people now call him Erik Slagbjørn."

Ålfgerd shook his head: "Not unless Erik was carrying a bow in addition to his sword, shield, spear and axe. Erik never carries a bow. The mortal wound that the bear suffered was an arrow through the throat. I think Erik was unconscious when the bear died, and you saved his life with your bow, which you always carry. Why do you not want people to know what a brave thing that you did? *You* should be the hero!"

Olaf realised he was undone, and Freya was looking at him with an intensity of admiration and affection so that he knew he must tell the truth.

"All right!" said Olaf, a little testily. "I ran into the forest in the direction of Sweyn's horn and arrived ahead of the others who had gone to fetch their weapons. I called out to my father and, as he turned, the bear caught him a great blow which knocked his helmet off and laid him out. I had one shot before the bear would have finished him off."

"And, clearly, quite a shot Olaf," added Freya whose eyes were now glinting in the light of the flaming torches.

"But why conceal it from everyone?" Ålfgerd's question was tinged with exasperation.

"My father is regarded as a great warrior, and he sees me as the runt of the litter for whom my mother, Alfhild, died giving birth. He would have hated it if he discovered that I, little Olaf here, had saved his life. I would have been toasted in the Mead Hall and he would have been ignored. Much better this way round. I'm no warrior and I found much better things to do on Midsummer Eve than get drunk with a load of boring, sweaty Vikings."

Freya snorted and suppressed a giggle which Ålfgerd chose to ignore.

Over the next few months life in the village returned to normal, although Olaf and Ålfgerd built an extension to the long-house where the two could stay with some privacy. Erik became something of a recluse and didn't seem to mind Olaf moving in with Freya. Olaf matured noticeably during this time and became popular in the village as his skills as a hunting archer proved him to be of great value in putting meat into the Mead Hall. He was also skilled at talking his way out of fights from lads in the village, jealous of his situation with Freya. He began to fill out a little, and, actually, managed to grow a few more inches, but still remained considerably shorter than the average young warrior. The boys in the village had little or no opportunity to display their warrior skills with raids or battles as in the sagas of old so they were destined to become farmers.

One rainy afternoon in October, a huge warrior covered in furs flecked with mud, walked his horse slowly into the village. At a glance, people knew he was a professional fighting man. His face was scarred, and his beard plaited with silver rings at the tip. His head was shaven but for a single plait which fell down his back. He carried a full array of weapons from a large hunting knife to a war axe attached to his shield. With surprising ease and athleticism, he slid from his horse and stood with his legs apart carrying a small coin between his fingers.

"Who will tend my horse?" Several boys rushed forward to catch the coin. "Have the blacksmith check his shoes". The boys nodded and led the horse away to the farrier.

"Welcome to our village, it is named *Dalby*. My name is Leif and I am the Ålderman here. You are welcome into the *ølbod* to sample our hospitality and you can tell us the purpose of your visit here."

"My name is Ødger (Edger). I am Huscarl (professional bodyguard) to the King, Harald Sigurdsson, known as 'Hardråda' (hard ruler) who has commanded that I come here. I have been sent to find the warrior from this village by the name of Erik Ohlsson known as '*Slagbjørn*'. His reputation has travelled as far as the *Kongsgård* (Kings Palace) at Nidaros, and the King is looking for new huscarls to recruit for his fight against the pretender; Sweyn

Estridsson, King of Denmark. Harald has accrued a great fortune in Byzantium and Constantinople and pays his huscarls well."

The Ålderman spotted Olaf among the throng of villagers come to gawp at the huge Viking. He was easily the size of Erik but leaner and harder. If he told you he had killed many enemies, you would have no trouble believing him.

"Olaf, go and summon your father and tell him there is a stranger in the village who wishes to speak with him."

Olaf trotted off to his father's long-house from whence came the sound of snoring and the stench of stale alcohol and an unwashed body. Without breaking stride, Olaf grabbed a full water bucket and let him have it. The results were instantaneous, a roar, some choice oaths and a swing of a huge fist that came nowhere near its mark. Olaf stepped out into the square and refilled the bucket. Returning to the house, Erik raised his palm:

"Stop! Olaf what are you doing? Can you not see I am sleeping?"

"You drink all night and sleep all day. You stink. A man sent by the King is here to speak with you. You must wash and change your clothes. I'll tell them you are bathing!"

Olaf trotted back to the hall and announced that Erik was bathing and would be with them shortly.

"Bathing?" said Ødger, with a touch of incredulity. "A Viking warrior bathing. Well and good, we huscarls are expected to bathe regularly at Nidaros!"

It was then that Olaf noticed the pungent melange of different aromas surrounding the big man. Horse-sweat, man-sweat, bearskin and wet leather.

Erik appeared ten minutes later, transformed by a set of clean clothes and a hairbrush. Together they entered the hall and sat at the long table at the far end. It was early October now and a good size log was crackling away. Some maids brought in goblets of *öl* and a plate of delicious reindeer that Olaf had shot recently. Ødger was clearly hungry and it was some time before he spoke.

"Erik Slagbjørn, there is a job for you in the service of the King should you wish to accept – as a huscarl."

"Huscarl?"

"On the proviso that you complete our training, which is rigorous, and get rid of all that fat! You look strong and the scars on your face give you a fierce aspect. You look the part, but you also look out of shape. Have you met King Harald?

"Yes, I took Olaf, my youngest, to Nidaros to get his Oath Ring from the King some five years ago. He is my last as my two older sons were both killed by the great bear. The same as gave me this," he said pointing to the fearsome scar on his face.

"As he is so young, he should stay with his mother, I think."

Erik shook his head,

"He has only me," which wasn't true as Olaf lived with Freya and the *Lech.*

"Anyway, Olaf is a gentle soul who doesn't care for fighting much but is useful as a crack bowman".

Ødger looked up, interested. "Archer, you say? Is he here?"

"Yes, he's the little Viking who came to fetch me. He is seated at the far end of the table. Olaf! Do you have your bow with you?"

"Yes *far.*"

"Show this man what you can do. Hit the centre boss on that yellow shield down the far end of the hall."

The light was fading, and the torches were not yet lit so the only light was from the smoking log in the centre of the Hall. Olaf stood up, strung his bow and slipped an arrow on the now taught string. Pulling back to his cheek and using the line of the arrow as a sight, he loosed. The goose feathers whooshed past the string to be followed by a metallic clunk as the missile embedded itself in the metal boss and wooden shield.

"*Herregud*! That boy can shoot. Bring him with us Erik, it will double the coin you receive. Hardråda has too few archers and we need them to shore up the shield wall if there is a breakthrough or anyone trying to go over the top."

"N-n-noooo!" wailed Olaf. I'm happy here, I'm not meant to be a warrior, let alone a *huscarl*!"

"Whaaat!" roared Ødger, rising, "you don't wish to be with your father and serve the King? Do you realise what an honour it is to be a huscarl? Besides", he said, his voice losing the sense of outrage, "you wouldn't have to fight until you reach your eighteenth birthday and the training you would receive would hone your already impressive skills, not to mention the generous stipend in coin. Hardråda is a very wealthy king, and he is not shy in sharing it with those who serve him well."

"Of course, he'll come with me" said Erik standing up, shoulder height with Ødger at six foot seven inches, and glaring at Olaf who, in turn, observed this colossal pair of killing machines and realised that there was to be no wriggling out of this one.

"Very good!" said Ødger, "I can give you one day to set your affairs in order then we leave for Nidaros by first light the day after tomorrow. Ålderman Leif, your small town will miss these two hunters and I am authorised to compensate you." With this he produced a leather pouch of the new coins that Hardrada had recently had minted, using his formal title of Harald III, and poured them over the table, where they glinted impressively as the maids lit the torches in the gloomy hall. The intake of breath was as Ødger had come to expect on these missions. This single Norwegian currency was now accepted across Scandinavia and its value guaranteed by the great wealth Harald had plundered from Byzantium and as far as Constantinople. Harald had, in fact, established a viable coin economy for trading with the Kievan Rus and the Byzantine Empire.

If Erik had any doubts, which he didn't, the vision of those glinting silver coins told him everything he needed to know about his King and new employer. Certainly, Leif was convinced. He clapped his hands and called to the maids to bring mead and more reindeer meat and invited Ødger to stay the next two nights at his house as his guest – a brave thing to do given the stench that pervaded this Viking. At the sound of revelry and the smell of cooked meat and bread, the warriors of the village began to congregate inside the Mead House and soon another feast was in progress.

The following day was a difficult one for Olaf as he now had to explain to Freya that he was going away for an indefinite period of time to take up service with one of the most feared men in Christendom. This was a man who liked to use mutilation to encourage his people to pay their taxes. This was also a man who, having fought right across from Byzantium to Sicily was not happy to settle down and enjoy his wealth but rather was recruiting fighters for his on-going wars against Sweyn of Denmark, a man who had been his ally.

Olaf had Freya's hand in his and was gently massaging her long fingers. Since before the arrival of Ødger, Freya had been decidedly off with him – particularly in the bedroom. She had told him she was not feeling well and had been subject to bouts of sickness. Now as he came to tell her his news, her head was turned away from him and, before he could begin, she interjected:

"I know Olaf, I know. Apparently, you impressed the big Viking with your archery skills in the mead hall. The lads told their girls and the girls told me. So, now you are going away on your big adventure, no doubt to create a great saga for the poets, if we had any in this dingy village, and you are leaving me with my father to bring up our child."

Olaf blanched: "Our what?"

Freya rolled her eyes towards the gods:

"Do you think it at all possible that I have let you plough me practically non-stop since Midsummer without thinking of the probabilities of any issue resulting - or did your father not tell you about these things?"

Olaf stood rooted, his jaw hanging open in an expression of utter stupidity.

"So, there it is," continued Freya, "you go off to Nidaros and come back in seven or eight-months' time, without getting killed, and I will present you with a son or a daughter."

Olaf found his voice: "I'll stay, I can't go now."

"Olaf!" A familiar roar announced the arrival of Erik Slagbjørn, into this awkward scene. "Get your boots on, I have coin and we are going to Lillehammer to buy a couple of horses."

"But I can't ride!", stammered Olaf.

"You'll learn, it's seven days to Nidaros and you don't want to be carrying all your possessions."

"Go!" said Freya adding a little shove and a smile which betrayed a gentle fondness which had not been there just now.

Both, father and son, tottered off down the slope to the great fjørd. Of the baby, Olaf made no mention, but it weighed heavily on his mind.

Hardrada Mynt

## *Chapter Four:*
## *The Trek to Nidaros - Ambush*

The following day the sun rose cold and clear. The whole village turned out along with a number from Lillehammer, including the horse trader, clutching two newly shod horses of the Icelandic pony breed – short of leg, sturdy and broad but with an exclusive trait found only in these animals, the ability to 'amble'. This made them comfortable and perfectly suited for long journeys on small rough roads. With the saddle being heavily covered in fur, it was rather like riding in a comfortable armchair.

Olaf, with no experience of horses sat astride his dapple-grey, grinning at this new experience and trying to bond with his new comfortable friend. He was docile enough and seemed happy that he had been chosen to carry Olaf's slight build rather than the massive bulk of Erik. Erik's horse was considerably larger and more powerfully built, which was just as well, as he had already laden the poor beast with his shield, sword, short axe and his great double-handed war axe. After much hugging and tears, Freya and Olaf finally parted and the three horses and riders rode out of the village amid cheers and waves with Freya resting her hands on where the baby might be, as a reminder to Olaf.

There had been some rain, so the ground was soft and easy going. The two warriors went ahead to leave Olaf to his thoughts. The mosquitos and the midges were long gone and there was nothing to disturb Olaf from thinking that this was an adventure after all and perhaps they could make it all the way without meeting another huge killer-bear.

For most of the first day, they followed the water on the Eastern side up from Lillehammer, heading due North-West along the great *Gudbrandsdalslågen* (Gudbrands river in the dale) towards the inland cross-roads at Dombås. It was a considerable trek and it had been dark for many hours when they left the main river to follow the right-hand tributary at Otta, where they stopped to stretch their legs and rest the horses for a short while. Erik had not been on a horse for some years and was feeling it. It was he who begged Ødger to stop for the night who, much to Olaf's surprise, agreed. There was, he said, a rough *ölbod* (Inn) that took in travellers. Between Otta and Dombås there was nothing except dark woods and, if they wanted a drink, then this ölbod at Otta, which served öl (ale), meat and bread, was the only place for many miles. Father and son could not have been more relieved.

It was a short ride to the long-house at Otta that acted as the ölbod and a convenient resting post for those going on the long trek to Nidaros. There was the smell of smoke wafting into the air which brought with it aromas of smoked fish and roasted game. The commotion from within was dampened by the fact that much of the long house was buried into the side of the hill with grass and moss growing over it.

Opening the heavy door, Ødger's huge bulk filled the entrance and with Erik behind him, the vibrant shouting and laughing died away almost at once. There followed one of the silence's where you expect someone to growl that they don't like strangers, but no one did and the three made their way to an empty table by the fire in the centre. The hubbub began to pick up again, but cautiously. A buxom serving girl came over and soon they were eating the most delicious smoked fish and game and washing it down with öl.

She returned shortly after to refill the goblets and Olaf tried to catch her eye and make conversation, but without success. She seemed distracted and kept glancing at the door.

Furthermore, a distant whinnying sound had aroused Ødger's suspicious attentions and instincts. Leaping for the door and knocking over the serving girl, Ødger made it in a couple of bounds and within a moment he was out into the cold night air, sword unsheathed and startling three *røvare* (villains or thieves) amongst their horses, one holding up Erik's silver drinking horn to see by the moonlight.

"*Oy, Herregud!*" yelled one as he struggled to pull out a hunting blade. Followed by another oath "*ah! fy Faen!*" as Ødger's blade ran easily into his torso. Erik and Olaf had followed hard on Ødger's rapid exit from the long-house and now, the second *røvare,* was about to bring the great silver horn down on Ødger's skull as he struggled to pull his blade clear.

The horn, instead of crashing into Ødger's uncovered head, fell to the ground and rolled in the stony mud complete with an arm, severed from the elbow, still clutching onto it. The original owner of this arm was currently staggering off into the night emitting terrible shrieks of distress.

"*Tusen hjertelig tak!*" (a thousand cordial thanks) said Ødger in mock courtesy to Erik's self-satisfied expression and clutching his bloodied sword. Both warriors then, simultaneously, remembered that there was a third *røvare* and, turning towards the horses, they saw he was in the act of making good his escape on Olaf's dapple-grey.

He was already a distance away and neither of the two big men were built for speed. Between the shouts there was an almost imperceptible sound of wind rustling through goose feathers and a sickening thud as an arrow struck *røvare* number three squarely between the shoulder blades. The horse stopped, sensing his rider was no longer in control, and after a few moments the grip of the rider's knees no longer held him in place and he slid off the fur saddle and onto the black mud outside the longhouse. There would have been silence then but for the distant shrieks and wails of the one-armed horn thief. Erik picked up his silver trophy and peeled off the fingers, letting the arm drop to the floor. The ground was now lit by a throng of villagers with torches, mostly from the ölbod, who had come out to watch the fun, but which was all over in the blinking of an eye.

Ødger turned to Olaf: "Nice shot boy, in the dark like that. Good idea to bring your *svein-stauli* (lad) with us Erik."

Erik humphed in agreement and turned to Olaf:

"Go fetch your horse then follow us into the longhouse."

Olaf's horse had already left the scene of his previous rider's demise and was walking back towards the lanterns and torches, pleased to be greeted by Olaf's affectionate stroking of his muzzle and neck. From inside the long-house came the noise of a further disturbance and turning, Olaf saw the other horses had gone and there was much shouting from within. It transpired that the serving girl had been complicit with the thieves as the one with the severed arm was her brother.

Ødger had walked his horse into the inn and had kicked over several tables to make room for the three mounts. The locals were not happy. Olaf entered and joined the others with their horses tied to the elk antlers on the wall. They removed the shields and weapons and enticed the horses to lie down on some straw that Olaf had collected. This afforded some protection should the locals feel so disposed as to try to steal from them again.

They did not, and the revellers mostly slunk off quietly into the night. But for the snoring of the weary travellers and the crackle of the logs on the fire, the night was peaceful. Olaf, ever a light sleeper, awoke to the hissing whispers and slaps of someone administering some late-night discipline. Stepping over the horses and shields he followed the sound until he reached its source.

The owner of the premise was blaming the serving girl for tonight's trouble and was taking it out on her by means of a leather belt. The girl, cornered on a bed, was whimpering and covering her head against a torrent of blows that stopped abruptly when Olaf grabbed the arm of her tormentor and spoke with quiet menace: "We are trying to get some rest here!" The slightly-built proprietor dropped the belt and, half bowing, left the room with profuse apologies. The girl looked up, her face red and bruised:

"I am so sorry, they told me to keep you occupied with öl so they could rob your horses. I am so sorry, please forgive me."

"I killed a man tonight for the first time. I hope it was not your brother?"

She shook her head and explained that her brother had survived and rushed back to her family home where they were trying to fix the wound. Olaf knew all about that. She continued that the three of them had made a living out of robbing travellers and often killing them.

"Otta will be pleased they are gone; they had no honour. You needn't go back to the horses just yet. Stay with me and let us console each other."

Olaf had a flash of guilt and an image of Freya standing, hand on womb, the next he knew he was pulled on top of the voluptuous and passionate body of the serving girl who managed to blow out the candle and pull off his shirt whilst planting kisses on his face. She might not have the godlike figure of Freya but it was cold outside and she had warmth enough for both of them.

The lovemaking was intense, brutish and short, after which Olaf slept the sleep of one who has travelled eight hours, eaten and drunk well, killed a man and had his way with a comely maiden whilst remaining ignorant of even her name. He was beginning to feel like a proper Viking!

Ulli, the serving girl

## *Chapter Five:*
## *Dinner in Dombås*

The morning cockerel was in full voice even though it was still dark. In the hall, the horses had slept well, as had Erik and Ødger. Torches were being lit and the fire re-kindled. Erik took the horses outside and found them some water and some oats. Ødger saw to the weapons and paid the proprietor a little extra for the damage of broken chairs who in turn brought them three steaming bowls of gröt (porridge) and some milk. It was at this point that they realised they were only two, with no sign of Olaf.

"Where's the boy?" asked Erik.

"I think you'll find him in a comfortable straw bed out the back sleeping very soundly after his exertions with Ulli, our serving girl, who tried to help those villains last night. I think it is her way of saying sorry," said the proprietor.

"He seems to have a way with the girls", said Erik, "it'll get him into trouble one day, that's for sure."

Olaf appeared a while later – his hair tousled and was in the final stages of dressing by doing up the buckle of his belt and hunting knife. Behind him, Ulli, the serving girl, scuttled off in the direction of the kitchen.

"Your porridge is nearly cold but get it down you as we won't be stopping to eat for quite some time. Dombås is a six-hour ride. I trust you made yourself comfortable last night?"

Olaf piled into the luke-warm gröt and drank a flask of milk, allowing him to ignore his father's remark.

"Where are Ødger and the horses?"

"They are all outside. Ødger is paying the Ålderman for the burial of the bodies. It seems that they won't be too badly missed around here – thieving *drittstøvel*!"

Olaf laughed and spat out some milk at Erik's use of the word meaning: 'something you have trodden in'.

The horses, having been fed and watered, the trio were ready to move off. Several of the villagers came to see them go and there was no animosity. Ulli leant out of a window, waving, the lace of her blouse improperly tied and baring her impressive cleavage for Olaf who shouted back laughing:

"Cover up you'll catch a death of a chill!"

At this she threw back her thick brunette hair and let out a laugh like Thor's anvil.

And so, the three riders set off on the next leg of their journey to Dombås, a ride continuing along the great *Gudbrandsdalslågen*, which might not have been the most direct route but ensured they did not stray and always kept the river to their left or West side. It was a journey of some forty miles, so another day's ride. The weather was cold but fine and the scenery breath-taking with the first snows settling on the mountains over to the East. On and on they rode with only a short break for the horses to eat and drink. Finally, as darkness descended, Ødger pulled his horse away from the river and the forest which flowed left and headed sharp right towards a meadow which showed signs of a farming community. Heading due North, they soon saw distant lights of a sizeable dwelling, much more substantial than Otta.

"That, over there," shouted Ødger, "is the town of Dombås where we will camp for the night. They are far more civilised than those barbarians at Otta. We should get a proper rest here as after this there are no rest houses for over a hundred and fifty miles up into the mountains until we arrive at the court of King Harald. So, four times as long as our journey today."

It had seemed strange to Olaf that Ødger had made a week's journey to a tiny village just to collect his alcoholic father but the fight at Otta had shown Ødger that Erik was still a good man to have watching your back and Olaf had proven himself in his first kill with unerring accuracy. Harald could not but be pleased to have Erik as a new huscarl and Olaf as a trainee archer.

Dombås was a pleasing town although, unlike Otta, it had no inn but a splendid Mead Hall in the centre. The protocol was to present yourself to the Ålderman, explain who you were and what your purpose was, who would then take you to the Chieftain or Jarl of the region. And so it was that Ødger, Erik and Olaf marched into the great ölbod to meet Haldor, who sat on a carved wooden throne covered with furs and flanked by two spear-carrying warriors dressed in armour as for battle.

The tables were filled with well-heeled unarmed townsfolk dressed in velvet and fur with finely carved brooches and rings. The people in this town certainly looked prosperous. The Ålderman, tall and thin, stopped a few yards before the Chieftain, and, raising his hand, called for silence:

"Jarl Halvar of Innlandet, may I present to you these two travellers and a boy who have asked for your protection and your hospitality before they continue their journey to the *Kongsgård* at Nidaros; Ødger 'Sköll' Hakonsson, Huscarl to King Harald III of Norway, Erik Ohlson called 'Slagbjørn' and his son Olaf…erm… *the Fair*?"

There was instant mirth at this humorous improvisation on behalf of the Ålderman who was known for his appreciation of good-looking young men and his sideways pout caused laughter all round. The Jarl suppressed his smile and addressed the two large warriors:

"Have you business with the King? I have sent him two of my strongest warriors for his household and I have paid my taxes for this year. If you see the King and he asks to shake your hand, don't give it to him – you may never see it again!"

Howls of laughter and a self-satisfied smile from the Jarl, pleased to have upstaged the humour of his Ålderman.

Having broken the ice, the trio of travellers felt they could relax a little in the knowledge that their horses were being tended to by the Jarl's men. The Ålderman finally introduced himself as Thorkel and ushered them to a bench with his arm around Olaf's shoulder so that he had to remove his bow and quiver and carry them. The food was fine compared with the rustic fare and wooden goblets at Otta and the meat was served with a deep red sauce of lingonberries, preserved from the Summer.

Thorkel, who sat himself next to a somewhat awkward-looking Olaf, was keen to tell Olaf what to watch out for when he finally reached the court of Harald Hardråda. He wasn't called 'Hard Ruler' for nothing and had a penchant for amputation for anyone who crossed him or was late with their taxes. He had two wives although he professed to follow the Christian faith. The first, Elisaveta Yaroslavna of Kiev and the second, a beautiful Norse concubine, Tora Torbergsdatter, a Norwegian whom he had married just four years later. Harald had written a poem bewailing the fact that Elisaveta did not return his affection although she did bare him two attractive daughters, Maria and Ingegerd. At this, Olaf's tired eyes lit up with renewed interest.

It didn't go unnoticed by Thorkel the Ålderman:

"Don't even think about it. You'll need both hands if you are to operate that bow!" Olaf laughed sheepishly, but the seeds of curiosity were now well and truly sown.

"Not only that", continued Thorkel, "but Elisiv, as she is known, and both her daughters are said to be practitioners of the *seidr*, or Dark Arts known to the Kievan Rus".

"You mean she is a *Völva*?" Olaf's eyes were now wide open.

"Ah you know this word? Yes, she is a witch and can converse with the spirits. She wears a hat and gloves of cat-fur, she carries a metal wand and a purse of henbane known as witches salve. Harald has used this in battle to cause hallucinations and bring on the craziness of a Berserker. Be very careful if you have dealings with Elisiv or her daughters, they are like sirens from the old Greek saga and they will try to lure you. Hardråda has been utterly brutal with previous young men who have succumbed to their flirtations. Obviously, Tora, who now sleeps in Harald's bed, and Elisiv hate each other so don't get between them or favour one against the other. In fact, my little blonde beauty, you are going to have to work very hard indeed just to keep out of trouble! I don't know who is more dangerous, Hardråda or the women!"

At this, Thorkel threw back his head and laughed in delight at the terror in Olaf's expression. A massive hand descended on Olaf's shoulder and the fire cast the shadow of Eric, his father, on the opposite wall.

"Come on now boy, we've a very long journey ahead and you need to get some sleep."

The three travellers thanked the Jarl and made their way to a guest room where there was straw for pillows but no beds.

# Chapter Six:
## *Wolves – Ødger's Saga*

The town of Dombås was just stirring when Olaf awoke to find Erik and Ødger already up and preparing the horses, who had been stabled and well-tended, as the night had been cold. A light snow was falling and it was starting to settle on the hard mud outside. Olaf threw some water over his face from a jug and flinched at how cold it felt. His hands though felt something new on his face.

The blonde, downy hair on his cheeks was starting to harden and he laughed at the thought that he was actually starting to grow a blonde Viking beard to cover his very boyish visage. Erik shouted at him to go to the ölbod to get some hot gröt and milk as they needed to move out soon.

Olaf gazed upwards at the grey sky and was concerned that the snow was definitely getting thicker. According to Ødger it was over a hundred and fifty miles over the mountains with absolutely nowhere to stay until they reached Nidaros. So, it would either be death by freezing, death by wolves or a bear or ending up in the company of a deranged mutilating monarch, a Kiev Queen of evil spells with two siren daughters and a beautiful concubine who was jealously guarded. The Ålderman was right, Olaf thought, I will have to work very hard to stay alive.

Ødger had been shopping amongst the town's market stalls and had returned with supplies for the journey. They did not need to carry water as there was fresh water all along the route. What he did buy was bread, meat, smoked fish and a present for Olaf.

"We might need you up there and I love reindeer meat."

With that he handed Olaf a quiver of well-crafted arrows from the local fletcher. Olaf was impressed. He made his own, but these were beautifully crafted from sycamore with bound and spliced fletching. This would give him far greater accuracy and range.

"Oh, I'll get you a reindeer if we see one! Thank you for these, they are wonderful. I need to learn how to fletch like this."

"Don't worry, I'm sure they'll teach you everything when we get to the *Kongsgård* at Nidaros."

They set off, just as the sun began to glimmer behind the snow clouds, offering enough light for them to see their way, ever Northward now and upward towards the grey and white rocks of the mountains. The Icelandic horses ambled up the pathways, sure-footed and uncomplaining and enjoying the soft snow under their hooves. Olaf huddled under his cloak of bearskin against the chill wind but Ødger and Erik seemed oblivious, as if they wished to prove to the gods that they were true warriors. After a few hours, however, even they succumbed and the three trundled onwards and ever upward.

By the end of the day, as the sun was setting, they had covered over forty miles and pitched camp in a deserted spot that Ødger referred to as *Kongsvoll*. They lit a fire and warmed up the salted smoked fish and the freshly baked bread from this morning. Erik had a flask of øl which he shared round gingerly, carefully, as if it were some precious ointments.

"We have to make this last" he said, with genuine concern.

Olaf laughed, but his mirth was immediately cut short by the familiar, but nonetheless disquieting, sound of a lone wolf calling to others in the pack. The howl rang off the rocks into the dark night and Olaf pulled his quiver closer, removed a single shaft and turned his back to the fire.

"Don't worry boy, he's a long way off even though he sounds so close," Erik tried to reassure his son. He knew and Ødger knew that the others in the pack may not be and the smell of the meat and the fish would not have escaped the highly developed sense of smell that wolves possess. One wolf would not attack with a fire to discourage him but a pack was quite another matter. Both Erik and Ødger did as Olaf had done and turned their backs to the fire whilst taking out their hunting knives and holding their short axes to cover the three possible attack points with the fourth being a sharp stony drop behind them. Ødger took three burning stakes from the fire and formed them in a triangular light just a few feet away from them.

He brought the horses behind them and used their shields to create a perimeter, but the ponies could scent danger and could not be induced to lie down. More wolf-cries broke out and the horses became threatened and disturbed. Olaf tucked in behind his dapple-grey, bow in hand and awaited the inevitable attack whilst stroking and consoling his mount. An hour passed, then another and still no attack came. The horses began to be less fretful and lay down to rest behind the shield protection and the burning fire.

They took turns in snatching sleep until the grey dawn broke over a snow-sprinkled landscape. They had survived one night but had slept little. Three more days and nights of this!

Olaf had not slept at all and was interested that Ødger had managed to sleep soundly for several hours and now was joined by Erik so that the two large warriors were both completely oblivious to any assault by a wolf pack. How had Ødger made this same journey alone without being attacked? After Olaf had made some warm milk to wake them, he put this point to Ødger.

"*Vagr!*" he growled. "Wolves are just pack animals who cannot operate without a leader. I have a god who watches over me. Did you not hear my name announced by that effete Ålderman in the Earl's presence?"

"I heard Thorkel announce you as Ødger Sköll....so what of it?"

"Ah! did you not listen to the sagas in the mead hall? Sköll and Hati are the two wolf-gods who chase the sun and the moon. I believe that the howl we all heard was indeed that of Sköll commanding the *vargr* to leave us in peace. My father had offered himself in sacrifice to the moon-God Sköll and was taken up to Valhalla during a great battle that I will tell you all about another time. For now, we must break camp and be on our way, there is still a great distance to travel. Wake up that idle oaf that you call your father and let's be going."

And so it was, that by the guidance of a glaring low rising sun, the three travellers continued to head North across the vast mountainous landscape that was known to mapmakers as *Kongsvol*.

Olaf had much to ponder on and was eager to hear in detail the story of Ødger's father, the wolf-God, and the great battle. Of the pretty blonde boy who liked to make flower wreaths with the girls last Summer, almost nothing remained. And so onwards and upwards, behind the grey ears of his ambling horse, that he had now named *Vanir* (after the Norse god of wisdom), Olaf struggled to stay awake. Finally, as the sun began to set, for the snow had stopped and the going had been good, Ødger called out that they were going to rest for the night. There was a tiny farming village ahead which Ødger referred to as *Fagerhaug*.

The path was clear, and the meadows were harvested for the long winter ahead. There was a homely smell of burning wood and, in the distance, a small, long-house emitted a whisp of smoke. There was also light visible between the beams. Ødger gave his walking horse a little nudge and it broke into its characteristic amble which the other two horses followed with no encouragement.

"Don't worry, the natives are friendly" and he made a strange growling noise which, for Ødger, passed as a laugh.

At this the door of the long-house creaked open and a gnarled-looking lady with plaits peered cautiously out.

"Hej?" she called out, questioning the strangers in the candlelight. "Ødger Hakonsson! Well, well. Have you come back for some of my mjörd or my cooking or something else, eh?"

Ødger laughed again: "Some food and mead would be welcome and I have coin to pay you for we are three people now, as you see."

"Well, two and a half!" shouted out Olaf as he nudged *Vanir* forward into the light.

"So, you had better come in out of the cold then *sveinn* (boy)! I am called Ålov Sigurdsdattor. My father was Jarl of Lade but fought on the wrong side at Stiklestad where Ødger's father was killed defending King Olav. Come in, come in and get some warmth on those frozen cheeks. Now who is this ugly brute? Oy, herregud! but you're another big one like Ødger!"

Erik also rumbled a growling noise, and the movement of his shoulders was the indicator that he too was laughing.

"I am Erik Ohlsson the one they call 'Slagbjørn'. I fought with a great bear that killed my two sons Sweyn and Magnus and gave me this pretty scar. The silver drinking horn and the title and adulation from my village were my reward for this great act of bravery.

The truth though, was told to me on the night I watched my beautiful brave boys sail out to Valhalla in a burning ship, was that the bear had knocked me unconscious. When I came to, Olaf told me that I had killed the bear with my axe. Ålfgerd, the village doctor, told me at the funeral that the bear had been killed, not by an axe, but by an arrow that had passed clean through the bear's throat. My little Olaf would never have told me as he wanted me to have all the glory. Olaf killed that bear with his bow."

A tear welled up in the big man's eye.

"Right, get your silver horn, tie your horse, and let's get to some drinking and telling of stories and sagas by the fire – I do hate to see a grown man cry!"

With the horses secured and given nosebags, they all made their way into the warm long house to join Olaf, who was already seated near the fire. Ålov was a perfect hostess who quickly provided an impressive table of mead and warm milk, öl, bread, freshly baked that morning, some chicken and even some smoked reindeer.

For a while there was no sound but the crackling logs and the rude noises of drinking and eating by three travellers who had not eaten but for a small bowl of gröt at sunrise. Erik belched contentedly and stretched out his boots towards the fire. Olaf was the first to break the silence:

"Thank you Ålov, that was better than perfect. You mentioned that your father was killed in the same battle as Ødger's. I'm in the market for a good saga so, between the two of you, perhaps you can tell me all about it?"

Ålov laughed and slapped her knees: "Well, I'll go first as my story is shorter and I haven't spoken to a soul for ten days. Back in 1030, when we were very young – not quite as young as you – this whole area of Trøndelag was known as Lade and was ruled over by a series of Jarls descended from Hákon Grjotgarösson who was made the first Jarl by Harald I of Norway (Harald Fairhair) for lending him his fleet of ships and created an alliance. Between them they managed to defeat the mini-kingdoms and turn Norway into a United Kingdom under one ruler.

But, after Fairhair died in 932 the alliance fell apart and for nearly one hundred years the Jarls and the descendants of Harald Fairhair would be locked in a bitter power struggle, which included religion, as Harald's descendants tried to convert the heathen Norwegians to Christianity. In 1015, Olav Haraldsson, descendant of Fairhair, landed back from a Viking raid, in Nidaros, and was proclaimed king, winning a great victory over the Jarls the following year at the battle of Nesjar – a naval battle off the coast of Norway. The Danes under Canute the Great were too tied up fighting in England so the way was open for Olav to secure himself as king and for the Jarls to keep a low profile or go into exile in Sweden. Olav brutally dealt with his internal enemies but was ousted after a massive sea battle at the Helgea against Canute the Great and the English navy in 1026, which gave the Norwegian Jarls a chance to vent their grievances against Olav, who fled into exile in Kievan Rus.

Canute appointed the Jarl Håkon Eriksson as regent. In 1029, however, Eriksson was drowned at sea and Olav wasted no time in marching an army across Sweden to attack the capital at Nidaros in 1030. He was met just seventy-five miles outside the capital by a vast army of farmers and Jarls, hastily gathered, but numbering some 14,000 men. My father was one of those Jarls opposing Olav, and Ødger's father was one of the huscarls in Olav's force of 6,500 men.  I'll let Ødger take over from here as I need some öl, I think!"

Ødger took a deep draught of öl and cleared his throat with a rumble.

"Ålov has told you the history and I couldn't improve on that. I have already told you why I am called 'Sköll' so I will now fill in some details. My father, Sigurd Hakon and I, were both in service with Olav, called 'the Stout', and we had followed him as huscarls on Viking raids as far as Spain, England and Normandy.

We were there when Olav went mad and had himself baptised in Rouen in Normandy. In 1015 he declared himself King of Norway. He was a violent and ruthless man, yet he liked to call himself a Christian whilst inflicting terrible hardships on many a good Norseman. By 1029 the feeling against him from the Jarls and Norwegian nobility was so strong that Canute the Great of England and Denmark was invited to drive us out, which they did, and we were forced to follow Olav into Kievan Rus where he had an ally in the person of Yaroslav the Wise. And there, in Novgorod, we stayed to gather strength and wait our time to take back Norway from the Jarls. Now here some strange occurrences happened about which I can only repeat what I have been told.

Although Yaroslav of Kiev and his wife, Princess Ingegerd of Sweden, were both committed Christians, they had a daughter, just six years old, called Elisaveta. Somehow this little girl had been born with the knowledge of the old ways and could foresee the future and commune with the spirits and the old Norse gods."

"A völga at the age of six?" Olaf could not help his interruption as his idea of a witch was an old crone.

"For sure" said Ødger nodding, "it is something you are born with. I was eighteen and was given the task of watching out for Harald, Olav's younger half-brother who was just fourteen but as blood-thirsty a warrior as you could hope not to meet. Trying to keep him safe was like trying to tell a bird not to fly. But, while at the court of Prince Yaroslav, he developed a fascination for this little girl who confided in him that the spirits had decided that Olav, the exiled King, my father and myself were to die in a great battle next year. She also told him that Harald himself was to be taken up but she had begged them to watch over him in battle.

Harald told this to me and of course I went to the little girl and asked her about it. She cried a little and promised to try and speak with the spirits. Several days later whilst I was with Harald, she suddenly appeared at our side, though neither of us had heard or seen her approach. She did not have the facial expression of a child but looked sternly and kept repeating the names Sköll and Hati. These were the spirits she claimed to be speaking with. They were the wolf-gods and they had, she claimed, agreed to watch over Harald and protect me for as long as Harald lived. Of King Olav and my father, she shook her head and said:

"It will be their time soon, and your father will be the sacrifice needed for your protection. I have spoken with your father and he has agreed. You may take the name 'Sköll' now as he is your new protector and his wolves will not harm you. At this she turned and drifted away and her character seemed to regain its childlike expression."

"And did that happen?" Olaf was impatient to hear the outcome.

"Let him finish boy and you'll find out," replied an irritated Erik who was also agog to hear the outcome.

"It happened just as she said. The following year, 1030, news reached the court of a shipwreck off the coast of Scotland and the Orkneys in which a Jarl of Lade, Håkon Eriksson was drowned. He had been acting regent in Norway for Canute and had the support of the non-Christian Jarls and the Norwegian farmers. King Olav got very excited and gathered us into what seemed like a great army, when in fact we numbered only around three thousand. But we were all loyal huscarls and better warriors would be hard to find. We left Novgorod and made the long march to the coast where a fleet carried us to Sweden. In the town of Uppsala, we were surprised when a sizeable number of Vikings offered to join our force for pay.

They were led by Dag Ringsson, a descendant of Harald Fairhair. These were not Christians like King Olav but proper Odin-worshipping Norsemen who I was very pleased to have join us. Another long march North through Sweden and then into Norway to take Nidaros from the East and proclaim Olav king once more. We were almost there, a day or two's march when we were caught in the open by a vast force of Jarls and farmers led by Thorir Hund and his bodyguard, the huge boat-builder, Torstein Knarresmed. Harek of Tjøtta and Kalv Arneson had also brought large numbers of men to the fight.

They were almost three to one of us but young Harald beside me seemed to relish these odds and his eyes blazed in a way I was to see so many times over the next twenty-five years. Harald wanted to be in the centre with his brother Olav who had my father there to cover him and so obviously I was there also to cover the young prince. We had the high ground so I watched with interest as the peasants and farmers tried to form a ragged shield wall and thought we could hold the hill against these men of the soil.

They were down there shouting and banging their shields with their weapons and the noise of fourteen thousand men shouting: 'Fram! Fram! Bonder!' (Forward farmers!) was really impressive. Olav encouraged our boys to reply with a more complicated 'Fram! Fram! Kristmenn, krosmenn, kongsmenn! (Forward men of Christ, men of the cross, men of the king!) but it didn't have anything like the volume of the farmers and the Swedish warriors on our side weren't going to shout any Christian slogans and risk the wrath of Odin in Valhalla. Olav sensed we were losing the shouting battle and, in a spectacular moment of madness, ordered that our tight shield wall charge down the slope into the farmers.

Harald was delighted and let out a great yell as our men surged forward. Olav shouted at us to take out the leaders so the others would break. Our men crashed into the farmers and with great skill reformed our shield wall. At first, we inflicted heavy loss of life and it looked like they would break. But these farmers were made of sturdy stuff and at three to one in open combat, a significant number of our men began to fall, suffering stabs and slashes from the side as they fought an opponent directly to their front. The more our men fell the greater the odds became until we were almost at five to one.

The fighting around the King was fiercest with Harald and myself covering his left flank and Sigurd, my father, covering his exposed right flank. Olav had elected not to carry a shield but instead was wielding a terrible war hammer with both hands. The cracking of shields and skulls before this instrument of death, opened a path for the King and his huscarls to get to Thorir Hund, one of the ringleaders. Olav squared up to Thorir who desperately tried to fend off a blow to his helmet from the great war hammer which shattered his shield and may have broken his arm.

Sigurd plunged a spear into the chest of Thorir's nephew attacking the King on the right and he fell, mortally wounded. On the left the huge boatbuilder, Torstein Knarresmed desperately tried to protect Thorir but was taken out by both Harald and I who inflicted wounds through his armour. This, however, did not stop him from falling between King Olav and Thorir. Olav was about to deliver the death blow when Torstein, falling at Olav's feet, managed to plunge a dagger just above the King's left knee. The hammer was suddenly used as a crutch to prevent Olav, screaming in agony, from going down next to Thorir, who had avoided death by a whisker.

Torstein regained his feet and looked to follow up his attack on the wounded King whilst fending off the swords of Harald and me with his shield. He had forgotten Sirgurd though who took the opportunity to plunge his sword into the huge man's back. Harald and I helped Olav back out of the immediate killing zone where he rested against a large rock whilst we removed the blade and attempted to bandage the wound. Back in the killing zone, Sigurd was fighting like a Berserker to protect the King and we saw at least four go down before his axe, as his sword was buried deep in the body of Torstein Knarresmed. Thorir had crawled to the body of his nephew to withdraw the spear from his chest that had killed him. His grief turned to rage as he saw Olav's standard bearer, Tord Foleson, rush to the side of his King and plant the royal standard into the ground beside the stone.

It was perhaps the worst thing he could have done. The enraged Thorir Hund regained his strength in his legs and using the bloody spear to get to his feet, rushed at the group surrounding the King. He was followed closely by his son-in-law, Kalv Arneson who had fought with Olav previously but was now his staunchest opponent. Running, bent almost double, to protect his broken arm, Thorir surprised the King's men, who mistook him for one of our own.

This enabled him to plunge the spear that had killed his nephew under the mail of Olav and up into his stomach. The King threw his head back in agony giving Kalv Arnesson the perfect opportunity to plunge his sword into Olav's neck. Sigurd appeared pursued by a throng of farmers and still fighting a furious rear-guard action. "Get the King out of here", he screamed. He was drenched in blood from his victims and from the multiple wounds he had received.

He and Tord Foleson held the position at the rock as we two lads ran backwards dragging the dead body of the King. Suddenly, the air went very cold even though it was late July. The screaming and shouting stopped as the light of day was replaced by a chilling blood red sun in a full eclipse of the moon.

Thousands of warriors looked up aghast at this apparition from the gods. The huscarls of the dead King took the opportunity to disengage and slip away and reform in a small huddle of less than a thousand men at the top of the hill, surrounding a cart carrying the body of King Olav II. Below, the farmers and the Jarls stood and waited as the sun slowly re-appeared to reveal the great slaughter of around four thousand dead on each side. By the rock, the King's banner flapped defiantly over the bodies of my father Sigurd and Tord Foleson surrounded by a great many dead farmers.

Harald recognised the uninjured tall warrior, Kalv Arneson who signalled to the farmers that the battle was over. 'I'll remember him!' muttered the prince.

The eclipse was clearly the work of the wolf gods, Sköll and Hati, chasing the sun and the moon and allowing Harald and I an otherwise impossible extraction of the body of the King - who was to become the Patron Saint of a Christian Norway! *Herrregud*! We buried the King just south of Nidaros by the Nidelva River. Harald had been badly wounded but had concealed it. After hiding in a farmhouse from the Jarl's men, there was nothing left for us few survivors but to head back to the safety of Novgorod and the kindness and protection of Grand Prince Yaroslav.

We told young Elisev of our story and the child just nodded and confirmed that it was indeed Sköll and Hati. The name of the farmland where we fought so hard a battle was called *Stiklestad* and this has now gone into Norse folklore as the most famous battle in Norwegian history."

The logs crackled gently as the great warrior concluded his story of his baptism of fire, in what was the most incredible saga that could never be surpassed…or so young Olaf thought.

"*Mikill Wotan*" (praise Odin) whispered Erik to break the silence of this awesome chronicle by Ødger. He had had no idea of his fame.

Ålov had been stirring during this amazing tale and now announced to the travellers:

"Do you have any idea how bad you three actually smell in my beautiful house? Luckily, I have had some Finnish visitors who have built me a sauna. It has been lit for some hours and the stones are hot and the room full of steam. Go and wash and get clean."

The three bathed in ice-cold water and entered the wooden hut of nearly boiling steam from the stones to cleanse their travel-worn bodies, through sweat pores, to emerge glowing and ready for the deepest of sleeps.

*Skōll, Viking Wolf God*

## *Chapter Seven:*
## *Nidaros*

The sun rose invitingly the next morning as the three travellers, now decidedly more fragrant, set off in the direction of Ulsberg. They bade their hostess a grateful and fond farewell and ambled along the path. The going was much smoother now with the worst of the mountainous and rocky scenery away to the Southwest behind them. Olaf hardly noticed as his head was still full of the incredible tale he had listened to last night. He was thinking that the young girl in Novgorod was now the Queen of King Harald and he would be meeting her in just a few days.

At Ulsberg they hooked up with the ferryman who took them and their mounts over the surging Orkla river. A long ride to the Soknedal valley followed and a night stop before setting off again on the final leg of the journey to Nidaros.

Olaf had expected the Kongsgård at Nidaros to be a spectacular palace. When they arrived, the whole town appeared to be more like a barracks with warriors everywhere and blacksmiths, farriers, fletchers, and armourers, all hard at work, creating everything that was needed for an invading army. Two soldiers approached, carrying spears, whilst two more covered them with bows from a distance and Ødger signalled for them to stop. A large Huscarl ran up with a roar and extended arms:

"Ødger Sköll! By the Wounds of Christ and Hammer of Thor! Put those spears up and replace those arrows before Ødger Sköll turns them into kindling and you into dog meat! This is the King's most trusted huscarl who protected King Harald at the great battle of Stiklestad when they were just boys. It was they who saved the body of Saint Olav!" The soldiers crossed themselves and, after mumbling apologies and bowing, melted into the distance.

"Is this the Bear-Slayer who is called Slagbjørn?"

"Bear fighter," replied Erik. "The bear had just killed my eldest son and had gravely wounded my second son and, although I had wounded the beast with my axe, it had just knocked me senseless and I would have been killed had it not been for my helmet and the accuracy of my youngest son, Olaf, with his bow."

Olaf gasped in amazement and Ødger stared in wide-eyed incredulity.

"How could you possibly know?" said Olaf, "You were not conscious."

"Ålfgerd, the village Lech, had inspected the body of the bear, before they cut it up, and noticed a single arrow wound in the bear's throat. He told me at the wake after the boys' funeral."

"I am Finn Arneson, the younger brother of Jarl Kalv Arnesson who helped to kill Olav at Stiklestad. It's a very dangerous name to have at this court. We have all made up now and Harald might be a hard ruler but he doesn't bare grudges."

"You hope!" said Ødger laughing and they all laughed but Finn not quite as easily as the others.

"Come now, King Harald has asked to see you the moment you arrive."

The party of four made their way to a covered wooden bridge which was the only way across the *Nidelva* (River Nid) which surrounds Nidaros and into the centre where the *Kongsgård* stood impressively against the setting autumnal sunshine.

Olaf was still aghast at his Father's confession and barely noticed the fabulously crafted bridge, the largest in all of Norway. Soon the horses came to a stop and Finn, who was on foot, signalled for a lad to come over and secure them whilst they slid out of their saddles.

Ødger put his arm on Erik's shoulder and looked him squarely in the eyes:

"You really should have told me, you know. You saved my life at that brawl in Otta and for that I thank you. But here we have no secrets. You are Erik Slagbjørn and you are the slayer of bears come to fight for Harald Hardråda, isn't that right Finn?"

There was a slight menace in Ødger's voice that had Finn Arneson nodding enthusiastically: "Oh, yes quite so. Now, let me announce you to the King."

Entering the Great Mead Hall of the King of Norway was quite unlike the hall of Jarl Halvar of Innlandet back in Dombås. That had been populated by wealthy merchants and their wives and the walls were covered with fine furs and tapestries. There was banter and humour and a sense of relaxed opulence. Here, however there was no trace of finery or soft living. Here, there was a tension as if everyone was acutely aware that they were in the presence of the most feared warrior in Europe.

Aware that at the top end of the hall sat a man who had slain twelve men at the Battle of Stiklestad, aged only fifteen, who had served Yaroslav the Wise as commander of the elite Byzantine Varangian Guard, campaigned from Jerusalem to Sicily, had blinded Michael V of Constantinople and had returned to Norway with a vast fortune and the daughter of Jaroslav as his wife. This man was a force of nature and his mead hall was full of powerful men with grim aspects. Olaf tried hard not to catch anyone's eye but, instead, looked around at the shields and weapons and animal heads that served as decoration.

Finn Arneson walked on ahead through the body of warriors to the far end where a small group of people were seated on carved thrones. Some warriors called out: *"Hej, Ødger Sköll, velkommen hjem!"* and he would nod in their direction. Finn stopped ten feet before the steps of the platform that contained the great throne of King Harald III which was lit with flickering lights from suspended Byzantine lanterns. On his right were three other smaller thrones and another single throne on his left.

All were occupied by women, the three on the right appeared to be dressed in silks and what Olaf thought to be 'foreign costume' with the elder lady wearing a 'coif', a white cotton cap that covered her head whilst the other two younger ladies had long, brown, flowing hair. On the other side of the King sat a tall upright lady dressed in conventional Scandinavian costume with a long single plait lying forward over her right shoulder. Olaf was at once struck with how she resembled Freya back at his home village of Dalby. All this he had taken in at a glance and was just awaiting the formal announcements of their names to the King when Harald suddenly jumped up with a roar:

*"Nej, Faen!* Ødger you great *drittsek* (shitbag)!" and leapt off the platform to wrestle with his boyhood friend. Olaf watched astonished as these two massive Vikings locked each other in bear hugs that would have crushed a normal man and the rafters resounded to their basso laughter. A great cheer went up from the warriors in the hall and all formalities were ignored as Ødger introduced Erik to Harald who administered a hearty royal slap over the shoulder. Olaf, who had always considered his father to

be a giant, was amazed to notice that the King was the tallest man there.

"You'll do well here Erik Slagbjørn but we don't have much time to get you fit as we are going to Denmark to teach that *rævhøl* Sweyn Estridsson who the real king is".

Olaf burst out laughing at hearing the King of Denmark described as an a-hole and it was then that Harald noticed him:

"And who is this pretty pixie who barely comes up to my sword-belt? This hall is for huscarls and royalty. Which are you?" Harald's face had darkened to one of mock menace.

'This is Olaf, son of Erik," intervened Ødger. "We brought him with us as he has a great talent with a bow and we need archers."

"How old are you boy?" Harald raised one eyebrow as the other was battle scarred.

"S-s-seventeen Your Grace."

"S-s-seventeen, eh? said Harald, mimicking Olaf's stammer. "Well, I think you can stay here and train as an archer-huscarl when you turn eighteen. My ladies will look after you as your father will be leaving for Denmark with the army in a few weeks."

Olaf had been aware of some giggling from the platform.

"Finn, take Ødger and Erik to show them their quarters and if they are not up to standard, they may take yours!" The hall erupted into laughter. It was clear that Harald did not like this man but this was as nothing compared with the hatred that he bore his elder brother, Kalv Arneson. Ødger and Erik made stiff bows and followed Finn out of the hall.

Olaf felt a huge arm around his shoulder as Harald guided him up the steps and onto the carpeted platform. Olaf had not seen a carpet before and marvelled at its luxury.

"You like my carpet, young Olaf? I took it from the Emperor of Byzantium; Michael V. I also took his eyes!" Harald laughed at the look of horror on Olaf's face who was remembering the warning words of the Ålderman of Dombås.

"This is Elisiv of Kiev, Queen of Norway whom I have known since she was six. She will tell you what you are thinking, what you will think and whether you will live or die. She didn't want to marry me but I had plundered palace exchequers on the deaths of three emperors and the wealth I brought back to my future father-in-law, Yaroslav of Kievan Rus, persuaded him. We now have two lovely daughters about your age. You may befriend them but if you once forget that they are royal princesses ready to be married to kings, I will cut off whatever part of you caused the offence, are we clear?"

Olaf nodded rapidly and, although the girls tried to cover their giggling with silk veils, their eyes glistened with tears of mirth. Olaf bowed to the Queen who said in a low voice:

"There is much to discuss Olaf, son of Slagbjørn, as you have a long future."

"This is my oldest, my first born, Ingergerd. How old are you, Inge?"

"I am seventeen *Far*, you know that. I was born while you shared the throne of Norway with King Magnus."

She spoke with authority and not a little hauteur and clearly was unimpressed at being introduced to a travel-stained, untitled, short Norwegian as a 'play-friend'. Olaf tried his most winning smile which was not reciprocated.

"Ahem, and this is my younger daughter, Maria."

"I am given to Eystein Orre and we are betrothed. He is the best of men but is the brother of the Queen Consort seated there," and she cast her eyes over to the tall Scandinavian lady sat on the other side of the King's throne. "Mother does not approve of the match."

"And over here," said the King, hastily stepping in to prevent Princess Maria from spilling any further royal secrets, "is my beautiful consort, Tora and mother of my young son, Magnus."

"Unfortunately, my young son inherited my husband's warlike features and not your gentle beauty," she smiled, and her eyes twinkled a mischievous blue wink at Olaf, whose heart skipped a beat at the resemblance of this older woman to his lovely Freyer.

"Right," said the King, "that's all done now, show him where he can sleep and keep his things and we'll see you back here for dinner."

"The stables?" suggested Ingegard.

"Pigsty more like!" added Maria and they both agreed and enjoyed their little amusement.

"Daughters!" The frail figure of Queen Elisiv stood with a white wand in her hand which she pointed at them. "When your father was just fifteen, he arrived at our family palace in Novgorod, dirty, tired, wounded and with no means at all. Your *morfar* (grandfather), Grand Prince Yaroslav, took him in and cared for him and he repaid my father with many years of loyal service. I think you both need to start behaving like princesses and show some courtesy and hospitality to a boy who has come here to serve your father. Now go and sort out his lodgings! Olaf go with them."

Olaf followed the two girls, who had been soundly chastened, to a corridor and a pleasant room with a bed, a bowl and a jug.

"See you at dinner? Said Olaf hopefully.

"Men only, oink oink!" and they both walked away making pig noises and laughing.

Olaf lay on his bed, utterly exhausted, thinking of Freyer, but also of the elegant Tora. Soon he was sound asleep.

## *Chapter Eight:*
## *A Testing Time for Olaf*

Olaf had slept for about two hours when there was a knock and the door opened to reveal the dark features of Elisiv.

"I'm sorry to wake you young Olaf, and I know how tired you must be, but the King has commanded that you attend the dinner next to your father and the King's closest friend, Ødger. I am sorry for the terrible manners of my daughters who have not yet learnt to behave like princesses but rather as spoilt brats. I have spoken with the spirits and they told me of your coming. There is a destiny for you which I cannot yet read but it involves the King that is and a King who is not yet, but is to be. Please get up and attend your father in the Great Hall."

Olaf arrived at the hall which was full of warriors all roughly the same size and build as Eric and Ødger. Finally, Olaf spotted the huge figure of Harald in the throng. Everyone was standing and drinking but Harald was a head above the others in height. Olaf pushed through the heavily built wall of testosterone and there, in a respectful clearing for the King, were his father and Ødger, clearly the favoured guests of the evening. Erik spotted his son approaching:

"Olaf, there you are! The King has heard from Ødger your feats with the bow back in the village and he would like to see you do this for him again here. Please go and fetch your bow."

Olaf always had a little of the gregarious show-off about him and agreed willingly, not understanding the dangerous path that Fate was leading him down. He thought it would win him the respect of the veteran huscarls and in that, he was not wrong. A short while later, Olaf was pushing his way again through the throng but this time with his bow and quiver of fine arrows given to him by Ødger at Dombås. Harald and his party ascended the platform and the loud conversation became subdued as they all sensed that something was about to be announced.

"Huscarls of Nidaros!" boomed the voice of King Harald. "Today we are pleased to welcome our brother in arms, Ødger 'Sköll' Hakonsson who has returned with a formidable warrior from Lillehammer, Erik 'Slagbjørn' Ohlsson." A huge cheer rent the air and a drumming of dagger butts on the tables started up.

"But!" the King's arms were raised for silence and the noise was swiftly quelled. "But" he continued, "there is a bonus in that he has brought another great warrior into our hall tonight." Harald signalled to Olaf to stand beside him and a great roar of laughter went up.

"Who is this *sansordinn*?" Shouted one. A few laughed but most realised at once that such an insult would mean fighting the boy's father, or even Ødger and the hilarity was at once subdued.

"Oh good!", said the King, "we have a volunteer. The insult you have just thrown at our guest in our hall is so severe that he has the right to kill you without any recriminations. But you shall have a fair chance. He is but a boy and, I hear, a good archer. You will have eighty paces between you and the arrow. He will have but one shot and, if he misses, then the quarrel is settled. You may have your shield and your helmet. Take him!"

Two large Vikings seized the miscreant and marched him to the back of the hall. They then released him to take up a defensive stance. He held his shield just up to the level of the nose-guard on his helmet. There was virtually no target but the legs. Olaf strung his bow, fuming with rage at the insult made against him by a complete stranger. He felt such a strong desire for revenge, not just to hurt this man, but to kill him and silence any further insults. At this moment, Erik suddenly shouted:

"Vita eista!" The immediate instinctive reaction of the target was to lower his shield to protect his 'manhood' and, at this split second, Olaf loosed his arrow which landed exactly where he had aimed it. The stricken warrior fell sideways, already dead, with the shaft protruding from his right eye.

There was a silence in the hall following the crashing of the shield to the floor: "Herregud!" Harald whispered, "you really can use that weapon!  Well, you have cost me one of my huscarls, so you are definitely coming with us to Denmark to shoot the eye out of Sweyn Estridsson."

"I-I don't think I'm ready for battle just yet. I'm not yet eighteen."

Erik interjected: "You've shot and killed two men this week, I think you're ready to serve the King."

"Two men?" Harald laughed heartily, "why, by the time I was sixteen I had already sent twenty-two warriors to Valhalla, am I right Ødger?"

"You are, indeed, my Lord and, since our days when you commanded the Varangian Guard, I have been unable to keep count."

"Good, well there it is, Olaf I hereby appoint you as 'Huscarl', which means you are sworn to protect me, Harald III of Norway who is called 'Hardråda'. Do you so swear Olaf, son of Slagbjørn by Thor, by Odin, and by he that is called 'The Christ' and on the bones of my half-brother Saint Olav of Norway?"

"I-I do so swear!" stammered Olaf.

"So now we feast!" roared Harald and a great commotion ensued of large men trying to sit on benches whilst grabbing the legs of roasted fowl before they were even seated, thereby knocking over the benches.

Olaf's great rush of adrenalin and the undeniable thrill of the kill had left him with a powerful thirst to quench and a hunger for food and something else. He was missing Freya and his thoughts dwelt on the impossible flirtation with Harald's younger Swedish wife Tora who had so impressed him earlier. He was vividly aware of what Hardråda would do to him if he found out.

Then he suddenly remembered the words of the King concerning Queen Elisiv and her knowing what people were thinking and he desperately tried to block out any impure thoughts where the Queen Consort was concerned. He looked nervously across at the King who was loudly sharing an anecdote with Ødger and Erik. Olaf thought how happy his father looked. He was completely in his element here and had found a good friend in Ødger. Olaf was still very weary and decided it would be safe to slip away unnoticed.

Olaf was housed in the ladies' quarters rather than in the barracks with the other men. He could hear the two girls laughing in a room they shared not too far from his and their girlish laughter irritated him as he was still indignant at the insults they had directed at him for his lack of breeding. It was this, combined with the unspeakable insult from the anonymous warrior he had killed, that had caused his red mist of rage. Walking back to his lodging, he had seen the body of this man lying on a flat cart, the arrow, still there, silhouetted in the clear moonlight, its feathers pointing to the stars.

He felt no remorse but wondered at why people he didn't know or had never met were prepared to dish out words designed to give such offence which would clearly lead to violence. He had been bullied by his two brothers from an early age and by the other boys in the village. But now, having been with Freya and having shown the warriors in the mead hall that he wasn't to be trifled with, he was feeling confident within himself as a fighter and a lover. The prattle from the princesses and the thoughts in his head made sleep impossible, so he went out onto the balcony to gaze at the stars on the clearest of nights before a full October Harvest Moon, as it was October 20th. Olaf stared up with awe at the immense space above him and amused himself by trying to name the constellations and all the gods.

The brightest of these stars was Saturn, which Olaf decided was in fact *Asgard,* that housed the palaces of the gods, made of gold and silver. Up there were Odin and Frigg, Thor and Freya and many gods of harvest and gods of war. Odin's great palace of Valhalla was only for the bravest warriors who died in battle, sword in hand. 'The piece of offal lying on the cart with one eye would not be going to Valhalla', he thought to himself.

A light snow began to fall over the Kongsgård, but Olaf was lost in his thoughts about the gods. He was brought out of this by his acute sense of smell. In the very near vicinity there was the unmistakeable aroma of a scent that Olaf had recognised as strange earlier in the day. He had never encountered it before, but he recognised it immediately as the musty perfume he had noticed on the King's concubine. Spinning round, he was thrilled to see the tall, elegant figure of Tora Torbergsdatter in a shawl. Her plaited hair gleamed in the moonlight, flecked with snow.

"Ha, I knew that smell!" laughed Olaf.

"Really, is that the way to address the wife of the King? I should call you Olaf the Oaf!" She laughed naturally in a manner Olaf found attractive, unlike the spiteful sniggers of the two princesses still audible up the corridor.

"I am so sorry, my lady, please forgive my clumsiness but I have never encountered this scent before as the women in our village had no such thing."

"No, it's not something that Viking women would wear. The King brought it back for Elisiv from Constantinople. It's called Jasmine and it is from a plant from Persia. She is a Völga, in case you didn't know, and prefers to make her own concoctions so I asked her for the liquid. She was glad to give it to me. It helps conceal the hideous melange of body sweat and bad breath that I have to endure from the King at close quarters.

"Oh, I know," said Olaf, "Ødger and my father both have it."

Again, the Queen Consort laughed her attractive laugh.

"Well, soon they will be gone off to battle and then perhaps we can get to know each other better. You need protecting from the witch and her two little she-wolves."

Olaf's eyes widened as he recalled the incident in the mead hall:

"No, but I'm going too, I have to, I've been ordered by the King."

"Oh dear, what a pity, and I thought we were going to be such good friends. You'll get killed like the rest of them. Such a waste." She ran a soft hand over Olaf's cheek, "goodnight, pretty warrior." She turned and, in a moment, was gone.

Olaf had considered following after her in a moment of utter madness but he was saved by the sound of male footsteps behind him. Turning round, he saw approaching, a handsome young warrior of about twenty years whose face was a sort of male version of the lady who had just left him in that it was finely chiselled and clearly aristocratic. He had a jaunt and confidence about his bearing that Olaf sadly lacked.

"Hello", he said, smiling to reveal beautiful teeth, "and who might you be skulking about here in the ladies' quarters?"

"I might ask you the same thing!" retorted Olaf with a touch of chagrin. "I am quartered here by command of the King as I am not yet of age and was to be looked after by Queen Elisiv and Queen Consort, the Lady Tora with whom I have just been talking."

"With whom?" he mimicked. "Well, you're very high and mighty, so why haven't I seen you round here before? Tora is my big sister. I'm Eystein Orre, son of Torberg Arneson, *Lendmann* to King Harald and engaged to his daughter, Maria."

"Lendmann?" replied Olaf, without proffering his own name, "what is that?"

"Ah, I see you haven't been in Court for very long, a Lendmann is the highest rank you can achieve in the *hird,* under the King and a Jarl."

"A hird?"

"Oh, Thor's trousers! Don't you know anything? The *hird* is the King's personal retinue of professional bodyguards, huscarls!"

Olaf's expression of blank stupidity quickly changed:

"Huscarls? But I'm one of them! King Harald swore me in this evening after I was grossly insulted by some stupid oaf."

"Now don't tell me. You are not the murderous archer who just shot the eye out of one of the King's warriors? Are you the half-measure that goes by the name of Olaf, son of that massive new warrior, Slagbjørn?"

"Yes, that would be me, Olaf Ohlsson."

"Ha! The whole barrack is talking about you. Fortunately, you killed the most hated man in the hird. Everyone wants to slap you on the back. On another subject, I've come here for two reasons and that, firstly, to say goodbye to my sister before we go to Funen and, secondly to try to sleep with my fiancée, Maria, to seal our betrothal. Elisiv has given it her blessing. Just one problem though, how to get rid of Ingegard?"

"No good looking at me, said Olaf, "she hates me already and suggested I sleep in the stables."

"Ah take no notice, they just love looking down their noses at people they think are beneath them, and that means everybody. I'll tell her that we are the closest of friends and that you are in your room unable to sleep for love of her. That'll impress her."

"All right," said Olaf, "I'll go to my room."

"Thank you," said Eystein, "I'm forever in your debt."

He shuffled off in the direction of the girls' voices and Olaf returned to his room, threw some water over his face, and climbed into bed. Within minutes he was sound asleep.

Olaf awoke in the dark to realise there was something warm and soft attached to his back. He remembered that he was supposed to be waiting for the young princess and so waited for her to say something.

There was no word uttered. Instead, a slender arm turned him firmly onto his back and then took control with skilled and precision love-making for ten breathless minutes until the slim, firm body threw on a cloak and slipped out of the door without a word.

Olaf lay there trying to regain his breath. He had seen Ingergard in the King's Hall and remembered her as being young, short and a little plump. The woman who had just ridden him in a frenzy of lust and without a 'bye your leave,' was firm of body and tall like Freya, but older, a woman in her prime. Did he dream it? No, it couldn't have been, surely not Hardrada's beautiful consort. Olaf broke out into a cold sweat at the thought and it was quite a time before he was able to sleep, fearing what the morning might bring.

His room had a strange musty smell as of some exotic perfume.

The morning broke, cold, and grey and, with great reluctance, Olaf ventured from his bed to dress. Stepping cautiously out into the hall, Olaf saw a hooded figure at the far end and he made towards it. He knew from the shape and height; it could be only one person.

"Good morning, Olaf, did you sleep well?"

"Well, my Lady although it was interrupted by a pleasant dream."

"I am pleased."

The Queen Consort went on to explain how last night had fallen into place: she had arrived at her room to find a message had been delivered that the King wished her to come to his chamber. She spent some time washing and changing clothes in the hope that he might have fallen asleep by the time she got there. Passing Olaf's room, she ran into Ingergard standing outside.

The Princess said she could not go to her room as her sister and Eystein were together there and that she had been told that Olaf loved her. Tora had told her that she could stay in her chamber as she had been summoned to the King's bedchamber, but she must not go into Olaf's room. Ingegard departed to Tora's chamber.

When Tora got to the King's bedchamber, she found Harald drunk, sound asleep and snoring. Much relieved, she returned to her room but not before she had enjoyed a beautiful young man who did not stink in body and breath nor was hairier than a brown bear. She said she hoped Olaf did not mind too much the imposition of having his sleep so rudely disturbed.

"It was no great imposition, my Lady," said Olaf coyly. The Queen Consort turned and walked to her rooms and Olaf, bemused, headed toward the noise of the barracks to try to hook up with Erik and Ødger.

Tora

# Chapter Nine:
## The Dragón Ship 'Ormen'

Olaf made his way to a great throng of warriors who were, variously, either eating gröt from wooden bowls, drinking water or milk in large quantities in order to appease a raging hangover or attempting to get into their chain mail. Given that he was about half the size of most of them, finding Erik and Ødger was not that easy. A voice called out:

"Hej, Olaf!" He turned towards the sound and there, walking towards him with his easy gait, was the tall thin figure of Eystein Orre, son of Torberg Arneson, fully kitted out with expensive chain mail armour and a beautifully crafted scabbard and sword hilt that stood him out as an aristocrat in the Norse world.

"Hej!" replied Olaf, "how did it go last night?"

"Ah, a bit awkward at first but we probably need practice. Poor Ingergard was standing outside your door trying to summon the courage to enter when she got bounced by my sister and banished to her chamber for the night. Sorry about that." Olaf knew all he needed to know about being '*bounced*' by Eistein's sister:

"Nothing to be sorry about, the King told me he would cut off any part of me that ever touched his daughters, so probably all for the best."

Eystein roared with laughter:

"And he is not jesting either!  Have you noticed the state some of these warriors are in? I thought they could drink."

"Some idiot induced the King to break out the wine he had brought in from Normandy. Have you ever tried drinking beer, mead and wine at the same sitting? There are piles of puke all around the mead hall."

They both turned around to match the basso voice of Ødger Sköll accompanied by a very grey-looking Erik Slagbjørn.

"Morning, boy," croaked Erik. "You left early last night?"

"Yes *far*, I needed my bed, it was a pressing matter."

"Anyone know what we are supposed to be doing in full fighting armour at this time of the morning?" Said Erik.

"Oh yes!" replied Eystein, my future mother-in-law is Elisiv of Kiev and she knows what Hardråda is planning before he does. We are going to take boats from here to a small town in the Southern part of Viken which King Harald established as a trading post from 1048. He has great plans for it and hopes to make it a capital city. The new Kongsgård of Norway.

"Does it have a name?" asked Olaf, ever inquisitive.

"Ánslo is what the natives call it and there have been Christians there since 1000. For reasons best known to him, the King tends to call it *'Oslo'* and if you'd like to correct him, you are very welcome! He sees it as the best and closest hopping off point to wage war against his arch-rival, Sweyn Estridsson, of Denmark.

A familiar face approached with another warrior and Eystein called out:

"Good morning, uncles! This is Kalv and Finn Arneson, my father's brothers."

"Ah yes," growled Ødger, "not someone I would forget. Jarl Kalv led the army against King Olav at Stiklestad and, I am pretty sure, helped strike the fatal blows that killed Saint Olav."

Finn smiled uneasily:

"Oh, but that was thirty years ago. Since then, we have been at court in the service of King Harald and he has even taken Torberg's daughter Tora as a concubine to keep the peace between the Jarls and the King." Finn was keen to make a point, but it was clear that Ødger still brooded on that day when his father and King Olav II had been killed and the young Harald had been badly wounded.

Kalv looked at Ødger with deep suspicion and then turned on his heel with a shout:

"Finn, Eystein, let's go, we need to be somewhere else."

A messenger arrived with a note for Ødger instructing his party of Huscarls to make their way down to the long jetty at Nidaros where he was to board the Dragon Longboat belonging to Hardråda. Olaf was supplied with an extra quill of exquisite arrows and off they all marched, with the Arnesons being in the second party.

Ødger's party numbered around seventy warriors including Erik and Olaf. They reached the levy where a great host of longboats waited along the River Nid. Olaf let out an excited yell when he saw their ship:

"Odin's breeches! *Fae Faan*! It's huge!"

Ødger laughed: "Ha-ha! This is the King's ship '*Ormen*' (*the* serpent). It is the finest ship on the water. On the stem is the golden dragon-head, and on the stern a dragon-tail. The sides of the ship are gilt. There are thirty-five rowing benches. Everything on this ship is of the finest; sails, rigging, anchors and cables. When the sail is unfurled you will see it is blood red."

The huscarls moved up the gangplank and handed their shields to a sailor who attached them next to the oars on the outside, giving the ship added protection against fire arrows. Ødger stood by the gangplank to greet the King. Erik took an oar, but Olaf was sent to the stern were there were other archers.

He noticed that most of these were not Norsemen but hard-looking dark, swarthy men that Harald had invited from the Varangian Guard of Byzantium. They had strangely small curly bows made of horn that could be fired from horseback. These bows were perfect for close quarter fighting but nothing like the range of Olaf's hunting bow. Olaf smiled at them and they looked back at him with cold expressionless eyes and drooping black moustaches.

"Oh good", thought Olaf, "it's going to be a long, quiet journey."

At this moment the King strode onto the jetty, flanked by two spearmen and a cheer went up from the huscarls. Running up the gangplank he called out to Ødger:

"Take her to sea and let's get down to Oslo whilst this fine weather holds!"

The oars were dropped and the great Dragon Ship, 'Ormen' glided out of the mouth of the River Nid where its huge red sail was unfurled and the course was set for Westwards before turning South down the coast of Norway to Bergen. At Bergen there was a short stop of a few hours to allow the other ships to catch up and Olaf counted ninety-eight long boats bristling with warriors.

He had felt very sea-sick for the first part of the journey, being unused to sea-travel, unlike Erik who had made many raids as far afield as Northumberland and Ødger, who had followed Harald from Kiev to Jerusalem and from Sicily to London. But Olaf was getting his sea-legs now and the brief puke over the side as they left Nidaros was ignored by all at the rear of the ship and unnoticed by the King.

After Bergen the journey continued Eastwards around the coast of Norway until a green church spire was sighted on the shoreline and orders were given to drop the sail and row into a village that Olaf heard was called Oddennes (Kristiansand). It wasn't so much a village as a clump of farms but it afforded some good flat open terrain for the three thousand warriors to pitch camp and light fires against the very cold night that was fast approaching.

The archers seemed to have their own little clique and camped separately from the others, but Olaf wanted to re-join the familiar and comparative safety of the company of Erik and Ødger who had camped next to Harald's almost palatial war tent. An aroma of roasted meat emanated from the tent, which smelt invitingly good. Olaf approached cautiously but was immediately stopped by the two tall spearmen who had flanked the King when he boarded the ship.

"And where do you think you're going, half-portion? Are you a Danish spy? Have you been listening in to the King's battle plans?"

"N-no" said Olaf when he could get a word in edgeways. "I'm looking for my father Erik Slagbjørn and Ødger Sköll."

"They're in there," said one, gesturing with a thumb over his shoulder, with Håkon Ivarsson planning for the attack.

"What attack? I thought we were sailing up to that boatbuilding place that the King calls *Oslo*."

"What in the name of Odin is going on here!" roared a voice emanating from a huge figure standing at the entrance of the marquee and blocking out the light from the lanterns.

"I-I'm sorry to disturb you my Lord, we caught this one skulking around the King's tent listening-in to the battle plans."

"Who are you?" said the voice "and what is your business here?"

I-I'm Olaf Ohlsson, son of Erik Slagbjørn and friend of Ødger Sköll......the King knows me!" blurted Olaf in a desperate attempt to identify himself.

"Oh, he does, does he? Well, we'll just check on that and I'm afraid that if you are lying, he will have your left hand, and nothing will give him greater pleasure, I can assure you."

The two guards chuckled to each other until a barked order had them scurrying back to their posts.

Olaf was pushed into the war tent where Ødger was poring over some maps with the King whilst Erik stood a few respectful paces behind.

"Håkon, where the Hades have you been? I need you here, don't you understand, we have to get this landing right to take them completely by sur…. oh hello, Olaf, your father is just here, come in and sit down and don't say a word."

"Sire do you know this boy?"

"Well, obviously as I've just called him by name, and a better archer than any of my Byzantine Varangian Guard. Now come over here and look at this. If we sail directly into the boatmaking yard in Odense they will see our ships from miles away as they have built a tall tower or lighthouse right at the tip of the scar and they have fortified the break-water so that only one longboat can get in at a time. They will let in several boats and then raise the chains trapping and exposing them to the mercies of fire arrows. No, we must sail down the coast of the Northern peninsula on the West side and stay out of sight of the lighthouse. Then we shall reach a beautiful sandy beach which is called the Bay of Dalby. Here we can land all our ships at one go and quickly assemble a crack killing squad to run to the village of Dalby and stop anybody trying to ride to the boathouses to warn the Danes. It will be a total surprise and a massacre."

Olaf was asking to speak urgently.

"What is it?" asked the King irritably.

"You said Dalby, my Lord. Well, we come from Dalby, near Lillehammer."

"Olaf, there are three villages in Denmark, two in Norway and two in Sweden all called Dalby. But perhaps it is a good omen from the gods. Ødger, you will lead the killing party with Erik and Olaf, and thirty warriors and ten archers. Take Kalv Arneson and leave Finn and Eystein Orre with me. We shall have two shield walls when, and if, we meet any Danish resistance.

Håkon will command the first and I will take the second with Eystein. The aim is to burn the boathouses and kill their boatbuilders and then leg it back to Oslo to recoup. We then leave half the army there to protect our boathouses and build up a fleet of three hundred ships for the final blow next Summer. I shall Winter in Nidaros with my family. So, there it is, let's eat!"

Håkon Ivarsson stepped out of the tent and instructed the two guards to tell the cooks and the serving boys to bring in the food. In a moment, there was a hive of activity as meat, vegetables, fruit and öl were brought into the King's war tent and placed on a long table.

"Tell the Jarls they may now come and join us," said the King and, before long a dozen of the Norwegian nobility began to fill up the marquee. Olaf noted the young Eystein enter with his uncle Kalv Arneson but of Finn, there was no sign.

As the noblemen quenched their appetites, Eystein shouted across to Olaf:

"Hey, Olaf what are you and your father even doing here? This table is for noblemen. I call you my friend because you helped me out but I cannot understand how you and your father are getting this special treatment?"

Ødger answered the question before Olaf could speak:

"I am the King's longest surviving friend and his closest bodyguard; I have chosen Erik as my partner in battle and his son is a bonus who can use a hunting bow with more skill than anyone I have yet seen. They are here by the King's consent. You are here by an accident of birth. Do not question the wisdom of the King! Be content that you are loved by the King and do not have the loyalty issues that hang over your uncles… talking of which, where is Finn Arneson?"

"I don't know," replied Eystein. He was with us on the second longboat. I haven't seen him since."

Ødger shouted down the table:

"Kalv Arneson! Where is your brother?"

"How should I know, perhaps he is eating with his men. Am I my brother's keeper?" He shouted, quoting from the Scriptures.

The Jarls went back to their food and drink until Håkon stood up and thanked the King for his hospitality and ordered them to return to their tents and get some sleep as they would be embarking at first light.

When only Ødger, Erik and Olaf were left, Håkon bid them *'God natt'* and left to go to his own tent. Ødger approached the King who knew him well enough to know when something was wrong.

"What is it Ødger? What did I hear about Finn Arneson?"

"He is gone Sire. I have questioned the guards on watch and they report that a small fishing boat left sailing South just after darkness fell. He may be going to warn Sweyn of our attack."

Harald's huge frame stiffened and stood erect, all seven feet of him with his face dark with rage. When he spoke, he spoke with a whispered suppressed voice quivering with anger.

"Ødger, on that day at Stiklestad, when we stood shoulder to shoulder, the traitor Kalv Arneson had killed my brother, King Olav and, although I didn't see it because of the eclipse, he and a killing party took out your wounded father, Sigurd, and the wounded standard bearer, Tord Foleson.

The only reason he is still alive is because I struck a peace agreement with Torberg and married his daughter Tora, who is the niece of those *drittsekker!* If I find Finn has gone over to Sweyn Estridsson, then I command you to immediately take revenge for your father and take the sword arm of Kalv Arneson, followed by one leg and then, finally, his head. He will not make Valhalla without a sword, nor can he walk there with one leg, nor can he see with no head. I would gladly do this myself but this way I can distance myself from blame from Tora. Erik and Olaf, I want you to watch Ødger's back, and tell of this to no-one. Now go and get some sleep as we sail at first tide."

The three bowed to the King and made their way to their own bivouac where some warriors were keeping the fire going for them against the cold. Olaf lay thinking for a while that tomorrow would be his first raid, maybe his first battle. He really was feeling like a proper Viking now.

# Chapter Ten:
## *Olaf's First Battle - Odense 1061*

Olaf awoke on a chill morning, to the shill cries of seagulls hunting for breakfast. A heavy mist covered the sea which was calm – perfect raiding weather. The army had been briefed the previous evening that they were not sailing up to Oslo but instead heading Southeast towards Gothenburg and down the Kattegat Sea towards Funen and finally beaching on the sandy Bay of Dalby. It was as darkness fell that the lookouts had spotted a small fishing boat with a lantern, heading out to sea towards Denmark.

The grey mist brought a chill to the faces of the Viking warriors, but they were all in good spirits as they were about to do what Vikings love best – raiding other countries. This was especially true of Harald whose drawn-out feud with his erstwhile ally had not brought him any closer to the throne of Denmark.

Olaf wondered how they would find their way through the mist but Ødger explained the magic of '*Vegvisir*', an Icelandic staff for guiding ships through rough weather.

"But how does it work?" asked the ever-inquisitive Olaf.

"Ha! It's a mystery!"

Erik laughed, "it's true, no one knows, but it works!"

By seven o'clock, all the longboats were crashing through waves with a favourable tide and the wind at their backs. Hardrada's great Dragon Ship '*Ormen*' led the way on an eight-hour journey to the coast of Denmark through the Cat's Gate (Kattegat). Harald stood at the prow holding the neck of the serpent with his long wavy hair blowing behind him. He was never happier than when leading a raid.

By four o'clock they had reached the Northern tip of the island of Funen, which was largely uninhabited. But they lowered their sails and rowed down the peninsula lest they be spotted from the tower on the Odense scar. *Dalby Bygt* was a wide flat bay with ample room for nearly a hundred longboats to land simultaneously. Within a short period of time Harald's raiding force of around three thousand warriors had disembarked and were formed up in two parties, lines of three ranks, ready to form a shield wall at a moment's notice.

Håkon took the front while Harald and his standard formed the second. Kalv was due to join the forty-man killing group headed for Dalby village to stop and kill any riders from the village trying to warn any Danish warriors but with Finn missing Harald ordered him to stay with the King's party. Eric and thirty warriors led by Ødger headed straight to Dalby village with Olaf and the Byzantine archers running ahead. It was expected that farmers would be out in the fields, but they were empty and the cattle untended. Four archers stood on the crossroad going south to take out any riders.... but there were none.

The others, including Olaf, checked the houses and the barns. They found women and children hiding and cowering but of horses and men there was no sign. Erik and Ødger's party arrived within a few minutes, blowing hard after the run. The Byzantine archers wanted to burn all the barns but Ødger stopped them as the smoke would be seen clearly from the boathouses at Munkebo Bakke or even Odense, where all the warriors would be.

"Is it possible that Finn Arneson made it here before us in that fishing boat?" said Erik.

"Well, he did have an eleven hour start on us and I expect by now he is standing behind Sweyn Estridsson telling him all our little secrets. I'll deal with him later but right now I have some urgent business with that traitor, Kalv."

They took up a defensive position at a crossroads by a pretty village and waited for the two main battle phalanxes to catch up with them. Håkon was the first to arrive with his fifteen hundred men:

"Did any men of fighting age manage to get out of Dalby?" he called out.

"Oh, only all of them" replied Ødger. "They left about six hours ago and with all their weapons. I expect they have joined the ranks of the main army coming out of Odense."

"You need to let the King know about this right away," said Håkon.

Behind him the noise of the second phalanx announced the approach of the King's party. They came to a halt some fifty yards behind Håkon's party. In the rear were some Jarls including Eystein Orre and Kalv Arneson. Harald ordered them to move forward to guard the left flank but ordered Kalv to remain behind with the standard along with the two bodyguards, Erik and Ødger and the archers which included Olaf.

The line, now stretching out for one hundred and fifty yards, marched straight down the road towards the boathouses at Munkebo, about five miles distance. Before they had covered this ground, they could see the colourful shields of the Danish army and the glinting sun on their spear points and on their helmets.

To the rear of this line was a small body of mounted men surrounding King Sweyn Estridsson and his banner. Next to him, also mounted, was the unmistakeable red hair of Finn Arneson. The line stretched from the inland Kerteminde Fjord on the Danish right to the Boathouses on their left. They were stretched out over a thousand metres, but Harald's army knew that the flanks were occupied by untrained farmers and only the centre had professional bodyguards like the Huscarls.

Harald turned to Ødger and said:

"Well, my friend, you know what to do."

Kalv instinctively raised his shield as Ødger's left-handed axe buried itself in the wood just above Kalv's shoulder. The axe all but split his shield as he went to draw his sword with his right arm, thereby exposing his bicep to a scything swing of Ødger's sword already in his right hand. The blade bit deep and Kalv's sword arm fell limply to his side held on by a fractured bone and some bleeding gristle. Ødger withdrew the blade from the screaming Arneson and struck again in the same place.

This time both the sword and the arm fell to the ground. Arneson staggered back raising his shield in a desperate attempt to protect his head. Ødger freed his axe from the splintered wood and, dropping onto one knee, swung the weapon into the left knee of Arneson who fell onto his backside at the feet of King.

"That was for Sigurd", said Harald, "but this is for my brother, King Olav." He swung his huge sword across Arneson's shoulder, and the head rolled neatly onto the grass.

"Someone go and throw that into the Danish lines as close to Finn as you can get. Tell him he is next!"

A warrior obliged and managed to get a good long throw into the Danish line where Finn could not but have seen it. This action triggered the start of the battle as the Danish line opened to release a horseman galloping in pursuit of the running warrior and speared him fifty yards from his own line only to be hit with a hail of arrows that felled both him and his mount. Most of the archers were placed on the left of the line to stop the longer Danish line from flanking them but Olaf and a few other chosen marksmen stayed with the King and his bodyguards in the centre.

The Norse Huscarls set up a tremendous rhythm using their weapons and shields as drums and chanting "Fram, Fram!" as they marched forward in time. The Norse right flank was protected by the sea and the tactic was to swing round and try to push the Danish line into the sea.

When the shield walls crashed together, the Byzantine archers, with great skill, fanned out on their left and did terrible damage to the lightly armoured bønder (peasants) armed only with spears, axes and pitchforks. In the centre the three-rank Norse wall was having a good effect on Sweyn's two- rank opposition and they were starting to be pushed round to the boathouses and the sea. Every so often, a horn would sound and the Norse wall would suddenly open allowing a killing party of Håkon, Ødger, Erik and some of the King's most impressively huge Huscarls, all carrying the great double-handed war axe, to smash a hole in the Danish line. Olaf and the other archers would then loose a flurry of killing shafts at the unprotected warriors who would fall, and their places be taken by warriors whose shields were still intact.

After two hours and much carnage, the Danes had formed a defensive semi-circular perimeter protecting the boat houses but losing the advantage of numbers. Harald's line was clearly gaining the upper hand and was now close enough to loose fire arrows at the Northern-most boathouse. The light was fading fast when a breathless runner approached Harald. He was one of the boys left behind to look after their ships. He told Harald that about twenty Danish ships had attacked them at their moorings and that, although those that had landed had been killed, he believed they were waiting to be reinforced as they had no idea how few had been left behind to guard the ships.

Harald swore every oath he knew and ordered a tactical withdrawal lest he be fighting on two fronts. This was done in a wedge-shaped formation with the archers and the warriors on the tips of the V turning and running back to the Dalby Bay. But it was dark now and the Danes did not pursue as most of them were just relieved to be leaning on their swords and panting in the knowledge that they had somehow escaped certain defeat.

The main army reached the bay in incredible time given they had just fought a battle. The archers were lined up along the beach with torches in the sand and the Danish ships appeared to have not received the reinforcements they were expecting. Hardråda, ran onto his Dragon boat with his seventy warriors and the others pushed the boat into water deep enough to row. With great skill the boat turned round to face the Danes and he sailed straight into the middle of them. *Ormen* crashed into two Danish vessels, smashing their oars, as archers poured fire-arrows into the rowers. Clamps fixed the two boats either side and Harald's men leapt into these, still very much in battle mode.

The Danes were sailors, not warriors and many of them were slaughtered or jumped overboard. The boats were set on fire and the sky was lit up for Sweyn's army to see. The remainder turned and fled behind the scar and the breakwater of the Odense Fjord. Harald's huge fleet of ninety-eight vessels lit their lanterns and followed their King through the night back to Oddennes (Kristiansand).

The great fleet arrived back in Norway as the sun was rising and, after a short stopover, they made their way up into the long fjord of Ànslo or what, by now, everyone had thought it wisest to call 'Oslo' rather than correct the King. Here, a great new town was being developed and a boatyard to rival the Danish one in Odense was already being built. Harald was determined to make this the new Capital of Norway.

## *Chapter Eleven:*
## *Olaf Winters in His Village of Dalby*

The King declared the raid a great victory and further declared there should be feasting in Oslo before everyone was paid and laid off for the Winter to return to their homes.

They would be recalled and prepared for the great final battle with Sweyn in the Spring or Summer when his fleet of three hundred ships would be ready for the last deciding match against the Danish king. Erik wished to return to Nidaros with Ødger and remain at the King's side. They would return on the great ship *'Ormen',* but Olaf requested that he be allowed to return to Lillehammer and the outlying village of Dalby where he was hoping that Freya would still be waiting for him with their unborn child.

The journey from Oslo to Lillehammer was surprisingly uncomplicated. It was a day and a half to Minnesund and from there he could travel by boat up the huge lake of Mjøsa and a distance of roughly one hundred and eighty miles to Lillehammer. Olaf had been well paid by Harald who had seen him fight at Odense and swore him to return to either Oslo or Nidaros by May at the latest when the snows had melted. So off Olaf set, having bid farewell to his father and Ødger and Eystein who were all staying with Harald. Erik was concerned for Olaf travelling alone but, as Olaf pointed out, he was no longer a boy but a *huscarl* with one battle and many kills under his belt - and soon to be a father. Olaf hired a guide and a horse and was soon at the edge of the massive lake where the guide left him and took back the horse to

Oslo. The boat Olaf took was a cross between a passenger ferry and a fishing boat, catching copious amounts of trout whilst dropping off travellers along the way.

After many hours on this rather uncomfortable vessel, the pilot announced that they would be stopping at Lillehammer within the next hour. Olaf began to feel an excitement in his stomach at the thought of seeing Freya again. He hired an ambling Icelandic mount from the horse trader and set off up the hill to his village. It was late afternoon; it was cold and wet and the going was slow. Finally, he began to smell the burning logs and see the lanterns of his home. But there was no one there to greet him as no one knew he was coming so, instead, he made for the ölbod and tied up his horse.

On entering he suffered flashbacks of that last Summer when he should have been looking after his brother Magnus but instead chose to leave him to go with Freya. The hall was full, with most of the villagers there to keep warm, eat and drink. Nobody looked up from their conversations and stories and Olaf was again ignored. Then Leif, the Ålderman spotted him and called out:

"Stranger, come over here and announce yourself if it is our hospitality you are seeking!"

Olaf was not the pretty boy who had left, half a year before, but rather leaner, his first beard beginning to show and an expression of a grim hardened fighter who has fought at the side of Harald Hardråda. His hair was flecked with mud as were his clothes and he smelt of horse and fish so that the dogs in the hall took an interest in him.

"I am Olaf Ohlsson, son of Erik 'Slagbjørn' Ohlsson, Huscarl to King Harald III and a native of this village of Dalby!" he announced in the swaggering style he had learnt from Eystein Orre.

"Oy Herregud!" shouted the Ålderman. "Olaf? Is it really you?"

Everyone stopped talking and the name Olaf was whispered in disbelief.

"Yes, it is me", said Olaf, "and before you ask, Erik Slagbjørn is not dead but has returned to Nidaros with the large Huscarl named Ødger Sköll as they are now the King's most trusted bodyguards. We fought a great battle in Denmark, but we were betrayed so we lost the surprise and had to withdraw without burning down the Danish boathouses in Odense. I can only stay here until the Winter has passed then I must return as I am also now sworn-in as a huscarl to the King".

There was much chatter and laughter with everyone not quite believing the incredible change that had taken place in Olaf. There was tremendous envy from the village boys his age for whom absolutely nothing of interest had happened since Olaf and Eric had left. One of the boys had run off to fetch Ålfgerd who was in his longhouse with Freya. When they entered the hall, a great cheer went up. Olaf dropped his things and ran at her to take her in his arms but she stepped back, stopping him with her outstretched arms.

"Be careful Olaf!" she shouted and it was at that moment Olaf realised that Freya was over six months pregnant and his face lit up with joy both at the sight of her condition and the fact of seeing her again. She looked radiantly maternal and Olaf could not resist going on tip toes to kiss her on the mouth.

"Olaf you smell of fish! Have you become a fisherman, or did you come here by fishing boat?" Olaf confirmed the latter and Freya laughed and took him out of the hall and into her hut where she prepared a large tub of hot water where Olaf was able to wash away several weeks of travel and climb into a change of clothes.

Ålfgerd was outside shouting for them to return to the mead hall as the elders had summoned the whole village to the ölbod to celebrate the return of the conquering hero. Olaf thought how much things had changed in their attitude towards him!

The feast went on through the night with Olaf the centre of attention having to tell of his adventures in every detail, which he did, although perhaps not *every* detail! At last, Freya said that she needed to sleep, and Olaf took that as a good excuse to take his leave. On returning to their small quarters which Ålfgerd had built for them, Freya stoked the fire and poured Olaf a flask of Mead and beckoned him to sit on the bed.

"Well, look at you," she said. "A proper little Viking!"

"Huscarl" corrected Olaf.

"Ah yes, huscarl. A warrior in the pay and service of the King at his beck and call. When are you commanded to return?"

"Not until the Winter melts, so around April or May when I'm needed to return to Nidaros, but I'll not go overland again, I'll travel down to Oslo and then take a longboat up to the capital where Erik and Ødger are with the King."

Freya nodded: "So did you kill lots of people and was there lots of rape and pillage?"

"I killed a man who was stealing my horse and I killed a man who greatly offended me in front of the King. In the battle at Odense, I don't know how many I killed – maybe ten?"

Freya's eyes widened in disbelief.

"And as for rape," continued Olaf, "well, there was one occasion."

"Oh no!" Freya put the back of her hand to her mouth, "I was joking, did the warriors rape you?"

Olaf laughed, "Not likely after they saw what happened to a warrior who made an offensive remark about my personal behaviour. No, this happened in the sleeping quarters at Nidaros when a woman climbed into my bed while I was asleep and took her pleasure of me and then left without a word."

"And you didn't resist?"

"Of course not, I thought I was dreaming and that it was you. She was so very like you only about ten years older. When I realised, I was not dreaming, I guessed who this person was as she wears a distinctive perfume."

"So, who was it?" Freya was intrigued.

"It was Tora Torbergsdatter, daughter of one of the most powerful Jarls in Norway and Queen Consort to the most ferocious killer in Europe. She is the mother of Magnus, Harald's son. If the King ever finds out he will chop me into very small pieces and feed me to his dogs."

"Oy, Herregud Olaf! are you insane! What if she is with child – your child?"

"Satan! The gods would not be so cruel, surely?"

"It has nothing whatsoever to do with the gods, trust me, I'm a doctor. What colour eyes and hair does the King have?"

"Err, I think his eyes are green and his hair is straight and long and a reddish brown and his eyebrows are a reddish blond."

"Well, you'll just have to hope that his next child does not have pale blue eyes and curly blond locks!"

They talked for a while further before curling up under a fur as the fire glowed warm against the howling wind outside. Many miles away a wolf was calling for his pack. Olaf sent up a prayer to the wolf-gods Sköll and Hati.

*Yuletide in Dalby*

# Chapter Twelve:
## Juletid (Yuletide) In Dalby

Life in the village of Dalby resumed along its uneventful way, but for the fact that Freya had imparted some shocking news to Olaf. He hadn't mentioned to her about his episode with Ulli, the buxom serving girl at Otta, but she had taken the scene with Tora remarkably calmly but for the danger to his life should Hardråda ever get word. Freya's great unveiling of her plans hit Olaf like a rock from a trebuchet.

She said that, much as she was very fond of him, she had no intention of being a traditional Viking wife who sits at home waiting in vain for his return, not knowing if he has been killed or captured or has taken another wife overseas. She revealed that a wealthy merchant from Lillehammer, whose wife had died childless, had taken a great interest in her and was prepared to adopt the baby and give them a safe home in his impressive longhouse across the lake.

Olaf was rocked by this news but gradually was able to understand her reasoning. He knew how much he missed the great travels and adventures he had enjoyed and was longing to return to the huscarls of Nidaros. This way, Freya and his son (as he was sure it would be) would be provided for. The merchant was almost her father's age but was of a kindly disposition who longed for the sound of young voices in his large and empty home. He would pass long before Freya and she would be free to marry again if she wished but with his fortune securely hers. Olaf marvelled at her scheming but couldn't fault the fact that her plans were for the safety and security of her and her baby.

"Shall I move back into Erik's hut then?" said Olaf sulkily.

"I think that would be best. The bed is no longer big enough for the three of us," she said resting her hands on her very distended tummy. I'll get a gang of girls in the village to help you clear it out as Erik left it in a terrible mess."

Of helpers there was no shortage and practically all the girls between sixteen and twenty were eager to help the good-looking hero to put his house in order.

As the time of the solstice was approaching and the snow lay thick on the ground, the girls decorated Olaf's hut as for the Season of Yule. Olaf cut down a fir tree and dragged it into the hut where the girls' made wreaths of mistletoe and winter flowers.

Mistletoe was of almost mythical importance in the Norse culture as it involved Balder, the god of light, who had been slain by an arrow of mistletoe. Just as Christians had their Easter resurrection, which Olav II had taught to the people of Norway around the coastal towns, those living in the inland dwellings still clung to their traditional pagan gods. Mistletoe represented the tears of the mother turning the berries red and bringing about the resurrection of Balder and looking forward to the end of Winter. Likewise, the tree in Olaf's hut was decorated by the girls with images of the gods and baked biscuits to please the tree spirits in the forest to wake up and bring about Spring.

As the Romans had introduced Saturnalia to Europe and the Vikings had celebrated solstice on December 25th, the Christian festival of Christmas and the pagan traditions all interwove neatly, but in Olaf's village there was, as yet, no Infant King. In the mead hall the Yule Festival was celebrated with feasting and drinking and singing of songs and telling of stories.

The Yule wreaths made by the girls were taken outside and set alight before being rolled down the hill in an effort to tempt the Sun to return to melt the snow. Erik was most missed at this time as it was he who always dressed up as 'Old Man Winter' with his white beard and hooded fur coat, his cart being pulled by two goats. He represented Odin and would hand out gifts, usually of wooden objects, carved with great skill by himself. In the hall, a great yew tree lay in the middle of the revellers, burning for many days. This was the Yule Log which had been dragged in and carved with runes to protect the village from any evil spirits. Olaf was as popular as ever as he had been out hunting and had managed to bag two wild boar with his bow so that spiced ham was served, as per the custom at this time, with öl and mjörd in abundance.

The story of Erik and the great bear-god was retold with great elaboration by those who were not there and Olaf, the only one who actually was there, was completely written out of the myth. Olaf caught Ålfgerd's eye who smiled and winked at him knowing the true story. Olaf smiled back with sad eyes, as Freya was seated next to her father and Olaf sat apart.

And so it was that the Festival of Yule was celebrated with all its pagan customs and the village waited patiently for the coming of Spring and the return of longer days. It was mid-February when Olaf received a messenger who said that he should come to Ålfgerd's longhouse right away. On approaching he heard screams that he knew to be from Freya. Breaking into a run he arrived just in time to be witness to the miracle of childbirth.

Ålfgerd, the skilled doctor, aided by the ample Hertha Blåtand (who had birthed more calves than you could shake a stick at) acting as midwife, had completed a perfect delivery of a baby boy. Freya, whose beautiful long hair was now matted with sweat, cradled the little pink baby in a shawl as Hertha dabbed her brow with a wet cloth. Olaf gazed at the exhausted but peaceful face of Freya. She opened her eyes and smiled at Olaf:

"Say hello to Olaf, your son. I have named him after you so we will never forget you. I have also prayed to Odin that he grows taller than you!"

Olaf laughed with the others and took the baby with its eyes still closed, gently in his arms with tears streaming down his face. He had never seen anything quite so beautiful.

In the coming months, Olaf visited Freya every day and watched the baby develop. First, his eyes opening to reveal the bluest of spheres, then faint blonde curls appearing and his grip on Olaf's little finger becoming ever stronger.

The weather that Winter of 1061 was hideous, but Olaf kept the village supplied with fresh meat and Hertha kept them supplied with fresh milk from her cows sheltering from the cold. Olaf could not contain his curiosity and one day, when it had stopped snowing for a while, he took a journey down to Lillehammer and enquired after a Bjarke Kjøpmann (the merchant). He was directed to a longhouse which appeared to be the largest in the town. Olaf banged on the door and a plump lady of middle years answered.

"Are you the wife of Bjarke the merchant?" asked Olaf without introducing himself.

"I am the house-keeper, and who might you be?"

"Err, I am Olaf Ohlsson and I should like to speak with Bjarke."

"I'll see if he's available, wait here please." She closed the door and left Olaf waiting in the hall where a small fire was lit. After a few moments she returned and ushered Olaf into a long room, richly furnished and with a large fire at the far end. In a carved chair a man was struggling to get to his feet with the aid of a cane.

"Ah, you are Olaf? Welcome! I expected a huscarl to be a huge warrior but you seem quite civilised. Please sit down."

Olaf sat opposite and was at once struck by the opulence of this man, his fine boots, clothes and fur. His face was as one who has lived life well and Olaf put him in his late fifties, but he did not look healthy.

"I have heard about you from Ålfgerd and his daughter Freya. They have been visiting me as I have not been well. Ålfgerd says it is my heart and I must stop drinking mead."

The housekeeper appeared with a tray and two goblets.

Bjarke's jowls shook with mirth: "well that's very unlikely to happen! But, on a serious note, I have asked Freya if she would like to come and live with me. Ålfgerd will visit me often as my doctor so she will still see him. She has a child now who she says is yours but you cannot or will not marry her because you are in service to the King.

I therefore propose that they both reside here in peace and comfort. I will marry her and she will live in Lillehammer as an honest woman. When the gods call my time she and her child will inherit as I have no children or surviving relatives. Is that fair?"

"More than fair," replied Olaf.

"She is a sweet creature, and more than that, she is a skilled nurse, so I do very well from the bargain."

Olaf and Bjarke talked for nearly an hour, by which time he was convinced that Bjarke was a good man and Freya had made a shrewd choice, if for all the wrong reasons. The snow had begun to fall again, and Olaf announced that he needed to be getting back before the track disappeared under the snow and he would get lost and be eaten by wolves! Olaf made his way back up the hill to the village content that Freya and son of Olaf would be comfortable and taken care of.

The Winter months passed slowly but at last the snow turned to rain and the sun began to make more regular appearances until small white flowers pushed through the thinning snow. Olaf said his farewells to Freya and baby Olaf as the whole village turned out to wave him goodbye. Some of the girls who had helped decorate Olaf's hut began to cry, but from Freya there were no tears.

On arriving in Lillehammer, the first thing Olaf noticed with relief was that the ice on the great lake Mjøsa had all but melted and he was clear to make the journey South to Minnesund. At Minnesund he hired a horse and made the twelve-hour journey down to Oslo. On arrival, he reported in and was allocated quarters where he could bathe and rest ready for the sea-voyage up to Nidaros

The following day, Olaf inspected the boathouses and to his amazement saw that work had gone on unabated throughout the Winter. There were literally dozens of new longboats being made and the small, scattered houses of the village were now joined up into a thriving new town. The harbour was full of vessels and the whole place was a scene of thriving activity. When Olaf enquired how many days, he must wait to take a boat to Nidaros, he was told that at least three left every day.

And so it was, in the Spring of 1062, that Olaf the huscarl-archer boarded a Viking longboat via Bergen, for his two-day journey to the court of Harald Hardråda with the news for Erik that he was now a grandfather.

## *Chapter Thirteen:*
## *Olaf Meets Astrid – Return to Nidaros*

The journey to Nidaros was slow as the weather was really poor and the sea extremely rough. At Bergen they put into port as the storm was in danger of breaking the ship apart. Olaf was very relieved to be on dry land again and went with several huscarls to the town's ölbod to dry out and grab a drink and some food.

Another buxom serving girl, in the mould of Ulli, brought them some bread, smoked fish and öl goblets which she filled from a goat's skin. Olaf smiled at her and the smile was returned with interest. Olaf thought at once of Ulli back in Otta.

"What news from the Kongsgård in Nidaros?" shouted one huscarl at the girl.

"We don't hear much down here but there is talk that the King is building an even bigger fleet as he wants another battle with Denmark. I don't see the point, especially as the Queen's going to be having a baby. He needs to stay at home and be a father."

Olaf started and spilt his beer: "Which Queen?"

The serving girl put her head on one side: "Well, the new one, obviously, the one from Kiev has passed the time for giving birth."

"Is this a recent event?" asked Olaf hopefully.

"Well, the rumour is that Queen Elisiv has declared that the baby was conceived during the time when King Harald was away fighting the Danes. Apparently, the King is very suspicious and is giving Queen Tora a terrible time and likewise any men known to the Queen who were not on that raid."

"Oh, well that lets me out then," Olaf managed a nervous laugh.

The three huscarls roared with laughter: "You? Ha! I think with the Queen surrounded by all those huge warriors you would be the very last person she would choose."

"Ha-ha, yes you're absolutely right," said Olaf with a sigh of relief.

"Well, I think you are very good-looking, if a bit on the short side," the barmaid was giving Olaf that intense 'I choose you' look that Olaf had seen before. "And if I wanted to sleep with a great hairy, smelly, brown bear then I would go out into the forest and find one!"

Everyone laughed this time and she topped up their mugs of öl.

"What's your name?" asked Olaf, starting to become intrigued.

"Astrid….it means 'beautiful goddess' in case you hadn't noticed. Will you boys be looking for a room for tonight?" One of the huscarls replied: "The pilot won't be going out again tonight or until that storm has abated, so 'yes' is the short answer."

"Well, you'll have to share, I can put three of you big smelly ones in the large room and the little one here can have my sister's room as she is away with my mother visiting our grandmother and my father has been enlisted by Håkon Ivarsson to make up the numbers for King Harald's big battle in the Summer".

They continued with their supper and Astrid left them to their banter, which centred around Olaf's attraction to other women, something Olaf was keen to discourage lest the subject of Queen Tora should resurrect itself.

It had been a long day and they had taken an exhausting battering from the storm so that it wasn't long before the warriors began to yawn and stretch.  Astrid re-appeared to clear the plates: "Would you boys want a sauna before you turn in?"

Olaf jumped up: "Have you got one?"

"We get loads of Finns and Lapps coming through here to trade. We had to build one as they kept complaining. It's out the back and its lit. Towels are inside."

The three big burly men and one much smaller one left their clothes and weapons by the back door and stood naked in the pouring rain outside a pine hut for about five minutes and then entered the hut lit by a small lantern. Olaf, the last one in, picked up the ladle from a bucket of water and threw it on the stones so that a great blanket of hot steam hit the warriors seated on the bench. Olaf laughed as they shouted in surprise.

It was their first sauna. After another session in the rain and then a final warm up in the sauna, the warriors picked up their clothes and weapons and headed upstairs laughing at this new cleansing experience. Astrid showed Olaf to a small room with a small single bed. Everywhere the walls were painted with flowers.

"I have to lock up now but if you need anything just knock on the wall as I am just next door."

Olaf, who just had a towel around him from the sauna, slipped, with tingling skin, under the fur and very quickly fell asleep.

Some while later Olaf awoke to hear the latch on his door lift gently and a curvy figure in a white gown slipped in beside him.

"Hej!" she said and giggled.

"Oh no, not again," sighed Olaf.

The next morning Olaf woke to the loud voices of the warriors down the hall. Astrid had left in the night to return to her own room and was now downstairs making up the fires and preparing the gröt, bread and milk for their breakfasts. The rain had stopped and the storm had passed.

In the cold light of day, Astrid was still attractive and bubbly as she attended to her guests. But her face fell as the pilot, who had slept in the boat with the other sailors, appeared and chivvied them to get going in order to catch the tide. The warriors had slept soundly after the sauna but now the *lemmer og kyss* (hugs and kisses) that Astrid was bestowing upon Olaf were a total give-away.

"We'll tell your father when we see him!" they all laughed but they paid her generously in coin for her hospitality. Olaf broke away finally and, with a sheepish smile he waved her goodbye and ran for the longboat.

"*Skynd deg elsker gutt!*" (Hurry up, lover boy!) shouted the huscarls and Olaf clambered aboard as the first oars hit the water.

The remainder of the journey was uneventful and then the pilot turned East past all the many hundreds of small islands and inlets and finally into the great fjørd of Nidaros (Trondheim fjord). It had been a further two days on the journey but the stop at Bergen had been very pleasant.

The huscarls disembarked and made their way to the barrack area to report. Olaf had only one thing on his mind, he had to speak with Queen Tora. He made his way to the palace and then to the ladies' quarters where he hoped he might still have a room. Two spearmen stood guard outside but they recognised Olaf and let him through with the remark:

"Careful who you talk to in there, it's all a bit tense."

Olaf was going to go straight to Queen Tora's chamber, but this remark quickly brought him to his senses. His room was still vacant, so he moved in and dumped his belongings and his bow onto the bed. He needed time to think.

After resting for a while, Olaf went for a walk to clear his head. A soldier came running up to him breathless: "Are you Olaf the archer, son of Slagbjørn?"

"Yes, I am Olaf, huscarl-archer to King Harald," he replied formally.

Oh! Thank the gods, I've been searching for you since your ship docked. The King had asked to see you the moment you arrived. He's not a man to be kept waiting."

"Faen!" said Olaf, "Did he seem angry to you?"

"The King is always angry these days. It has been a long Winter and we have all worked very hard trying to get his army and his ships ready. It's best not to catch his eye."

Olaf followed the breathless soldier at the trot to the Great Hall and up to the platform where the King sat alone with two large hunting dogs and two spearmen standing behind him. The other thrones stood empty and there was no sign of Ødger, Erik or his general, Håkon Ivarsson. Olaf felt his heart pounding and fear in his stomach. Then Olaf noticed a dark figure in the shadows wearing Byzantine costume. Olaf stood and waited.

Harald stood up with arms outstretched:

"Where have you been *mitt lille fjelltroll* (my little mountain troll)? Welcome back!"

The foot soldier looked astonished having never seen the King in a good humour.

"Come here Olaf, we need you here with us. It is nearly time to complete our final battle against Sweyn Estridsson but you are the critical chess-piece. I want you to meet Urbicus Acropolites. He commanded my left flank at the battle of Odense and caused great damage to those bønder that Sweyen had arrayed against me. This time we will all be on boats and the archers will be crucial. I want you and Urbicus and the other Byzantine archers to train up at least two hundred more archers for my ships. You have two months before we leave."

Olaf was thinking the same as Urbicus, that it takes years to master a bow and to try to train two hundred conscripted men of the land was a very tall order.

He was, however so delighted with the fact that Hardråda was not going to feed him to his dogs that he agreed enthusiastically. He remembered Urbicus from the sea voyage to the island of Funen but, whereas before, his gaze was met with an icy scowl, it was now met with a smile of mutual respect as between two professional warriors. Urbicus bowed and left the hall leaving Harald and Olaf alone with the two dogs and two spearmen.

If Olaf thought he was out of the pan he was wrong. Harald sat back down again and spoke softly but without any perceptible menace: "Olaf, we have a problem and it's of a personal nature. I don't quite understand it either. How many times have you met my daughter, Ingegard?"

Olaf could reply with honesty: "Just the once with you and Queen Elisiv."

"And in that time did you do or say anything to make her believe that you had feelings for her?"

"On the contrary, Majesty, I was the butt of their unkind jokes regarding pigsties, and I was a little offended, but Queen Elisiv apologised for their behaviour."

"Ah yes, I think I remember. It was just before we sailed. So why does she think that you are in love with her?"

"Ah, I think I can explain, Majesty, it was a deception by Jarl Eystein to get to Princess Maria as he wanted to see her alone before we sailed to Funen."

And where did Ingegard go that night?"

"I could not say, Majesty, I did not see her."

"Tora says Ingergard slept with her in her chamber. So, Olaf, you are in the clear, which is just as well. I need Ingergard to marry an Olaf but certainly not you. I mean Olaf, son of that dog Sweyn Estridsson, to join our nations so that my family will rule Norway and Denmark whether we win or lose the battle. Olaf, you are free to go but understand that Ingergard must not be touched by anyone on pain of death. Am I clear?"

"Very clear, Majesty."

Olaf bowed and left the hall. His heart was beating, he had broken out into a cold sweat, but the King suspected nothing.

Stepping out into the Spring sunshine, Olaf made his way to the barracks where Erik and Ødger were trying to train the bønder the skills of a shield wall.

"Hej, store kriger! (Hi, big warrior!), what news? Am I a grandfather yet?"

Olaf sized up the huge frame of Eric, who had lost a lot of weight but now was more like Ødger where muscle had replaced the fat of his previous alcoholic lifestyle. He and Ødger could easily be brothers, they looked so alike.

"Hej, Far or rather Morfar. (*Father or rather Grandfather*) Freya has had a beautiful strong son who she wanted to call Olaf!"

"Oy Herregud! Too many Olafs," growled Erik.

Ødger came and joined them as Olaf explained how Freya was going to live with a rich merchant in Lillehammer and Erik furrowed his brow.

"Is that what you want, boy?"

"It's what she wants and it makes good sense as I won't be there to take care of her and the baby."

Ødger butted in: "Come now Erik, let's finish with these *gårds hender* (farm hands) and get on with wetting the baby's head. Eystein, put up your sword, you won't teach anymore to these *pløyere* (ploughmen) today. Olaf's had a baby boy! We're going to the kriger ølbod (warriors' beerhall) to thank Odin for Olav's new son."

Eystein Orre sheathed his sword: "Skål for deg! (Cheers to you!). You can count me in. Are these bønder really going to fight on our side? They'll just get in the way!"

The two young warriors and the two great veterans made their way into the smoky and rowdy mead hall set aside for the huscarls. Ødger roared the news that Erik has a grandson rather than that Olaf had fathered a son and a great cheer went up with serving girls appearing with trays of *øl og mjød.*

Back in the village of Dalby, Freya made her way with baby Olaf and her meagre belongings on a cart with Ålfgerd leading the horse on the three-mile journey to the lake and ferry at Lillehammer. On arriving, they made their way to the centre of the town to the longhouse of Bjarke Kjopmann. It was Friday or *Fredag* meaning Freya's Day, on this occasion, both the goddess and the bride.

Freyer's golden hair had been skilfully plaited by her girlfriends in the village and a lovely *blomsterkrans* placed on top. A crowd of people stood outside the long house and clapped as she arrived. The *blomsterkrans* was carefully removed. Normally, a bride would wear a *krans,* a small gilt wreath worn by Norse girls as a symbol of their virginity but, as that ship had already sailed, she wore a flower wreath instead. Bjarke came out of the house with the aid of a stick with a beaming smile on his chubby face.

Freya climbed down from the cart and Bjarke placed a gleaming silver crown where the flowers had been. The town Völga placed the rings on each of their fingers and then pulled out a long knife and turned to the unfortunate goat tied up behind – a sacrifice to Odin was outmoded but still practised in Lillehammer. Bjarke turned and quickly led Freya into the house where a long table had been set and beautifully decorated.

The guests followed in behind Ålfgerd, who was carrying the baby and handed the bundle over to the housekeeper. At the top end of the table was a beautifully crafted *barneseng* (rocking crib) filled with furs. Into this young Olaf was placed and quickly fell asleep amidst the reassuring hubbub. The guests stood and raised their goblets to Bjarke and Freya with a great shout of "Skål!" Freya was now a married lady of Lillehammer.

At the same time away in Nidaros, Olaf was getting incredibly drunk and trying to explain to an equally drunk Eystein how his uncle's head was missing from its body and discovered behind the

Danish shield wall as they retreated before the Norsemen to the boathouses. It was going to be a long night.

Staggering back to his room late, and even in the condition he was in, Olaf recognised a familiar smell. It was Jasmine and he knew without a doubt that she either had been there very recently or she was still in the vicinity. Olaf went to the balcony, where he had stood before, gazing up at the Harvest Moon. It was now Spring, and the stars were shrouded in low clouds so that it was quite dark. Sure enough, as Olaf had guessed, a tall, hooded figure appeared behind his left shoulder.

"Hello Olaf, I heard that you were back, but it seems that you have been celebrating." The fumes from an inebriated Olaf hadn't gone unnoticed.

"I hear you are with child?" said Olaf coming straight to the point.

"Yes," said Tora quietly, "I told the King that it was conceived that night before you all went to fight King Sweyn. He was so drunk he wouldn't know. But then that *heks*, Queen Elisiv, put her hand on my stomach and declared that it was conceived in the King's absence. The child is ours Olaf without a doubt. She is, of course wrong in the date but she knows something is not right. If the child is born beautiful with blue eyes and golden hair you will need to be out of the country…. shhh! Who is there?"

A shrouded figure moved quickly from the shadows and away down the hall. The figure was small but even in the darkness Olaf could make out a white coif as worn on the head of Elisaveta of Kiev. Tora slipped silently away and Olaf likewise but not quite so silently as his shoulders kept hitting the wooden walls as he sought to steady himself.

## *Chapter Fourteen:*
## *The Battle of Niså - August 1062*

Olaf woke with a thumping head and the shocking realisation that all his worst nightmares were coming to fruition. If Queen Elisiv had heard Tora's whispered words he was as good as dead. And if Tora was right about the golden-haired blue-eyed baby he was as good as dead. Olaf thought the only decent plan was to die in battle. But the battle wasn't scheduled for another two months. Olaf felt bitter that Tora had put her wanting a beautiful baby, that did not look like the rough and fiercely ugly Harald, above her own safety and what was much worse, *his* safety.

Olaf decided the best way to avoid attention was to do nothing.

Each morning, he would rise early and meet with the trainee bowmen. To his surprise some of them were quite used to a hunting bow and progressed quickly whilst the Byzantines under Urbicus learnt the art of sea warfare as an archer. Not a day went past when he didn't expect a messenger from the King to summon him to attend an inquest followed by a horrible death. But the weeks passed quickly and, on the few occasions that he saw the two Princesses, Ingegard and Maria, he would just nod politely in the form of a bow and move swiftly on. Ingergard would gaze at him, expecting some look or glance of affection or confirmation of what Eystein had said to her, but Olaf was giving nothing away.

The time for the final battle arranged between King Harald Hardråda of Norway and King Sweyn Estridsson of Denmark was fast approaching. Harald had three hundred ships but only half his fighting men were full time professional huscarls.

Sweyn had about the same number of ships and men but many more were not seasoned professionals. The ensuing battle was evenly poised but Harald was confident and had no time for anything other than his battle plans with Håkon Ivarsson, his chosen general.

It was mid-July and Tora was due anytime soon. She sent for Olaf to visit her and dismissed her maids. She explained that on their return he must say that he was visiting Lillehammer as would be allowed after a battle.

In reality, he must flee to England, and she gave him letters of introduction in Northumberland and also in the Orkneys in a sealed leather pouch which chinked with the sound of heavy gold coins.

Half the great fleet were waiting down in the shipyards of Oslo and the other half were ready to sail from Nidaros with the forces of Trøndelag that Ødger, Erik, Olaf and Urbicus Acropolitis had been training for the past two months. The great Dragon Ship *Ormen* led the fleet of one hundred and fifty longboats out of Nidaros and down through the islands of the Norwegian coast.

Pausing at Bergen to take on more supplies and fresh water, no one was allowed off. Olaf thought of Astrid, whose father must be in one of those ships behind, though he never found out who he was.

The fleet sailed around the coast of Norway and back up the long fjord into the new town of Oslo. The town was absolutely bustling with as many ships and warriors again, the greater part being professional huscarls. The order to disembark and make camp was given.

This was a huge undertaking of some ten and a half thousand men. The weather was warm and the mosquitos not as bad as in Olaf's village surrounded by forest. There was swimming and fitness training during the day as well as battle-craft and close quarter fighting in the confined space of a long boat.

"Why do we not just attack them?" Olaf asked Ødger one hot afternoon. "Surely, we are as ready as we will ever be?"

"Ah, I asked Håkon Ivarsson the same question. It appears the two kings have been sending each other messages and have decided that this is all going to be organised at an appointed place and time and on an appointed day. That day being 9th August at the mouth of the Niså River on the Swedish side down the Kattegat."

"Jarl Håkon is a good man to have on our side," said Olaf.

Ødger growled, "He has a habit of changing allegiances as the wind blows. He used to work for Sweyn Estridsson, you know, who gave him land and titles and he repays him by captaining Harald's army against his former boss."

The two weeks went quickly and on August the 8th the order went out to have everything prepared to sail. The night was clear, and the waters were calm as the fleet slipped out of Oslo at around midnight.

The tide was with them and by eleven o'clock next morning, they were off the coast of the settlement of Göteborg and heading South towards Halland, a Danish province which bordered onto the coastal waters of Kattegat. By two o'clock the Norwegian fleet had arrived at the mouth of the Niså River where Harald formed his ships to face out to meet the Danish fleet sailing from Odense.

His own great *drekkin* (dragonship) 'Ormen' he placed in the centre.

Harald waited and scoured the horizon for any sign of the Danish fleet. Three hours passed and still no sign. Harald was storming up and down decks roaring every colourful description of the King of Denmark that he could think of, much to the amusement of the warriors on board who laughed and cheered the fouler the inventive insults heaped upon Sweyn Estridsson became. Finally, the King shouted an order:

"Those miserable cowards are not coming. We had an agreement to settle this thing once and for all. Right! All ships not containing huscarls, or professional warriors are to return to Oslo where you will be paid. All huscarls and warriors will raid the shores of Denmark until we have looted the equal sum of the cost of this voyage, and maybe more."

Half the fleet containing a relieved force of *bønderkrigere* (farmer-soldiers) set off North towards Norway, happy to be able to return to their farms alive, to bring in the harvest for their families. The huscarls watched them go in silence:

"They would only have got in the way," muttered Ødger.

"What's to do now?" said Erik, "the King's not happy, so don't catch his eye!"

In that Erik was not mistaken. He waited until the farmers had sailed out of sight then, just as he was about to order the fleet to set sail, a lookout called from the top of the mast.

"Sails approaching from the Southeast!"

Harald looked across: "*Satan!*" The whole of the horizon was now filled with square sails as the three hundred Danish longboats, who had watched the departure of half of Hardråda's fleet, were now descending on the Niså Estuary. They were just one hundred and fifty ships but containing some of the fiercest and experienced warriors in Europe.

"Time to go Sire?" asked Håken Ivarsson.

"*Fy Faen*! I'm not running from that *Drittstøvel*. Fasten the boats together, no gaps. Archers in the centre. Håken, you take Erik and Ødger and watch the flanks with your Trøndelag thugs and make sure they don't get round us. Olaf, you stay in the centre with Eystein and Urbicus and his dark murderers."

Because the Niså was not that wide, Sweyn was obliged to shorten his line considerably so that his fleet was now three ranks deep. He had appointed Finn Arneson, the traitor to Harald, as his Captain but kept him close in the centre. When Sweyn saw that Harald had bound his ships together, he decided to adopt the same tactic, so that when he collided with Harald's fleet, they would create a floating platform where his superior numbers would tell, after a time.

At first there was a stand-off with the two armies firing arrows at each other to no great effect so that after about an hour Sweyn got his rowers to row his fleet into the Norwegian ships where they crashed together, and a floating land battle ensued. The sun was beginning to dip now and soon it would be dark. The superior fighting quality of Harald's huscarls was matched by the superior numbers of Sweyn's forces.

There appeared to be no advantage on either side, except that, whilst Sweyn's archers were targeting the armoured and shielded Norwegian warriors, Urbicus with his Byzantines and Olaf with his newly trained archers were targeting the unprotected Danish archers and with great effect.

Olaf was picking them off almost at will until those who remained lost heart and fled to the third rank of ships and hid. The rain of Danish arrows had all but stopped and every time an archer appeared on a Danish deck, he was hit with a hail of arrows from Hardråda's ship. But the deadlock continued until something quite inspired occurred.

Håkon, who was protecting the right flank, disengaged his large ship from the main body and rowed around the Danish flank and engaged a number of smaller ships guarding Sweyn's left flank. These ships were no match for that which came at them containing Håkon, the two huge figures of Ødger and Erik and three hundred of the largest and most experienced huscarls in Hardråda's force. The small boats managed to pull away, leaving the whole of Sweyn's flank exposed to a side-on attack. Håkon pulled alongside the first of the ships and piled in with Ødger and Erik either side.

Within fifteen minutes the ship had been cleared with the occupants either dead or swimming for the shore. This tactic was repeated to even greater effect as they moved to the next ship and the next in the near darkness.

The second and third ranks could just see the devastation on their left flank and determined to untie themselves from this withering attack. Some fifty boats from the front line had been cleared and there was no stopping a force of three hundred each time it boarded a ship containing around seventy. The river was crowded with bodies and Danes trying to swim to the banks. The ships in the centre were engaged with Harald's centre and, by now were aware of their second and third row disengaging and pulling out of the fight.

Eystein had seen, just before the light faded, the great work that Håkon had done in demolishing Sweyn's left flank and put his own similar action into effect on Sweyn's right. Some seventy ships were emptied in total, nearly a third of the Danish fleet, with the others sailing away as fast as they could. Håkon's group of warriors were making faster progress than Eystein's which was just as well otherwise Eystein would have come up against Finn Arneson, his uncle. As it was, it was Håkon who came up against Finn behind a shield wall fending off Hardråda's men in front.

Finn was aware that Håkon's group would be attacking from the side of the ship tied next to them and all but Håkon and Erik were engaged with the enemy in emptying out the boat next to Sweyn and Finn in the centre. Finn made a huge, desperate swing at Håkon, which was parried and held. Erik bought the edge of his shield down on Finn's wrist with such force that he broke the bone and the sword clattered to the floor.

The other warriors around Finn threw their swords down in capitulation as they were now completely surrounded. Sweyn had taken off his crown-helmet and replaced it with one from the body of one of his warriors and was trying to jump overboard. It was to no avail as Håkon recognised him and shouted to Erik to grab him. Sweyn nearly made it to the edge but suddenly felt a massive and powerful hand grab the back of his cloak and jerk him off his feet.

He landed next to Finn on the floor where Håkon and a number of others, who had now cleared the previous boat, were guarding those who had surrendered. Ødger appeared, panting, to say that the previous boat was now secure with its warriors dead, swimming or surrendered. At this Håkon, strangely, ordered Ødger and Erik to stay put while he dragged King Sweyn across the whole line of empty boats, talking to him all the time. Ødger was shocked when Håkon returned alone.

"Where is the Danish King? Did you execute him?"

"No, he is swimming right now without his cloak. I've done a deal. He will make peace with Hardråda now. Neither of them can afford this senseless war any longer and when Ingegard marries

Sweyn's idiot son Olaf Estridsson, Hardråda's grandson will be King of Denmark. It makes diplomatic sense."

Ødger shook his head doubtfully. He had known Harald a long time and he didn't imagine for a minute he would see it that way. Not when he had Sweyn within his grasp.

The battle of Niså concluded by torchlight and burning ships. Because of the darkness, many of the Danes were able to either sail away or slip over the side and swim for the shore. It was, clearly, a great Norwegian victory and Håkon Ivarsson was heralded as the great hero of the battle because of his decisive flanking move. Håkon explained that they had Finn captive, but that Sweyn had got away. Harald seemed exhausted and nodded with irritation that they hadn't got the Danish King, but Finn was some consolation. They slept in rotation on their ships whilst the others watched the prisoners and waited for the sunrise.

# The Battle of Niså 9th August 1062

## *Chapter Fifteen:*
## *Return to Bergen and Astrid*

The sun rose bright and clear on August 10th, 1062, over the estuary of the Niså River. The water was still infused with the blood of so many warriors floating lifelessly or, more often, sunk by the weight of their armour. But for the carnage, it was a beautiful morning at five o'clock and the King ordered the fleet to sail out into the Kattegat and head North to Oslo and home.

Harald was content that he had Finn Arneson captive and in much pain with a broken wrist but could not quite understand how Sweyn had managed to slip away when he was, quite clearly, surrounded. Ødger knew of course but chose to keep this gem of information to himself until they reached Nidaros and Håkon, who was the hero of the day, had had a chance to explain his actions to the King.

The Norwegian warriors put their captives as hostages back into their own long boats and towed those in seaworthy condition back with them to Norway. Harald's fleet of one hundred and fifty ships now grew to two hundred with the captured enemy vessels plus the hundred and fifty ships he had sent back to Norway.

The waters were calm and after a day and a night they reached the port of Bergen. They made a two hour stop and some of the warriors who lived there disembarked. One such warrior was a man of middle years who possessed neither proper armour nor a sword. He had received a leg wound from an arrow and was using his somewhat rustic axe to help him walk.

"You're no huscarl," Olaf put to him, "why didn't you leave with the other *bønderkriegere*?"

"I tried to," replied the wounded man, "I was used to relay a message to Håkon Ivarsson and, when I tried to return to my boat, I saw that they had already left. At least now I can get back to my ølbod in Bergen and get my leg seen to. My daughter, Astrid, is quite skilled with healing herbs, and she'll see to it that this wound is properly cleaned and bandaged."

"Astrid?" said Olaf. "You have a daughter called Astrid?" The man nodded. "Curvaceous and with reddish hair who works at the ølbod in Bergen?"

"Oh, do you know her then? She's, my daughter!"

Håkon shouted across to hurry up and get the wounded men off so they could load fresh water and supplies. The King was impatient to move off as he had heard the word from a messenger that Queen Tora had recently given birth to a baby boy but, at just seven pounds, was surprisingly small given the fact that his father was one of the largest men in Europe. Olaf needed no further prompting:

"I'm going to help this injured man back to his home. Don't wait, I'll come over on one of the boats behind us when I've got him safely with his nurse-daughter in town."

"Come and see me when you get back Olaf," shouted Erik, "we'll celebrate in the *Krieger Ølbod*."

Olaf marvelled at being addressed by his own name by Erik. He always called him 'Boy' or something derogatory like 'Liten

Øl' (small beer). He had finally earned his father's respect and he felt good about it.

"So, what do they call you," asked Olaf.

"I am Anders, and my inn is called 'Andershus'."

"Oh yes we sheltered there during a violent storm and Astrid looked after us very well, we even had use of your fine sauna."

"And what do they call you?" said Anders as he hobbled painfully, leaning on Olaf's shoulder.

*"Olaf den kjekke!"*

Anders roared with laughter: "and who calls you 'Olaf the Handsome' then?"

"Astrid does!"

There was silence. Then Anders let out another roar of laughter followed by a howl of pain as his wounded leg touched the ground. "Steady!" advised Olaf. "Sit here on the jetty and I'll see if I can sort out a cart to take us."

Olaf returned with a cart and a mangey-looking donkey and its equally mangey owner.

"Hej, Anders! You're back then?" shouted the mangey owner.

Anders scowled: "All the folk in Bergen and you have to come back with the town idiot. Hello, Aksel. How much to take me to my inn?"

"Just a full goblet of mjørd and a kiss from Astrid!"

"You can have the mjørd but we have enough injured people here right now without you trying to kiss Astrid. She would throw you out of the window without opening it!  Olaf I'm alright with this fool; you can make it back to your ship now. Thank you for your kindness."

As he spoke, there was a great splash as seventy oars hit the water and a creaking as the great dragon-ship 'Ormen' turned and headed out to sea.

*"For sent! du har gått glipp av båten!"* (Too late, you have missed the boat) shrieked Aksel hysterically, and began dancing crazily, almost overcome with mirth.

"You are very welcome to shoot him in the leg Olaf. I promise you; it really hurts."

"I was hoping to stay at your inn tonight if you have a room. I can pay. I need a good strong ship to take me to Northumberland in the morning."

"Let's go and ask Astrid. *Aksel! Dra i det jævla eselet for Tors skyld!* "* (Aksel, pull that bloody donkey, for Thor's sake!).

They arrived at Andershus to be greeted by Astrid, absolutely delighted that her father had returned, albeit wounded, but alive. More than that, she was absolutely thrilled to see he was being helped by Olaf, whom she was sure she would never see again. Unfortunately, all the rooms were taken but Astrid assured Olaf that that was not any kind of a problem once she had sorted out her father's wound and given him a draught to make him sleep. Olaf was hoping for a good night's rest after the long voyage, the late-night battle and the journey back. Astrid had very different ideas as she blew out the candle in her white nightshirt with a giggle that he remembered well.

"Not again!" sighed Olaf.

# *Chapter Sixteen:*
# *Olaf and Astrid Sail to Orkney*

The morning dawned bright and clear in Bergen and a sleepy Olaf awoke to find that, once again, Astrid was up and about her chores: lighting the sauna, baking the bread, making the grøt and collecting the milk from the *'melkepike'*. Astrid had also washed Olaf's clothes whilst he was in the sauna that morning. They dried quickly by the sauna stones and soon he was able to emerge for breakfast outside in the morning sunshine.

"How is Anders?" asked Olaf

"He is in some pain. He asks that you go and say goodbye to him before you go. He wishes to thank you. My Stepmother and my sister are coming back today, and I don't want to be here when they get back. They treat me like their servant, someone who just works here. They can look after my father. Can I come with you, Olaf?"

Olaf's eyes widened in astonishment.

"I don't know where you are going but I can look after you, I can cook for you and sew and take care of you in so many different ways!"

"Ah!" said Olaf with a distinct lack of enthusiasm. "I'm afraid I'm going across the sea. I have a letter of introduction to the cousin of Queen Tora to Thorfinn Sigurdsson, who is Jarl of Orkney. He is to help me get down to Northumberland and enter service with either Edwin, Jarl of Mercia or his brother, Morcar.

But Tora says I should seek service with a powerful Jarl in the South called Godwin, Jarl of Wessex once I have a command of their language.”

“Earl,” said Astrid, “in England they are called ‘Earls’, I have had many Saxon and Viking ex-patriots stay here and I have picked up quite a lot of their language. I can be of use to you.. take me with you?”

A call came from upstairs: “Astrid! Am I to die up here? Come and change my bandage and bring that small huscarl with you.”

Olaf followed Astrid who bustled up the wooden stairs clutching some clean bandages. When she was done, Anders sat up:

“Astrid, I couldn’t help hearing your conversation just now. I think Olaf is a very lucky man to have won your affection. Olaf, my wife is not Astrid’s mother, and they really don’t get on. If Astrid wishes to go with you, I will miss her terribly, but it will save me the cost of a wedding with all my terrible Christian neighbours eating me out of house and home and the strife between daughter and stepmother will end and there will be peace in this house.” He leant to a cupboard by the bed and lifted out a heavy leather bag and rattled it so the coinage chinked.

“Better to spend this on each other than my gluttonous neighbours. Take this with you to England and send word when you are settled and have children and perhaps, I will come and visit. Now, go before your terrible stepmother returns.”

“Thank you *far!* Thank you!” As she leant forward to kiss her father’s forehead there was a crash downstairs. The door had been kicked open by a man carrying a lot of bags. Behind him was a large lady holding the hand of a small child.

"Astrid!! Where are you? Come down here and give this oaf a hand with the bags and pay him a single *Harald-mynt.*"

"But we agreed three," whined the overloaded cart driver.

Astrid pulled Olaf with her down the stairs with orders to fetch his bow and quiver. When he returned with his few belongings, the heated conversation was brought promptly to an end by Astrid, who opened the door, pushed Olaf through it and shouted up the stairs, "Goodbye *far!*" and then, very quietly, "Goodbye mother, goodbye little sister, we are going to see the Jarl of Orkney."

On closing the door behind them, Olaf could hear a bellow of "Anders!", almost drowning out the remonstrances of the cart-driver: "But we agreed three!"

Returning to the jetty, ships from the battle were still docking and leaving, a day later. Olaf asked each ship if any were headed to the Earldom of Orkney.

After a few hours, a ship pulled in and declared that their onward journey was, indeed to Northumberland, via Orkney.

And so it was, on 12th August 1062, that Olaf, son of Slagbjørn, boarded a sizeable longboat, carrying his bow, a pouch of gold coin, letters of introduction, and an unexpected self-appointed fiancé who was so excited she could not stop talking to everyone about Olaf's business. This was the last thing Olaf wanted, who wished to travel fast and light and as inconspicuously as possible.

The oars crashed into the water and the boat set a course for *Skalpafloi* (Scapa Flow) some thirty-six hours away.

# Chapter Seventeen:
# Dubious Company

Considering it was August, it was pretty choppy, and the salty spray was cold and harsh against their cheeks. Olaf huddled up with his newfound bedwarmer under a fur provided by the sailors. After an endless day and a half of being thrown about, the cry of '*land fremover!*' (Land ahoy!) finally went up and the small group of islands '*Orknøene*' appeared on the horizon.

Within half an hour the oars were back in action and the sail was furled. The longboat slipped silently into a thriving fishing port which the crew referred to as Kirkjuvagr (Kirkwall), the second capital of the Orkney Isles. Finally, the longboat was tied up and they were able to disembark and stretch their legs, although the jetty itself appeared to be still moving. Some soldiers stood idly by, leaning on their spears, and watching with indifference as the ship unloaded its cargo.

"We are looking to find the Jarl Thorfinn. Where might we find him?" The two soldiers peered down at the bedraggled pair.

"Well, you won't find him here. He's up North in his palace called Birsay, it's about six or seven miles. You can hire someone to take you there if you've any coin."

"We certainly have, *Hardrada-mynt*" chirruped Astrid.

"*Shsssst! Vaer stille!*" hissed Olaf. Alone in a strange land that is the last piece of information you would wish people to know.

The two lanky guards perked up at this news:

"For just four pieces, we can get you a cart and driver and we can ride escort behind you to make sure you don't get robbed by brigands. There's a few Scots on the island and they are not to be trusted - cut your throat soon as look at you."

Every instinct told Olaf not to trust them but too late, Astrid spoke:

"But that's a marvellous idea, yes please, we'll do that."

Olaf's eyes narrowed as he took stock of these two 'bodyguards'.

"So do you work for Thorfinn Sigurdsson?" asked Olaf. He needed to know a bit more about these two.

"Well not exactly," answered the shorter of the two. He seemed to do all the talking and had a very curious accent. Not Nordic at all.

"We've been in the pay of Mac Bethad, King of Alba – 'Macbeth' in your language. He was killed a few years back at the Battle of Lumphanan (1057) by forces loyal to the present King, Malcolm III. Some of us fled here to the Orkneys to escape any retribution and though we help out, we don't work for the Viking, Earl Thorfinn."

The tall thin soldier had slipped away during this exchange but soon returned with a shady-looking cart driver. He was a hunchback with greasy black hair and a large, hooked nose. He was ugly in a way Olaf had never seen in Norway. He took an immediate dislike and mistrust of this character which reinforced his mistrust of the two soldiers. He could smell trouble. Of any of this, Astrid remained oblivious and bubbly.

"Oh, look Olaf, we've got transport and an escort!" She climbed onto the cart, pulling Olaf by the hand who steadied himself with his bow. Astrid pulled out her heavy leather pouch of coins, but Olaf prevented her and spoke quietly:

"Not until the job is done."

The two soldiers had procured mounts from somewhere, two worn-out spavined creatures. Both horses looked unequal to the task of a twelve-mile round journey and the nag pulling the cart was in no better condition.

The small group left the quayside and shortly the clopping of hooves on cobbles was replaced by the dull thud of grass as they moved into open ground. There was a track which was marked 'Old Finstown Way' but, apart from that, it was just open country with a biting wind blowing in from Iceland to the Southwest.

Astrid could not contain her excitement at this adventure and gabbled non-stop at the cart-driver who looked ahead and not once acknowledged that she was speaking to him. Olaf had been scouring the treeline on the left side for any sign of movement but now turned his attention to the rear.

"Astrid Look!"

Astrid turned around to look at where the two riders had been following at a distance of some fifty yards. There was no sign of them. Instinctively, Olaf slid the bow from his shoulder, placed an arrow on the string and a second in his belt. Astrid tugged at his arm and pointed to the copse on the left where there was movement in the bushes and between the clump of trees.

"We need to go faster!" Olaf shouted to the driver and Astrid translated into English, to which he replied with a Gaelic curse which neither of them understood. A loud shout went up and a group of five men with broadswords emerged from the trees. The fact that the wind was behind the attackers and the dye they used to colour their tunics yellow was from horse urine, made them very difficult to miss. Olaf loosed a shaft that knocked one of the Picts clean off his feet.

The four survivors stopped in their tracks as the body on the grass twitched in his death-throes. They quickly retreated back to the comparative safety of the copse. The silence was disturbed by a dull thumping as the two riders desperately whipped their reluctant horses to charge at the cart with lances couched and lowered for the kill. Olaf strung the second arrow and loosed it in a moment.

As he felt over his shoulder for his quiver, a boney, but steely strong arm grabbed him by the throat and stifled any air to his lungs. Olaf struggled, eyes bulging, knowing he had only a very short time before he would pass out or be run through by the on-coming lance fifty yards away.

Suddenly, the cart driver gasped, loosened his vice-like grip on Olaf's throat and, emitting a Gaelic oath, fell from the wooden bench, clutching his bleeding side, to stain the grass below. Olaf hadn't time to think but managed to string a third arrow and aim it at the surviving rider.

In the second before release, he managed to focus on the look of horror in the eyes of the smaller, more talkative of the two soldiers. The arrow struck just below the left shoulder with enough force, at such close range, to pierce the tunic and the left atrium of the heart. The rider fell backwards over the back of the horse which, deprived of its unwanted passenger, immediately slowed to a gentle walk towards the cart. Olaf swung round to see Astrid holding out his hunting knife with two fingers as far from her body as she could reach as blood dripped from it.

"I don't want his horrible blood all over my clothes if I'm going to meet the Jarl of Orkney," she said with an expression of disgust.

"Where did you get my hunting knife from?"

"In its scabbard where you left it. Well, I wasn't going to let that filthy cart driver mess up my little Olaf now, was I?" She smiled her most seductive smile and Olaf melted for a few seconds before being distracted by shouting from the copse.

"All right laddie, ye'v won fair and square. Leave us one of the horses and we'll noo trouble ye nor the lassie agin, ye'v ma worrrd on it."

"You'll not get far on that broken-winded creature!" shouted Astrid.

"We're noo gonna ride the poor beastie. We're gonna eat it. We're starving oot here!"

Olaf tied the one horse to the cart and, with a flick of the reins, spurred on the carthorse leaving the other nag to its unfortunate fate as it stood oblivious, chewing on some mossy grass with four dead bodies scattered randomly around.

## *Chapter Eighteen:*
## *Hospitality of the Jarl of Orkney*

The cart bumped along the pathway towards Finstown for almost an hour with neither of them saying a word. Olaf was deep in thought and was mightily impressed at how Astrid had composed herself in a crisis. He had been very reluctant to have her tagging along as he held firmly to the view that she would get in the way and slow him down. He had to admit to himself that, far from slowing him down, she had most definitely saved his life.

He tugged at the reins and the horse came to a halt. He turned to Astrid who had been brooding on the fact that she had just killed a man. Olaf kissed her cheek and put his arms around her in a warm hug of affection and whispered his thanks in her ear. Astrid blushed prettily and was about to kiss Olaf in return when a shout came across the landscape and the horse tied to the back of the cart threw his head up with a nervous whinny.

Two riders were approaching from a distance carrying spears and helmeted just like the two Olaf had brought down an hour ago. Olaf passed the reins to Astrid and jumped onto terra firma, bow in one hand and his left arm reaching across his chest instinctively to produce an arrow from over his shoulder. One of the riders held up the palm of his hand but Olaf did not lower his bow.

"Keep away from us!" shouted Astrid in Norse.

The reply came back in the same language: "Vi er ikke røvere, vi er Jarlsmenn!" (We are not robbers; we are the Earls men).

"Don't trust them, shoot them off their saddles!" was Astrid's undiplomatic advice. But Olaf had eased off the draw although the arrow remained strung.

"I can't be shooting the Jarl's men when we've come here to ask his favour," came Olaf's well-reasoned reply.

When the two riders were fifteen yards away, they both dismounted and approached, walking their horses. One called out: "That cart looks very much like the one used by Einar of Brodgar. He and two henchmen, dressed like soldiers, use it to offer transport to guests and visitors to the Jarl who they then kill and rob and dump the bodies in the sea."

Astrid could contain herself no longer:

"Yes, yes! That's exactly what happened to us, and they had a mob of Picts hiding in the bushes, all trying to kill us and steal our money and everything!"

"So, how then did you manage to steal Einar's cart and outrun the mounted soldiers and the gang of savage Picts?"

"Well Olaf shot one of the Picts and one of the soldiers and then the cart-driver tried to strangle Olaf, so I killed him with Olaf's knife, then Olaf shot the second soldier and then we gave one of the horses to the Picts as they were starving, and they let us go on our way to see the Jarl!"

The two soldiers stood open-mouthed as Astrid rattled off the story without drawing breath.

"So, *you* killed Einar of Brodgar? Well, I've got some good news for you, young lady, the Jarl has put a price on his head and half as much for the two henchmen. If you make your way to Birsay and the Jarl's palace, he'll make it good after we have identified the bodies. Then we have to find and escort a huscarl who is sent here by Queen Tora from Nidaros."

"But I am that huscarl!" said Olaf.

The soldiers laughed heartily: "You're about a foot and a half short of being a huscarl," said one, "but if you've left four bodies back there, including the most wanted villain in Orkneyjar, then I'm not going to argue with either of you!"

His colleague laughed again: "So if you were the huscarl sent by Queen Tora, you'd be carrying a letter of introduction with her seal, would you not?"

Olaf went to the bag in the back of the cart and produced the parchment complete with Queen Tora's unbroken seal and red ribbon.

"Like this, you mean?"

The soldier's mirth was immediately transformed to incredulity at the sight of this royal document:

"Oy herregud! Oh well, more good news. We can provide you with the escort we were sent to be, and we can take your word on Einar as the whole island will be talking about it in no time. Shall we go?"

The two riders flanked the cart as Astrid passed the time by telling them her life story. Soon, the crashing of waves became audible as the fortified palace, perched on the cliffs of Birsay, hove into view. Astrid became very animated:

"Thank Odin for that! I am starving, in fact I am so hungry I could eat a horse like those horrid hairy Picts back there."

One rider raised his eyebrows in warning: "Don't let the Jarl hear you using any pagan oaths in his presence. The old gods are strictly forbidden here since King Olaf I threatened to slay the then Jarl on the spot if he and his people did not convert to Christianity on pain of fire and sword. The Jarl agreed."

Two expensively dressed tall lads of about Olaf's age and a bit younger came out through the archway. The two riders touched their knuckle to their eyebrow by way of salute.

"Father said you would be escorting one of the King's Huscarls from Kirkwall and you come back with these two stragglers. Who are they?"

"Paul and Erland Thorfinsson, may I introduce you to Olaf Ohlsson son of Erik Slagbjørn, Huscarl to King Harald III. Olaf himself is an archer-huscarl who has recently fought alongside the King at the battles of Odense and at Nis\u00e5 where your grandfather, Finn Arneson, fought against the King and is currently in chains at Nidaros.

Olaf is carrying papers for your father from Queen Tora. The lady here is Astrid Andersdottir from Bergen. She claims the reward for slaying the murdering cut-throat Einar of Brodgar. Olaf here killed his two henchmen and a marauding Scotsmen. I think your father would like you to treat them as honoured guests."

"He certainly would!" The two boys turned together as each felt a hand on his shoulder. These were the sons of Thorfinn the Mighty, Jarl of Orkneyjar.

"Huscarl Olaf, son of Erik Slagbjørn, though slight of stature and young as my sons in years, your reputation already precedes you."

The Jarl was tall, and well-built, carrying natural, aristocratic manners and an impressive warmth and charm of a good host. His two grandfathers were Malcolm II of Scotland and Thorfinn 'Skull-splitter' and he moved with ease past his two gangly sons to greet his guests.

"I heard this young lady has slain the evil Einar of Brodgar….is this true?"

Olaf interjected: "It is my lord. We were outnumbered and ambushed and whilst I drew a bead on a rider with couched lance, the villain driving the cart caught me around the throat with such strength I should have died swiftly but for the fact that my companion, Astrid, had the foresight to quickly pull out my hunting knife and plunge it into his side in a mortal wound, leaving me gasping but free to take down the rider."

"Sweet Jesus be praised!" said the Jarl, smiling, "but there is enough here for a saga already! Come inside in the warm, bathe and we shall see you for a celebratory feast in one hour. Do you have clothes for a feast? No? Then the maids will seek out some clothes that might suit. We don't want our people sneering at your travel-worn attire, do we boys?"

The boys shook their heads dubiously.

Astrid and Olaf were taken to a beautiful oak-panelled room overlooking the angry sea, crashing against the rocks below the Earl's Palace. Astrid was beside herself with excitement as maids appeared with a large tub of hot water and fragrant soap. They held up cloths of gauze to hide her modesty as she washed the sea and the dirt from her hair and her body, all the time giggling and laughing and shouting to Olaf to come and join her.

Olaf looked at her travel-stained clothes and then noticed for the first time the great smear of blood from the side of Einar, the cut-throat. It could all have gone so differently, and their bodies would now be food for the seabirds. Astrid stepped out of the tub, still giggling, and was wrapped in a towel and led away by two maids, leaving Olaf alone to use the fragrant soapy water still in the tub.

The door creaked open, and a voice called from outside that Olaf half-recognised in its effete, sing-song intonation:

"Huscarl Olaf, I am here to attend upon your dressing. Might I please enter your chamber?"

"Yes of course, please come in", shouted Olaf, washing the soapy water out of his blonde beard.

"Oy Herregud!! It's you! You're the Ålderman Thorkel from Dombås. What on earth are you doing here?"

"Well, well, if it isn't Olaf the Fair! Might I ask you the same question? I have left the service of Jarl Halvar of Innlandett and am now working for Jarl Thorfinn. So here I am. You even remembered my name! I am here to help you dress. What a delight that will be….my, how you have grown this past year, and a beard too."

Olaf grabbed a towel and quickly wrapped it around his waist.

"So, you survived the witchcraft of Queen Elisev and her two poisonous daughters? Well done, Olaf. My master, Thorfinn, is an old family friend of Jarl Torberg, the Queen Tora's father, and we have been hearing how you have managed to impress everybody – especially Queen Tora! Is it true you shot out the eye of one of Harald's huscarls on your very first night there?  Impressive indeed.

Things are very difficult at court now and there are things that you ought to know.  I have been at court seeking work after I left

Jarl Halvar. I have enjoyed the protection of Queen Tora who secured me this post here. I have seen her new son whom she has named, Olaf and, do you know, there really is a striking resemblance!" Thorkel pouted mischievously as he had done at Dombås and handed Olaf some leggings and a rich velvet jacket of emerald-green to put on.

"These were for the boys, but they grew out of them before they were ever worn. When I left, you were in the clear with Harald as he was incandescent with rage when he discovered from Ødger that the hero of the Battle of Niså, Håkon Ivarsson, had captured Sweyn, King of Denmark and then let him go. Even though he did take the traitor, Finn Arneson prisoner, many of the Danish ships escaped and the battle was inconclusive. Finn is in chains and there is talk that Harald will throw him into the snake pit. Did you see what happened to his brother Kalv at Odense?"

"I did," said Olaf, now dressed like a young aristocrat, "when he saw Finn mounted next to King Sweyn behind their shield wall, he nodded to Ødger who hacked off Kalv's sword-arm then severed his left leg before Harald took his head from his shoulders with a great double handed-sword. I was standing a few feet away and was spattered with blood."

"How disgustingly gruesome," said Thorkel putting a kerchief to his nose, "but you must know, of course, that Kalv Arneson killed Harald's half-brother, King Olav, at Stiklestad and probably killed Ødger's father, with the help of about five others, during that strange eclipse."

"Yes, Ødger had told me the whole story. But the difficulty as I see it, is that Thorfinn, your new lord, is a great ally of Harald Hardråda, who needs these Orkney islands as a staging post for any attacks on England he may wish to make. But if he throws Finn in the snake pit, he will be killing Thorfinn's father-in-law and the grandfather of his two boys, Paul and Erland."

Thorkel added: "He has put out word that Kalv was killed in the fighting but most of his army saw the Arneson head being thrown over the Danish shield wall and frankly, the Norse Jarls are a bit twitchy around Nidaros and the King is keeping his huscarls close."

There was a gentle knock at the door and one of the maids announced that the Jarl Thorfinn would be pleased if he would join them for dinner.

# *Chapter Nineteen:*
# *Three Bishops at Dinner*

Thorkel quickly finished dressing Olaf and having brushed his blonde hair and beard, sent him off with the maid looking for all the world like the son of nobility. Descending the great oak staircase, Olaf met Astrid coming down from the other direction. He hardly recognised her.

Her red-blonde hair was skilfully plaited, and she wore a flowing dress of sky blue which glistened with tiny pieces of silver woven into the gauze and silk material. Her cheeks glowed after the hot bath and her eyes glistened with excitement. As the two staircases joined into one, the young couple descended into the great Mead Hall of Thorfinn 'The Mighty'.

The first thing that struck Olaf was not the abundance of men-at-arms (including their two friends from this afternoon) but the abundance of what appeared to be high priests. Olaf's knowledge of Christianity was limited and, he guessed, that Astrid's was closer to non-existent. Thorfinn came over to greet them as servants brought them goblets of Rhenish wine from the Rhineland. It was a very new taste to both Olaf and Astrid but clearly not to a portly priest who was drinking enthusiastically and thereby achieving red upturned stains on either side of his mouth like two devilish tusks.

"Olaf of Dalby, son of huscarl Erik Slagbjørn, and his partner Astrid Andersdottir of Bergen, slayer of Einar of Brodgar!"

Thorkel was standing on the upstairs balcony and made the announcements. An elegant lady of similar height and looks to Queen Tora, but considerably older, approached with a beaming smile:

"My dear how brave of you, it is not often that we get lady heroes here. The days of the shield-maidens are long gone, and we are all expected to behave ourselves."

Jarl Thorfinn introduced his wife:

"May I present to you Ingebjørg Finnsdottir, Lady of the Orkneys."

She turned at once to Olaf: "I hear you have letters from Queen Tora? I hope there is news of my father. We are all very worried that King Harald will do something terrible."

"Let us talk of these things after we have eaten," said Jarl Thorfinn and Astrid nodded enthusiastically. They took their places near the Jarl at the top end of the long table where he had placed them, beside Ingebjørg, as the priests intoned a Latin plainsong grace:

*"Benedic, Domine, nos et haec tua dona quae de tua largitate sumus sumpturi. Per Jesum Christum Dominum nostrum. Amen"*.

Everyone except Olaf and Astrid crossed themselves. They had much, if not all, to learn about Christianity at a time when not following the Faith could incur the death penalty. Thorfinn leant over and spoke to Olaf.

"We are honoured to have three Bishops dining with us tonight so this will be the holiest food you have ever eaten! The one consuming wine at such a rate is Henry, Bishop of Lund, who was sent here by the Archbishop of York, to become the first Archbishop of Orkney.

That fellow there is Thorulf, the present Bishop of Orkney and helping to build my church here at Birsay. It was he who brought this fine wine as a gift from the Archbishop of Hamburg. And, finally, the third Bishop is Egino, Bishop of Dalby, who is currently, with the help of Sweyn, King of Denmark, building the first stone church to be erected in the whole of Scandinavia."

Olaf was going to ask what a Bishop was, but he thought it best just to nod. Then Egino called out in a Germanic accent.

"Did I hear you announced as 'Olaf of Dalby'?"

Now this was a subject he knew something about.

"Oh yes, I am from Dalby, just outside of Lillehammer in Norway and I fought a battle in Denmark at Odense when we landed in Dalby Bay near a village named Dalby. King Harald says there are many such place names, even some in England."

"Is that where my uncle, Kalv Arneson, was killed?"

All eyes turned to the Lady Ingebjørg.

"Er, um, yes, it was there by the shipyards in Odense on the island of Funen," stammered Olaf.  Astrid knew nothing of this, but she could tell that Olaf was rattled.

"But Kalv was an old man, too old to be in the shield wall. He would have been at the rear with the King."

"He was my lady, but when the King saw his brother Finn, your father, mounted on a horse next to Sweyn and his standard, his rage was terrible to behold. He ordered his most trusted huscarl, Ødger, to cut off Kalv's sword arm and then the King took off his head with a single blow. A warrior was dispatched to hurl the decapitated head of Kalv over the Danish shield wall, close to where Finn and Sweyn were mounted.  And now, as you have already heard, your father, Finn Arneson, is captive of King Harald."

Ingebjørg's expression was one of abject horror:

"He cannot harm my father; he is the uncle of Queen Tora."

"So was Kalv, my Lady", said Olaf quietly.

Thorfinn interjected,

"Yes, but Finn did not fight against him at Stiklestad, nor kill his half-brother, the recently sainted Olav of Norway. Finn went over to Denmark because he was offered the title of Jarl of Halland. A difficult offer to refuse. If Harald wants the use of my islands here and me as an ally, he must not harm my wife's father. I will send a messenger in the morning. Now, let's feast."

Astrid helped herself to half a chicken before the servants could help her and the Bishop of Lund called loudly for more wine.

Bishop Thorulf was still looking troubled as everyone else at the table tucked into the roasted meats and fish:

"I am somewhat concerned by what I have heard, Olaf. May I ask you why Harald instructed this warrior to cut off Kalv Arneson's sword-arm before he beheaded him. King Harald is probably the most feared warrior in Christendom and beyond. He would have had no trouble dispatching the aged Jarl without any help at all."

"Well, two reasons that I can think of," replied Olaf. "Firstly, Ødger was nineteen at Stiklestad and he told me that, when the eclipse cleared during the battle, it revealed Arneson standing over the body of his dead father, who had fought a fierce rear-guard action along with the standard bearer allowing Ødger and Prince

Harald to recover the body of King Olav. So, it was revenge for Ødger's father.

It was revenge for Harald too, who had seen his stepbrother, the King, run through with a spear and Kalv Arneson finish him off with a sword blow to the neck. In keeping with Viking vengeance, he ensured that Arneson did not die with his sword in his hand and would not enter Valhalla."

Bishop Thorulf smashed his goblet onto the wooden table: "Whaat! Are you suggesting then that Harald III of Norway is not a Christian king? He is the stepbrother of Saint Olav!"

"Yes, and he also has two wives!" added Ingebjørg

The three Bishops conversed with each other in muffled voices.

At the end of dinner, Thorfinn signalled to Thorkel who accompanied Ingebjørg and himself out of the hall as everyone stood in respect to the hosts.

Olaf was then summoned, via Thorkel, to the Jarl's chamber with the letters from Queen Tora. It turned out that they were just letters of introduction, but Thorfinn did detect a note of urgency in her writing.

"It seems that Cousin Tora wishes that I send you to England at the earliest possible opportunity. What have you done that she is so keen to put a lot of sea between you and King Harald? You didn't have dealings with either of his two daughters, did you?"

"No, no, nothing like that! King Harald made it clear what the consequences would be."

"Indeed? Well, I am instructed by Tora to give you a promissory note which you can redeem once you get to England.

The reward for the killing of Einar of Brodgar and his two henchmen I can give you in coin in two saddlebags.

Tomorrow my men will escort you overland to Stromness where a boat will take you to John O'Groats and thence down to Whitby with a stopover at Lindisfarne to collect some books for the bishops. Breakfast will be at six o'clock when I shall give you a short briefing as to your introduction to English nobility. So, sleep now, you have a long couple of days ahead."

Thorkel ushered Olaf out of the room and led him to his bedroom. Olaf looked about him:

"Where is Astrid?"

"I will make enquiries, but I think I can guess." Thorkel went out onto the landing and was gone for just a few minutes. "It is as I thought; Lady Ingebjørg has three bishops staying tonight and the idea of you two sleeping in sin under the same roof as them is a total impossibility. Astrid is not happy at all!"

Olaf chuckled and began to undress in the knowledge that he might get his first decent night's sleep for some time.

## *Chapter Twenty:*
## *Lindisfarne Priory*

The sun rose bright and clear over Birsay at around half past five and with it came a respectful knock on the door followed by a polite suggestion by Thorkel for Olaf to get up. The sea had subsided and was glinting peacefully around the rocky cliffs of the Earl's Palace.

Olaf splashed some water over himself and dressed quickly in his eagerness not to miss breakfast. Descending the staircase, he found the maids busy preparing a delicious breakfast of bacon and eggs rather than the grøt usually served at a Viking longhouse.

Astrid was already down and apparently had helped the maids make up the fire out of force of habit. Jarl Thorfinn sat at the head of the table with a large wolfhound stretched out by his feet after a mornings' walk. Behind him stood Thorkel and by the door stood the two bodyguards who had escorted them to Birsay.

"Morning Olaf! I trust you slept well?" Olaf half nodded, half bowed and looked well-rested.

"Good, well this is the brief for your travels; when you land at Whitby, you will be half a day's ride from York. Buy yourself a horse and cart and make your way there. Ask for an audience with Morcar or his brother Edwin, Earl of Mercia.

They should be at York trying to broker the peace between the good people of Northumbria and Harold's insane brother Tostig. King Edward, known as *'The Confessor'*, has made him Earl of

Northumbria instead of Morcar, and he is ruling with a very heavy hand. Tostig should be in Durham trying to raise money to fight the Scots and pay his huge retinue of Danish huscarls that he needs for protection against his own people.

We have an interest in de-stabilising Northumbria and getting Tostig and his Danish Huscarls removed or killed. We are sending you as a diplomatic gift from Queen Tora and King Harald to forge an alliance with England against Denmark. Good luck, young huscarl and take good care of this remarkable young lady."

Olaf had been paying more attention to his bacon and eggs and didn't understand half of what was being said and had no idea what a diplomatic gift was. Astrid, however, was suppressing squeals of excitement at the prospect of such an adventure and the prospects it offered for her beloved boy and, she hoped, her future husband.

A cart, of far greater comfort than the one which brought them to Birsay, was waiting for them outside with the two bodyguards mounted and fully armed. The saddlebags of coin were loaded, and the Lady Ingebjørg came to join the kindly Earl in seeing off their young guests on the next leg of their perilous mission. Olaf, with his hunting bow slung over his shoulder, thanked them both for their kind hospitality and the cart driver clipped the powerfully built horse into a brisk trot.

As the journey progressed, Astrid asked the name of the first settlement they passed through:

"Twatt," replied the nearest rider. "It's quite famous in the Orkneys as having the greatest number of village idiots in either Scotland or England so that the word has been adapted as an insult to mean *an idiot.*" Astrid shrieked with laughter as Olaf, mindful of the events of their previous journey, scoured the tree line for any unwanted Scots.

The remainder of their two-hour journey to Stromness passed peacefully in the August morning sunshine until the picturesque fishing port hove into view. The harbour was empty but for a full-sized Viking longboat flying the crest of Thorfinn the Mighty. The boat was manned, loaded and ready to sail.

"Are you coming with us?" Astrid asked of the two riders.

"No, ma'am, this is where we part company, but the crew are all the Jarl's men with strict instructions that you are very special cargo and must be landed safely in Whitby at all costs."

They boarded the longboat which was about two thirds of the size of *Ormen* but big enough to seriously impress Astrid who was thrilled when the captain bowed to her like a princess and welcomed her on board. The bodyguards waited by the dock until the ship was under full sail and heading out into the open sea to Scotland. Astrid waved furiously to the riders who raised their spears in salute. She was having just the best time ever.

Both Olaf and Astrid had been kitted out in warm travelling clothes and did look like the nobility they were supposed to be. The crew treated them with great deference and brought them bread, cheese and fruit to sustain them on their journey. At around midday they sighted the Northern tip of Scotland which the sailors said the natives referred to as *John O'Groats* for reasons they did not understand.

"Well, at least it's better than *Twatt*!" shrieked Astrid and the sailors joined in the hilarity. Olaf remained somewhat reserved as his head was full of the serious nature of the mission he had had thrust upon him. He held no illusions of the danger that would be attached to any attempt to oust Tostig, the son of Earl Godwin, with a reputation for extreme violence against his enemies and, indeed his own people.

Letters to Malcolm, King of Scotland, were dropped at John O'Groats and the longboat continued on its way South for Northumberland. Sailing conditions were near perfect and a Southerly wind took them briskly down the East coast of Scotland, past Berwick and the Northumberland coast to the Holy Island and the religious settlement at Lindisfarne where they put in for the night.

Lindisfarne in 1062 had recovered from the terrible raids from Danish Vikings in 793 and a great priory had been built to house the Benedictine monks for their fine work, illuminating books. The great Lindisfarne gospels had been completed around 720 but the early Viking raiders had no interest in Christian books other than to remove a jewelled metal cover. The Gospels survived.

The captain told Olaf and Astrid to leave their coin on the ship where it would be safely guarded by Thorfinn's men and to travel with him to the Priory by cart. Two sailors loaded a heavy chest onto the cart and horses appeared for the men-at arms who had been on the ship. The light was starting to fade now as they trundled their way towards the silhouette of the great Abbey. The Prior and a handful of monks lit torches to guide them through the twilight.

"Why are there so few in this great building?" asked Olaf.

"Ah, they have only recently returned, such is the fear they have that the Danish pirates might return. But Denmark is a Christian land now. They think they have nothing to fear from Vikings. This great chest is full of gold coins from the bishops staying at the Earl's Palace. It buys them illumined books and contributes to the re-establishment of St Cuthbert's legacy on this Holy Island."

The white-haired Prior with his tonsured head beamed at the sight of the great wood and metal chest:

"Splendid, splendid! We have the books and scrolls for you to collect in the morning. But now you must dine with us and thank God for your safe passage here. Ah, I see you have a girl with you? Well, she can't stay here after sunset. Brother Peter, would you guide this young lady to the Sisters and ask them to take care of her until tomorrow morning after Prime or Matins."

"Not again!" shrieked Astrid as she was led away.

Olaf, the Captain and the soldiers were led to the refectory which was designed for a great many monks to eat in and, although it was all but empty, the kitchen seemed to be fully staffed. The food was brought out with great drafts of ale followed by magnificent plates of food that even excelled the fine table kept by Jarl Thorfinn of the Orkney Isles.

The fire and candles lit their faces and the monks were indefatigable in their questioning of Olaf as to his mission or purpose and stating that their great fear was that of Tostig, the Earl of Northumbria, who regularly robbed from the Church and whose brother Sweyn had even kidnapped a beautiful nun whom he kept as a sex slave.

The great drawback was that Tostig kept a retinue of two hundred Danish housecarls to protect his back and that he was also a favourite of Edward the Confessor and brother of the great warrior son of Earl Godwin, Harold, who was tipped as being the next king of England. Olaf tried to keep up and as most of the party were bi-lingual in Norse and Anglo-Saxon, the language was very similar and could be translated when required.

Olaf got the picture that England, as things stood, was in a very precarious position. Canute the Great had ruled England, Denmark and Norway in an amazing Northern Empire but his offspring had died out with alarming expediency leaving a totally denuded dynasty of a devout King Edward (the Confessor). Earl Godwin had even got him to marry his attractive twenty-year-old daughter, Edith, in an attempt for Edward to father an heir, but he stuck to his vow of celibacy.

Worse than that, Edward had got this idea into his head that England should be left in the hands of the Christian Normans and had begun to import a whole host of Norman noble and clerical immigrants to whom he granted lands and titles and even banished the great Godwin dynasty to Flanders.

Olaf sat with eyes agog as he tried to take in this enormous amount of information from the monks who seemed to know everything about the political situation in Europe.

Every problem for the monks and the Church had seemed to stem from 1051 and the appointment by King Edward of a Norman cleric named Robert de Jumièges. According to the monks he was a truly evil man whom Edward had made Archbishop of London then Archbishop of Canterbury – the first Norman ever to hold this title. He successfully managed to get Edward to banish the Godwin's but, on their successful return in force, fled the country.

He didn't go quietly. On leaving his palace in 1052, he slew two random and innocent by-standers in his rage and snatched two young royal princes as hostages to give to William of Normandy.

One was *Wulfnorth*, Harold Godwinson's youngest brother, and the other was *Hakon*, son of Sweyn and Earl Godwin's grandson. Robert had given these two boys to the Duke of Normandy known as William 'the Bastard' (with good reason) to keep as hostages and informed William that Edward had asked him to relay the message that the childless King had chosen William to be his successor ahead of the rightful heir, Edgar the Ætheling, the only survivor of the English royal dynasty.

Edgar was twelve years old, born in Hungary whilst his father, Edward was in exile, having been deposed in 1016 by Canute the Great, King of Denmark and England. Edward the Confessor was now in failing health and was making no attempt to support Edgar's legitimate claim to the throne of England.

"I'm not sure I understand the word *Ætheling*," said Olaf.

"Ah, it's an old Anglo-Saxon word meaning a royal prince next in the dynastic line to succeed," answered the Prior. "So you see, with what interest Duke William of Normandy, King Sweyn of Denmark and King Harald of Norway are looking at our rich and prosperous country. The only man strong enough to hold the country together now is Harold Godwinson, the late Earl of Wessex's boy."

The conversation went on long into the night but Olaf, fatigued by the journey, was led away to a dormitory used by the monks and quickly fell asleep.

## *Chapter Twenty-One:*
## *Bacon and Eggs and on to Whitby*

Olaf slept soundly and was awakened by the sound of plainsong - singing monks, as it was six o'clock in the morning and Prime was the first service of their Benedictine routine before a light breakfast of bread and ale. Olaf had never heard plainsong before and was soothed by the lilting melody of the Latin words.

Outside, the whole island was covered by a mist rising off the sea and Olaf thought how very peaceful this was. The peace was abruptly shattered by a loud female voice coming through the mist who was accompanied by a distressed nun trying unsuccessfully to hush her.

"Olaf! Olaf where are you? These mad women have been up half the night singing, they put me in a cell with bread and water and a wooden bed and now they are trying to get me to go to church!"

Olaf ran down the stairs with his finger on his lips: "Tust! They are at prayer; you will offend them."

"Oh no, they're not singing as well now, are they? Go and wake the captain and tell him we need to go soon and get off this madhouse of an island. Tell him we need to go somewhere where they serve bacon and eggs."

The captain appeared on cue behind Olaf, alerted by the noise.

"Ah Astrid, good morning. Do I take it that the nuns did not treat you to the same lavish supper we had last night?"

At this the escorting nun turned on her heel with a scowl and a muttered: "Ours is a nunnery not a guest house," and headed back to her religious commune.

The singing of plainsong stopped, and a brown-robed figure appeared who they recognised as Brother Peter:

"Good morning brothers and sister in Christ. The Prior and in fact all the brothers could not help but overhear that the nuns did not extend the same hospitality as we did to our guests.

You will be pleased to hear that the Prior has given instructions that, as you have come here on a Godly mission and have brought a great fortune for our commune, last night and this morning have been declared a Feast Day and therefore there will be bacon and eggs before we load up your books and scrolls to take back to the bishops. Sister Astrid, as it is daylight, you too will be welcome to join us."

Astrid's face, which had been like a thundercloud, was now a ray of sunshine. By half past six the refectory was filled with the smell of bacon and fried eggs and Astrid sat face down and elbows squared in full concentration of the plate before her.

This special treat had all the monks in high spirits and, after breakfast they began to load the beautifully illumined scrolls, books, psalters and missals for the Orkney bishops and the Abbey at Whitby. Astrid had by now completely transformed from her previous petulant state into her usual positive, happy and bubbly disposition, much to the relief of Olaf. Returning to the ship, they found everything just as they had left it with their small fortune carefully guarded by the Jarl's men.

The weather was set fair and the Prior, Brother Peter and a few of the Benedictine brotherhood sang a *non nobis* from the quayside and waved them off. The boat dropped sail and proceeded South down the coast of Northumbria towards Whitby and the Benedictine Abbey there with their precious cargo of books and scrolls.

"They are still singing, Olaf! Do they never stop?" This time Astrid was amused and waved as the monks' voices became fainter and the ship picked up speed.

"At this rate we'll reach Whitby by seven o'clock tonight," shouted the amicable captain, pleased at the Southerly breeze.

And so, it transpired. The Benedictine monks were there to take their cargo but had made no plans to put up the travellers for the night. The Abbey was not nearly completed and there were no rooms, not even a roof. They lit a fire on the beach and managed to procure some fresh fish and ale from the village which were delicious under a clear starlit sky. Astrid was happy that she could cuddle up with Olaf under a blanket and a fur and there they slept with the crackle of the logs, the chatter of the sailors and soporific lapping of the waves.

At daybreak the captain woke them with some urgency to warn them that a high tide was about to engulf them. And they scurried back to the safety of the ship.

"This is where we part company, I'm afraid. Olaf and Astrid, it has been a pleasure. We won't be leaving until the tide changes, so I suggest you go into the village, find a blacksmith or a horse dealer and get yourself a cart to take you both to York. You can have one of my men as protection though I don't think you'll need it. Then come back here and collect your things."

In less than an hour they had returned with a pretty cart and a frisky black pony.

"Good job I tagged along", said the man-at-arms, "young Astrid here was going to pay the first price he asked. We got it down to half when he saw we had gold coin."

"As long as that doesn't get round the town," said Olaf. We remember what happened in Orkney."

"Yes, and a lot of the first part of your journey is through the Forest of Dalby. It's very beautiful by day but you don't want to be there after dark as it is a favourite haunt for outlaws. I suggest we hide these saddlebags under the seat with furs. I can see you have plenty of arrows so if you are ambushed, Astrid you take the reins and leave Olaf free to discourage them with some accurate archery. Don't shoot any of Tostig's men who may be patrolling. I think they are all in Durham protecting him. They are Danish Huscarls and very dangerous."

"The Forest of Dalby?" said Olaf, "is every place I go named after my home village?"

They said their goodbyes to the loyal captain and his men and set off at speed towards York. On a bright and warm morning their first experience of the breath-taking scenery was combined with all the live murmurs of a Summer's Day. The little trap pony positively danced along the well-used path as the butterflies and bees filled the air.

Olaf was amused to come across a small village at a fork in the road called Low Dalby, where they stopped to water him and buy two flagons of cool ale from a little inn called, by coincidence, *The Prancing Pony*. Astrid went in to order as she spoke Anglo-Saxon and Olaf guarded the cart.

"You got a strange accent their girl, you aren't with one of those Danes that Tostig likes to keep by him?"

"No!" laughed Astrid. "We are sent from Norway by Queen Tora to see the two earls Edwin and Morcar."

"What for?" said the yokel.

"None of your business," replied Astrid, laughing. "Just pour the ale and I will give you a silver Norwegian coin."

At the sight of the gleaming *Harald-mynt* the yokel filled a sizeable leather jug and gave them two pewter mugs with half a loaf on a wooden plate with a few slices of ham. They enjoyed the stopover and the yokel seemed delighted with his side of the bargain.

Rested and replenished they set off out of the woods and into open ground where they found the road much improved and their pony made very good time. In less than three hours they had sight of the walls of York or Jorvik as the Vikings called it. Approaching slowly, a guard called to them from the wooden parapet.

"What is your business?"

"We have business with the Earl of Mercia; we have letters from Queen Tora of Norway and Jarl Thorfinn of the Orkneys."

The cart trundled slowly into the foul-smelling muddy streets of York even though the road from Whitby had been bone dry. Just then a window overhead opened and a bucket full of excrement was hurled onto the streets. The pony shied away as a young soldier grabbed at the reins to steady him.

"I've orders to take you to see Edwin and Morcar, the two sons of Ælfgar, Earl of Mercia."

"Oh, I thought Edwin was Earl of Mercia," said Olaf remembering what Jarl Thorfinn and the Benedictine monks had told him.

"Tread carefully young stranger, Earl Ælfgar has only just recently passed away and his sons are in mourning. But you are right in that his title will pass to Edwin."

"Understood," said Olaf.

The soldier led them to a gated arch and from there to a beautiful courtyard which smelt of flowers and newly scythed grass. A stone manor house at the far end of the garden was their destination with a wooden staircase leading to an upstairs room. A groom appeared from a stable under the manor house and the soldier gave instructions for the nervous pony to be fed and watered. Olaf slung his bow and quiver and helped Astrid down from the cart.

"You won't be taking that in with you, young lad," said the soldier. "It'll be right here when you come back down."

"I'm an Archer-Huscarl to Harald III of Norway, I even sleep with it," protested Olaf with a touch of pomposity.

"I wasn't referring to the girl," replied the soldier and Astrid shrieked with laughter. Even Olaf twitched with amusement.

Above them a heavy wooden door clanked open and a young but imposing figure stood at the top of the stairs. He was dressed in blue velvet with a gold chain around his shoulders and, with wavy golden hair and fine features, there was no mistaking his aristocratic lineage.

"Are you come from the Orkneys? *Ha du kommet fra Orknøyene?*" he asked again in Norse.

"*Ah, du snakker Norsk?*" replied Olaf, impressed.

"Ha, only a bit, living in this Viking town we all get along bi-lingually. I'm Morcar, the younger son of Ælfgard, Earl of Mercia, who died in July."

"My Lord, my name is Astrid of Bergen and I speak your tongue. This is Olaf, Archer-Huscarl to Harald III and, although he has been learning very quickly on the voyage, I can translate anything he doesn't understand and also anything in the letters that he is carrying from Queen Tora and Jarl Thorfinn."

"Excellent, then you'd better come up right away."

Olaf could follow quite well what was said and moved towards the stairs, complete with bow and quiver, and clutching a leather satchel. The soldier moved forward to prevent him but was waved down by Morcar.

"It's alright Renweard, they're on our side, I think."

Renweard, whose Anglo-Saxon name meant 'guardian of the house', stood down like a guard dog being told to sit and stay.

Olaf, (complete with bow) and Astrid were invited into the great hall over the stables, which was lavishly decorated with tapestries and hunting trophies. There were large carved oak chairs with cushions. Something you would never see at Nidaros. In one of these chairs sat another elegantly attired nobleman with similar features to Morcar although older and more serious in his demeanour. His hair was slightly darker and longer and his face harder and leaner under a thick blonde beard.

"Brother, may I introduce you to Olaf, an Archer-Huscarl to Harald III, and his companion and useful translator, Astrid of Bergen. This is my elder brother Ēadwine or Edwin, as we call him, who should be, and will be, Earl of Mercia despite that thug

Tostig withholding his inheritance from him on the orders of Edward, probably as the Godwin clan held a knife to his throat.

Now let us see these letters of introduction and we shall see how or if you may be of use to us."

Opening the leather bag, Olaf removed several scrolls: one very travel worn and the other two more recent. Morcar clapped his hands and a steward appeared from a side door before being ordered to return with ale, bread, fruit and meat.

The two brothers broke the wax seals and spread the letters over a large oak table and asked Olaf and Astrid to sit at the far end where maids were being chivvied in by the steward, carrying silver trays of delicious strawberries, apples and pears which had ripened early in the fine weather. Pewter mugs were filled with North country ale, better than anything they had tasted in Norway, and finally, a whole roast chicken flanked by some guinea fowl with some hot bread rolls. Astrid had lost all interest in the letters and was intent on doing justice to this magnificent spread.

They were even given linen napkins to wipe the grease from their hands and faces. Before they had started, a maid approached them with a bucket of water and a towel and gestured that they must wash their hands before they ate, something that they had never encountered before.

"I love it here", exclaimed Astrid to Olaf, who had more than half an eye on the two brothers poring over the documents. "The ride here was just so beautiful. No wonder they call this 'Eng'-land; the land of meadows." Olaf ate without speaking, wondering what could be in those letters.

After what seemed an age, the two noblemen rolled up the scrolls and carefully tied the red ribbon around each. Edwin took a wax stick from the drawer and melted the green wax over the broken red wax on each. He then removed his signet ring and resealed the scrolls and placed them in a strongbox which he locked. The two walked to the far end of the table and Morcar poured himself and his brother a flagon of ale.

"Well," he sighed, "you have been a busy boy! The letter from the Queen of Norway is quite a surprise. I dread to think what would have happened if that had fallen into the wrong hands."

Olaf's eyes were wide with astonishment and Astrid sensed that something big was about to break.

"What does it say?" asked Olaf with beads of perspiration forming on his brow.

"Well," answered Morcar, "perhaps we should ask Astrid to leave if she is your wife, she won't want to hear this."

"She is my companion, not my wife but we have no secrets except, perhaps, this one which happened before we had met." said Olaf, shaking.

"All right then, I shall tell you both. It says that Olaf must be protected from Harald Hardråda who will kill him if he finds out that Olaf is the father of a child expected in July or August. The letter is, of course, out of date but we have word that on 9th August, Queen Tora gave birth to a beautiful blue-eyed boy two weeks after her time. The boy was born with golden curls and guess what she has named the child?"

Olaf gulped, "Olaf?" he whispered.

"Oh yes indeed! According to this very frank letter to my brother and I, she came to your bed chamber whilst the King was drunk and took her pleasure with you in order to conceive a child that wouldn't grow up to be as ugly and violent a tyrant as her husband and first child!  That leaves your bastard son as second in line to the throne of Norway. It's too fanciful!"

"Herregud!" Astrid exclaimed after the pause.

"So, what did the letters from Jarl Thorfinn have to say?"

"Ah", said Morcar, "well they were not altogether about you except to say both you and young Astrid had left a body count of four on his small island, including three wanted criminals and that Astrid had killed the ringleader herself. Impressive! Most of it was about the situation in Nidaros regarding his stepfather, Finn Arneson, who was captured at the Battle of Niså and his commander Håkon Ivarsson who allowed the captured King Sweyn of Denmark to escape."

"Yes, I know, I was there. He didn't allow Sweyn to escape, he actively assisted in his escape."

"You were there? My God, you are full of surprises! Do you know what's happened to either Finn or Håkon?" Edwin was astonished.

"I can only say that having cut off the head of Kalv Arneson, there is every chance he'll do the same to Finn for his treachery, or even worse, the snake pit. As for Håkon, he was brilliant at Niså and, with my father Erik Slagbjørn and Ødger Sköll, led a killing party that totally outflanked Sweyn's superior numbers and was the hero of the fight. Remember Håkon had also served under Sweyn so wasn't exactly a traitor like Finn. Håkon may escape with exile."

"Queen Tora said that Hardråda valued you as a marksman with a bow and that we should keep you on to try to help depose Tostig and restore Northumbria to my brother Morcar. They hate him here with a passion as he is cruel, over taxes and keeps a large retinue of Danish huscarls to fight his pointless wars against the Scots. My father hated the Godwins and we have inherited that. I suggest you stay here for a while in safety and learn the language and local customs. Things will start to get very violent around here in the not-too-distant future. We will give you a small cottage in the courtyard where you should be safe.

Tora and Thorfinn both say they have given you money and I have a promissory note for your keep. They will send more if necessary. So, there it is. I'll send for the steward and the maids to make you comfortable. You will be treated as minor nobility now under our protection. We will speak soon." They all rose and Olaf and Astrid thanked the two brothers for their kind hospitality in taking them in.

Olaf and Astrid couldn't believe the comfort of the little cottage in the courtyard and they were given Renweard to guard them and a maid to take care of their needs.

The Summer had been a warm, dry one and the leaves started to change colour mid-September as Olaf and Renweard became good friends and often went out to Dalby Forest to shoot deer, boar or some other game. Olaf's Anglo-Saxon was coming on as he was a quick learner. Astrid kept house as well as she had in Bergen and gave orders for a sauna to be built in their garden.

On the outside things of great pith and moment were brewing in and around England as powerful men, with great ambitions, plotted and schemed their ways to more power and even greater wealth than they already possessed.

## *Chapter Twenty-two:*
## *Tensions in the lands of the Norsemen*

The Autumn in Nidaros was not a happy place to be. Tora, with great courage and strength of purpose, had weathered the storm of gossip and suspicion and, despite the machinations and accusations of Elisiv, Tora had skilfully managed to appeal to Harald's vanity that he was, in fact, the father of such a beautiful baby boy. Tora was happy and radiant, Elisiv scowling and resentful because she just knew something was wrong, but simply couldn't prove anything.

Jarl Håkon Ivarsson was riding high on a great wave of popularity as the hero of Niså with neither Ødger nor Erik feeling comfortable in speaking up against a man whose great courage and leadership had turned the tide of the battle so decisively against his former employer, Sweyn of Norway. During the Winter, songs were sung about his bravery in the Great Hall. None of the Huscarls who had been there on that ship were prepared to say a word. Håkon averted the gaze of Ødger and Erik who surmised that he was living on borrowed time.

Finn Arneson was the unlucky one. Having defected to the Danes, after accepting Sweyn's bribe of the Jarldom of Halland, he gave away his countrymen at the Battle of Odense and then turned out for the Danes at the Battle of Niså.

In Harald's eyes, he was a full-on Judas and deserved nothing less than the snake pit. But here was the problem. His wife concubine, Tora, was the niece of Finn and cousin to Jarl Thorfinn of the Orkneys whose wife was Finn's daughter. He had already received dispatches from Thorfinn insisting that his father-in-law not be harmed in any way. He threatened to withdraw from an agreement allowing Harald to use the Orkneys as a staging post for any plans he might have for attacking England.

Furthermore, his best loved young warrior of noble birth was Eystein Orre, who was Tora's younger brother and therefore also nephew of Finn. Eystein it was who often asked what had happened to his young friend, the archer-huscarl, Olaf. He had even asked Erik Slagbjørn who could only say he had last been seen at Bergen helping a wounded man and had heard nothing since. So, there it was, a dilemma for King Harald.

Over in Denmark, Sweyn was also in a dilemma. He had a good claim on the throne of England given that, not only had he been born there, but his mother was sister to Canute the Great of England who was therefore his uncle. His information was that England was in a state of near civil war and the aged King Edward was childless and not long for this world. However, Harald had mauled his fleet at Niså and he had only escaped himself due to the help of Harald's commander.

He had lost a lot of ships and, as things stood, was not strong enough to launch an attack on England. This was especially so as he was still at war with Harald, which would leave Denmark wide open to attack from Norway if he attempted to take his fleet against England.

Further South across the English Channel was a Viking colony where the Norsemen had attacked the churches and abbeys in France and, in 911 at the Battle of Chartres, the Frankish King, Charles the Simple, sued for peace and signed over Rouen and lands across the coast to the Danish Viking leader, Rollo, thus establishing the Duchy of Normandy.

Like Guthrum in England, Rollo was baptised Christian. In 1062, William, Duke of Normandy, the illegitimate and only son of Robert the Magnificent whose father was Richard II, Duke of Normandy (Richard the Good) had stood as godfather at Rollo's baptism. Hence, William, present Duke of Normandy, was known as *William the Bastard*. His father had died on a pilgrimage to Jerusalem but had called a council before he left and named William as his successor, legitimate or not.

William had a tenuous claim to the throne of England. Edward the Confessor had grown up in exile in Normandy before being placed on the throne of England with the not inconsiderable backing of the Godwin clan. Edward had been importing Norman nobles and clergy to England including the unspeakable Robert of Jumièges whom he appointed as Archbishop of London.

William's claim by lineage was through his grandfather Richard the Good who was Edward the Confessor's maternal uncle. But the real claim, that William said justified his right to the throne, was that the ousted Robert of Jumièges had returned to Normandy with hostages and a forged letter claiming that Edward had named William as his successor. But a far greater opportunity would present itself in 1064 via an abortive diplomatic mission by Harold Godwinson to release his brother and nephew held by William.

## *Chapter Twenty-three:*
## *Meeting Tostig*

In the years before Olaf and Astrid arrived in York, England had sustained a certain amount of peace and prosperity, but for the odd raid over the Scottish border and a complete thorn in the side of the King from the other border, over in Wales.

From 1053, a Welsh leader, Gruffydd ap Llywelyn had been defeating his own rivals and enemies at home and had begun to unify Wales as a kingdom. He formed an alliance with Ælfgar of Mercia, father of Edwin and Morcar, who had a strong grievance against the Godwin brothers who had seized Ælfgar's Earldom in East Anglia.

Gruffydd and Ælfgar made a formidable partnership and marched on Hereford, on land belonging to Harold Godwinson and defended by the Earl of Hereford who brought his army of mounted soldiers to meet Gruffydd and Ælfgar. The Earl, known as 'Ralph the Timid', lived up to his name and Hereford was sacked and its castle destroyed. Diplomacy prevailed and Ælfgar's lands were restored.

Gruffydd made peace with Edward the Confessor and for seven years Wales had a single king and was at peace, not only with itself, but also its English neighbours.

Then in 1062 Ælfgar of Mercia died, depriving Gruffydd of a powerful ally. Harold had not forgotten nor forgiven the sacking of Hereford and sought Edward's permission to go after Gruffydd. Letters were sent to Tostig to collect men from Northumbria, especially archers and to attack by land from the North of Wales early in 1063 while Harold attacked by sea from the South.

Returning from a hunting trip with a small deer over his shoulders, Olaf and Renweard were alarmed to see a group of armed men outside their cottage banging on the door.

"We are Huscarls to Tostig Jarl of Northumbria, and we have business with Olaf the Archer!"

Astrid's voice was audible from inside:

"I don't care who you are, you sound like nasty Danes to me and you're not coming in until Olaf gets back."

Throwing down the dead roe deer, Olaf ran towards the cottage, bow in hand. Behind him, Renweard followed with drawn sword. The Danish huscarl was astonished when an arrow struck the door two inches from where his fist was banging it. He jumped back to be confronted by a diminutive Norwegian who had already threaded another arrow which was now aimed at his right eye, just past the nose guard. His four colleagues fanned out, two on either side, hands on sword hilts without drawing them. One of the four raised his hand and gestured to Olaf:

"Put up your bow, Olaf. We are not here to cause you any harm. We are here because we are sent by the Earl of Northumbria, Tostig Godwinson. He is very aware you have been staying here without paying any taxes but is prepared to overlook this on the understanding that you lend your expertise to Harold Godwinson's expedition to the land of Gruffydd ap Llywelyn, the self-appointed Welsh King. Tostig will be invading in the Spring, but he wants to meet you."

Olaf lowered his bow: "When does he want to see me?"

"Right now," said the Dane, who seemed to be in charge. "He's upstairs with Edwin and Morcar in the manor house."

Olaf called out to Renweard to look after Astrid who was hanging out of the upstairs window, desperately try to hear what was going on.

Olaf crossed the grassy close, now with an extra carpet of dead leaves, accompanied by the one Danish huscarl, to the wooden staircase leading up to the hall of the manor house. As he reached the top of the stairs the heavy door opened from the inside to reveal two more burly Danish huscarls. At the far end of the long table sat the two brothers Edwin and Morcar but at the head was someone Olaf had not seen before. He stood up to reveal himself as a tall, lean and hard-looking aristocratic warrior of Anglo-Danish descent and an expression that Olaf recognised from Hardråda, as of one having no pity.

"Ah, so you're the young huscarl-archer from the court of Harald III. I am Tostig, son of Earl Godwin and appointed Earl of Northumbria by King Edward. I need you to lead my small group of not very good archers against the Welsh. I am also keen to hear everything about King Harald. He is the most famous warrior in the world. Have you fought alongside him in any battles, or are you too young?"

"No, my Lord," replied Olaf when he could get a word in, "that is to say, yes, I have fought alongside King Harald in the attack on the boatyards at Odense and the following year in the great sea battle of Niså when we destroyed half the Danish fleet and captured King Sweyn only for one of our commanders to release him. It was still a great Norwegian victory over the Danes though."

The two massive huscarls by the door glowered and rumbled like two bears growling. Edwin and Morcar could barely conceal their amusement. Tostig was unmoved:

"Good, so you have some idea of what is required in battle. You stay close to me and direct your arrows where I say. The huscarls are all staying here in Northumbria to keep an eye on the locals who don't care for me overmuch, am I right in thinking that, Morcar?"

"You do tax them until the pips squeak, my Lord, and you are very harsh with them as does not pay. What's more, you are a Southerner and people round here don't care for Southerners overmuch."

"So, there it is. I shall be taking an army of local recruits to help my brother Harold who is still crying because the Welsh sacked his beloved Hereford. Tell me, Olaf, how did Harald of Norway deal with those who did not pay their taxes?"

"Mutilation is his preferred method, usually a left hand."

Tostig, roared in approval, "I'm starting to like this hard ruler! Olaf, you must stay put in York until the New Year when I shall send for you to join the rest of the army. Right, we are back to Durham tonight, good day, gentlemen."

Edwin and Morcar stood as the door opened and the huscarls followed Tostig out as he strode into the close and mounted his horse.

"I think you've just been enlisted," said Edwin.

"Why doesn't he ask you both to supply men and go with him?" asked Olaf.

"Ah, you see it's complicated. Our father, Ælfgar of Mercia, had his Earldom in East Anglia, given whilst the Godwin's were in exile, removed after Harold returned. Ælfgar joined forces with Gruffydd and defeated the King's army at Hereford and did terrible things to the citizens there as well as destroying the castle.

Harold was sent with a large army, but our father fled back to Mercia and Gruffydd into Wales. The matter was settled diplomatically when Godwin died, leaving Harold as Earl of Wessex and the most powerful earl in England. Ælfgar's land was restored to him but our sister Ealdgyth is married to Gruffydd, so, you see, we cannot go to war against him."

"Ah, yes, complicated indeed!" Olaf laughed. "Gentlemen, forgive me but I have some fine venison, lying on the close outside, that I should like to get prepared and hung in time for Yule. It shall be my gift to this hall. I also have the unenviable task of telling Astrid that I shall be going to war in the Spring. She won't take it well."

"Goodbye Olaf."

Olaf returned to the spot where he had dumped his roebuck, but it had gone. However, a small track of blood led him to the cottage and there, out the back, were Astrid and Renweard skinning the deer with much giggling from Astrid.

Olaf thought that they seemed to be having too much fun together, but he set aside any thoughts of jealousy. Olaf, in answer to Astrid's questions as to the meeting with Tostig, explained that he had been enlisted to fight for the Godwin family in the Spring of 1063. To his amazement, Astrid took it remarkably calmly.

The Autumn passed without incident as things brewed in England. Harold, on the early death of Ralph the Timid was now caretaker and Godfather for his son also called Harold, of the

Earldom of Hereford. In the Winter of 1062, he took a powerful army there to contain the Welsh border and await the pincer attack with his brother Tostig in the Spring. The castle was rebuilt and the fortifications strengthened as everyone hunkered down for the cold weather.

In York, as Advent approached, Olaf and Astrid began to get caught up in the excitement that was growing with the approach of the pagan festival of Yule and the Christian festival of the twelve days of Christmas.

*Astrid kept a fine table.*

## *Chapter Twenty-Four:*
## *Jul in Jorvik 1062 - (Christmas in York)*

Since their arrival in York in August, Olaf and Astrid had lived comfortably and, apart from the unexpected arrival of Tostig's huscarls, nobody had troubled them in any way. Renweard had become very much a part of their lives as they carried out their daily routines as a threesome, but with Renweard stopping just short of actually moving in. As a soldier in the employ of the Earl of Mercia, Tostig was unable to enlist the services or any of Edwin's men.

Olaf was happy about this as it meant that Astrid would have company in York and, if anything happened to him during the invasion of Wales, she would not be left alone. Nobody had asked any questions regarding the fact that they were not married, nor did they attend church on Sundays or even understand the Christian faith. But Yule, they did understand as it was a pagan festival very similar to the Christian one.

It was the First Sunday of Advent on a cold afternoon and Astrid was about to serve up a delicious stew to Olaf and Renweard by a roaring log fire when there was a knock on the door. Opening the door, Olaf took a step backwards as there appeared to be a huddle of cloaked and hooded men standing in the freezing rain in his porch. The tallest figure spoke first:

"Olaf the Archer?"

"Who wants to know?" answered Olaf defensively.

"Ealdred, Archbishop of York and these two distinguished clerics are Bishops Wulfstan and Æthelwig. May we come in out of the rain?"

"As long as you don't start all that singing again," shouted Astrid from inside.

"Yes, of course," said Olaf, standing to one side as the three figures ducked in through the low door and removed their dripping cloaks to reveal fine woven costumes underneath with heavy bejewelled crucifixes fashioned in gold.  Renweard immediately got to his feet and moved towards Ealdred who proffered a large gold and ruby ring which Renweard duly knelt before and kissed: "Your Grace."

Æthelwig was far more interested in the contents of the cauldron on the hearth and also, it must be said, in the buxom pink cleavage which was generously protruding from Astrid's smock.

"Do you like dumplings?" asked Astrid with a mischievous twinkle. "I make mine in the Viking way using boiled bread, berries and carraway seed. The meat is venison in beer with red cabbage."

"What? Oh, erm yes, I er do indeed like dumplings," stammered the red-face, ogling Bishop Æthelwig. Astrid giggled.

"There's plenty here if you'd like to sit down, I can serve you. Renweard, could you fetch some beer for our guests. Olaf you can pass the plates."  Astrid was absolutely in her element as if she were back in her inn in Bergen.

"But you must promise me not to sing or it will get cold!"

Archbishop Ealdred of York administered the shortest grace:

"Benedictus, benedicat, Amen," as Olaf placed the pewter plates and wooden bowls, they crossed themselves rapidly before tucking into the delicious smelling venison and dumpling stew.

"You keep a fine table here Mistress Astrid," was Bishop Wulfstan's summing up with a mouthful of food. Astrid beamed and there was no more conversation until the plates were cleared and the flagons topped up.

"Thank you all so much for your kind hospitality," said the archbishop. "I expect you would like to know why we are here?"

"I had wondered," said Olaf, "unless word of Astrid's cooking has spread in York."

Ealdred laughed, "Not yet anyway and we shall keep it secret. No, the reason is quite serious. What is that amulet around your neck Olaf?"

"Oh this?" he said tugging at the leather string around his neck. "It's Thor's Hammer. It gives protection if you are at sea."

"Ah yes, indeed, and that is exactly the problem we have come to see you about.  You see, Olaf, and you Astrid, you are living here together in the diocese of York and not only are you not even married, but you are also not even registered as having been baptised into the Christian faith. For centuries the Christians and Pagans have co-existed here in York, living and trading together.

But now, Norway, Denmark and Normandy are all Christian countries. The King will not have any pagans here in England. You both must be baptised and, if you wish to live together, married in the Cathedral."

Astrid, wide-eyed, put her hand to her mouth with an excited intake of breath.

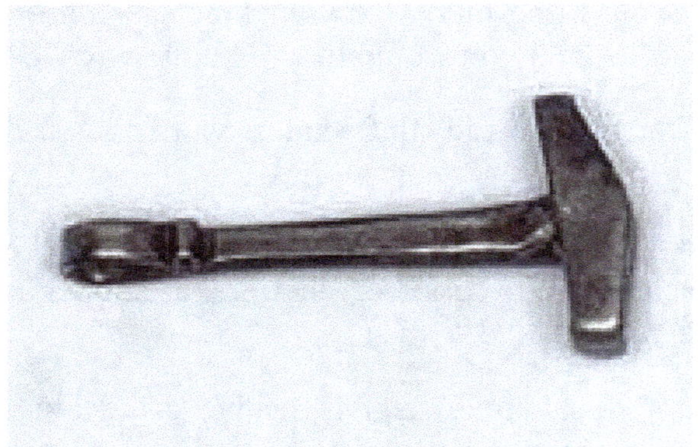

"I'm going to give you an ancient coin," continued Ealdred, "not as payment for the fine supper, but to remind you that you may still hold to your Norse gods in private but, in public, you must be seen to be Christian. It's called a St Peter penny and was minted here in York. The Latin name Petri or St Peter has the T in the shape of Thor's hammer. On the reverse is also the hammer of Thor.

I was ordained as Archbishop of York on Christmas Day 1060 so this will be my third anniversary and I should like to baptise you both at midnight mass on Christmas Eve, and then we can really start the feasting!"

"Well, I don't mind," said Astrid, clearly quite excited by all the attention.

"Well, if we are to stay in England, I suppose we are going to have to adopt all its customs including Christianity. But I will forfeit my place in Valhalla for the Kingdom of Heaven, which doesn't sound like half as much fun," Olaf added.

"Excellent!" said the archbishop, clapping his hands. Father Æthelwig and Father Wulfstan will see to your instruction, you have just three weeks."

Each day either Father Wulfstan or Father Æthelwig would summon them to their school in the Church of St Peter with a kindly monk. It was a futile attempt to teach Olaf and Astrid the Catechism, or Christian catechesis, which took the form of instruction in and memorising of the Apostles Creed, The Lord's Prayer, and basic knowledge of the sacraments.

Since both Olaf and Astrid were already working on their second language of Anglo-Saxon English, the learning of great chunks of Latin and taking in practically incomprehensible theology such as the Great Mystery of the Incarnation, seemed really just too much.

The gentle monk, Brother Lar, had instructed many children in his time and was able to make the story of the Nativity come alive with colour. Astrid loved it but Olaf didn't perk up until Herod ordered the Massacre of The Innocents. Olaf thereafter referred to him as Herod Hardråda.

On the 22$^{nd}$ of December, Olaf and Astrid were asked to attend the great Church of York as rebuilt by Saint Wilfrid in the 670's. It boasted the most substantial school and library in Northern Europe. It was built entirely of stone and had a beautiful font at the West end. This was just a rehearsal so that Olaf and Astrid knew what to do. On Christmas Eve, the church was full of the good people of York looking forward to the feasting and high jinks that was traditional at this time in the Christian calendar.

Olaf and Astrid sat together at the front of the nave whilst up in the Quire sat the clergy, robed in rich and beautiful garments. Behind them sat the monks in their brown Benedictine sackcloth robes and sandals. Also in the Quire, before the Great Altar, sat members of the nobility: Tostig, Earl of Northumbria, Edwin, Earl of Mercia, his brother Morcar son of Ælfgar, and an array of wealthy thegns in order of importance.

The light was of a thousand candles and the monks sang the plainsong *Hodie Christus Natus Est* in two-part harmony. Ealdred,

The Archbishop of York came forward down into the Nave, accompanied by acolytes carrying great golden candlesticks. The air was heavy with the scent of incense, which partly concealed the smell of the great unwashed horde standing behind Olaf, Astrid and Renweard. Suddenly the singing stopped and the archbishop began speaking in English.

"Beloved in Christ, on this auspicious night, when Christ was sent down to live among us as the Son of God and was born of the blessed Virgin Mary in a humble manger, we will all celebrate the coming of our Saviour. I have a small celebration too as it was on this night four years ago when I was ordained as your Archbishop to the See of York. I should also like to celebrate this by bringing two young pagans from Norway into the family of Christ."

The thurifer moved forward, swinging a great silver thurible and causing the heavy censer to billow incense and carve a path, through the people standing to where the marble font was situated. Edwin and Morcar, Renweard and Father Wulfstan with Brother Lar all followed the archbishop to the font. An acolyte guided Olaf and Astrid to join them. Astrid was dressed in white which Olaf found amusing. Apparently, Edwin was going to act as godfather to Astrid and Morcar was to be his godfather. After the godparents had agreed to guide their charges in the Christian way and Olaf and Astrid had agreed to 'turn to Christ', they were baptised with the sign of the cross from the font and duly welcomed into the Christian Church with much cheering and clapping and the monks breaking out with 'Gloria in excelsis Deo' in emulation of the angels on the hillside to the astonished shepherds and, no doubt, equally astonished sheep. Olaf and Astrid followed the clergy back to the High Altar to take their first communion.

*If only my father could have seen this*, he thought to himself.

"The Mass is over, go forth in peace, and may I wish you all a very Happy Christmas," declared the archbishop. The great West doors were thrown open to display a thick blanket of white on the frozen mud and large flakes of snow falling peacefully onto the rooftops and streets of York. Ealdred approached Olaf having removed his mitre and passed his crozier (shepherds crook) to an acolyte.

"This is a small but very precious baptismal gift which I hope will protect you in the forthcoming conflict in Wales. You may wear it next to your Thorhammer!"

He handed Olaf a small golden cross on a chain.

"Now I must join my clergy for our first feast of Christmas and you must go straight to the Manor House to join Edwin and Morcar, your new Godparents, where all the Earls and Thegns in the region have been invited."

Archbishop Ealdred blessed them both and departed in the direction of the vestry.

"Is this where we get to eat?" asked Astrid.

"Yes, this is the good part of having wealthy godparents. Come on Renweard I'm sure you can come too."

"Absolutely not Olaf," said Renweard, "remember I am just a soldier in the pay of Edwin, Earl of Mercia. I'll go and join the lads and drink a lot. You go and have fun with your aristocratic friends." And with that he turned, pulling his cloak around him, and disappeared into the snow.

It was a ten-minute careful walk in the snow to the courtyard and the Manor House. The candlelight from the windows lit their path, as did the noise of laughter, raised voices and a strange musical instrument being played with someone hitting a drum. Gaining the stairs, the door opened as before but this time it was a smiling maid rather than a growling huscarl.

Astrid squealed in delight as she saw how the hall had been decorated in the Norse style she knew so well. The great central table was now on one side and had been joined by a second against the opposite wall with a top table across the far end. The centre was now taken up by a great burning 'Yule Log' over which a deer was roasting. There were holly wreaths, and also decorations made from ivy and mistletoe.

A man was blowing a Northumberland bagpipe and another beat rhythms on a tabor with a single stick. Maids attended to the guests with great jugs of ale and mead. Wine was served to the Earls.

Olaf spotted Morcar down the far end waving to them to approach. Two spaces had been reserved for them at the top with Olaf seated next to a beautiful lady who Edwin had introduced as his sister, Ealdgyth, who introduced herself as Edith, wife of the Welsh King, Gruffydd ap Llewelyn. Olaf asked curiously why she chose not to spend Christmas day with her husband in Wales.

"Do you know who that man in the centre is," she asked.

"Yes, I know him, that is Tostig Godwinson, Earl of Northumbria and quite a warrior I gather. Not much liked around here by the people, I have been told."

"Well, my brothers had me brought here for safety as they say he will be attacking Gruffyd's palace at Rhuddlan. He was away fighting at the time so didn't notice that I had gone until he returned a week ago. I don't suppose he is very happy as I brought the children with me for their safety too."

Meanwhile, Astrid was making great headway with Morcar who was flirting with her and asking probing questions about her future intentions with Olaf. As a thegn of high standing, the idea of marriage to anyone not titled would be out of the question but he could not help but drop in the provoking line:

"It's a good thing they didn't ask me to be your godfather, that would have been awkward as I find you far too attractive."

Astrid blushed and turned to look at Olaf who seemed far too tied up with the raven-haired beauty beside him. Astrid needn't have had any concern as Olaf was earnestly milking Ealdgyth of all information concerning her warlike husband and his defences.

And so, the Christmas of 1062 drew to a close in York with roast boar and venison, spiced ham and figs, laughter and strange music. Who could have guessed that Olaf and Astrid, from tiny Norwegian backwaters, would be seated as guests of honour in the midst of some of the most powerful families in England?

## *Chapter-Twenty-Five:*
## *War Against Wales*

The Twelve Days of Christmas had no sooner past, with all its strange antics and traditions when word reached the camp of Tostig that his brother Harold had marched a surprise attack into Wales in an attempt to try to take Gruffydd captive. No one knows for sure, but it did occur to Olaf that the intelligence held by Ealdgyth would have been mighty useful to Gruffydd holed up in his fortress at Rhuddlan, not a great distance from Tostig's army camped on the English border at Chester.

Choosing not to use his brother's forces, just a thirty-mile distance from Chester, Harold took his army from Hereford, in the South and sailed North to surprise Gruffydd's army and very nearly captured him. Gruffydd had clearly been tipped off and escaped by ship before Harold's men could close in on him.

Tostig's army rushed the five-hour march to Rhuddlan and found a very small army there to oppose them. Olaf remained close to Tostig with a few mounted knights. A body of foot soldiers, about two hundred strong, were sent forward to prevent anyone leaving the fortification and trying to make it to the ships. They remained at a safe distance, some three hundred and fifty yards back, out of the range of any archers.

Suddenly, from behind the palisade came a great whistling sound as a black cloud which flew up and then descended on the line of Tostig's men. As the arrows thudded home on the astonished foot soldiers there was much screaming, much spilt blood and much running away. Some thirty soldiers were left behind on the blood-stained grass, writhing in agony or twitching in their death throes.

"Herregud!" whistled Olaf. "That is just not possible!"

"How did they do that?" Tostig shouted across to Olaf.

"I have never seen such a range from a bow. We must try and capture one so I can see for myself," replied Olaf.

The castle at Rhuddlan was well positioned at the top of a steep bank leading down to the river Clwyd offering a clear view to the archers. Given the minor massacre he had just witnessed, Tostig withdrew his forces to a thousand yards and waited for reinforcements. Olaf was beside himself with curiosity regarding the extraordinary range of the defending archers and wondered how they were going to take the castle without any siege equipment. Just then, from the direction of a tiny fishing village called Rhyl, Olaf spotted a sail and then another and then a whole fleet of ships approaching the Clwyd estuary. A great cheer went up from Tostig's army as they realised it was Harold with his forces.

"That'll be my brother no doubt come to sort out our little problem here," said Tostig. Olaf nodded, intrigued to meet the most powerful Earl in England. Sure enough, after about half an hour, riders were seen approaching Tostig's camp led by a tall powerful warrior. On dismounting, Olaf could see clearly the family resemblance. Harold was taller and more powerfully built and carried with him an air of natural authority. He swaggered into Tostig's encampment with a cheery:

"Greetings, brother! I see you have just discovered the killing power of the Welsh war bow. They call it a longbow. How many have you lost already?"

"How are we going to take this castle with those damned things cutting us down," was Tostig's frosty reply.

"Ah well, let me introduce you to a friend of mine. This is Cyan ab Iago, a Welsh prince whose father was king of Gwynedd but was killed and the throne was seized by Gruffydd ap Llywelyn in 1039. Cyan believes Gruffydd killed his father and is going to get his revenge and his throne back with our help. Now, I think we are going to have a little chat with these bowmen in the castle."

"Take Olaf, my archer with you as he wants a look at these bows." Olaf looked at Tostig incredulously at being volunteered for this suicide mission.

"All right, young Olaf, saddle up and let's get up that hill."

The party of six was made up of Harold, Earl of Wessex, Cyan ab Iago, Olaf and his hunting bow and three housecarls from Harold's force. From the sea came a smell of burning ships as the Welsh escape route was destroyed. One of the housecarls carried a white cloth on a spear. As they got within range, archers heads appeared on the parapet but they did not loose. Harold and Cyan continued forward to about seventy yards and stopped. For a moment there was silence broken by Harold's strong baritone voice:

"Archers of Rhuddlan, we are destroying your ships, and you are surrounded. You may starve in there and we will cut off your hands, your ears and your noses when we take you. Or you can put down your bows and walk out unharmed."

This was followed by the lyrical tenor voice of Cyan, translating:

*"Saethwyr Rhuddlan, rydyn ni'n dinistrio'ch llongau, ac rydych chi wedi'ch amgylchynu. Efallai y byddwch yn llwgu yno a*

*byddwn yn torri eich dwylo, eich clustiau a'ch trwyn i ffwrdd pan fyddwn yn mynd â chi. Neu gallwch chi adael eich bwâu a cherdded allan yn ddianaf."*

From the parapet an audible hubub broke out as a disagreement was clearly in progress between whoever was in charge and those who valued their body parts. There was an angry shout in Welsh and a bowman stood up and pulled the feathered missile on his bowstring slowly back to his ear in the great effort of strength required to use this weapon.

Olaf had seen him and had strung an arrow and loosed it between the heads of Harold and Cyan as there was no time to go around them. His arrow flew upward  and true, hitting the longbowman in the shoulder as he was pulling the bowstring. The force made his elbow jump upwards and the arrow was realeased in all its velocity into the grass in front of Harold's mount, who shied his head but otherwise stood still.

There was clearly a struggle going on in the castle and amidst shouts and screams, the body of the wounded bowman was flung from the walls. If Olaf had only winged him, his own colleagues had done the rest as there was no head attached to what thumped onto the grass outside the wall.

There followed a noise at the gate as of a great wooden beam being lifted from the iron brackets and the heavy doors were swung open. A severed head was thrown out and there followed a host of archers, probably about fifty or more walking out dejectedly towards the six riders.  A large contingent of Harold's mounted knights galloped up in protection but they weren't needed. One of the bowmen, appointed spokesman as he spoke English, walked up to Earl Harold and removed his leather cap:

"If it please your grace, the boys here would like to accept your kind offer to surrender, except Gruffydd's captain was a bit of a glory hunter, see, and wanted to get us all killed so we took him out, see? That was a fine shot and no mistake young archer!"

"And what is *your* name, archer?" asked Harold.

"I am Rhys, Rhys of Prestatyn, if it please your grace, and I'd be happy to help get that Gruffydd who took all the supplies and provisions and left us with six arrows a-piece to die here."

Harold called out to the other archers and asked Cyan to translate:

"You may keep your bows if you join my army against Gryffydd."

*("Cewch gadw eich bwâu os ymunwch â byddin Harold yn erbyn Gruffydd?")*

They held up their bows and cheered:

"Le! rydym i gyd yn cytuno!" (Yes! We all agree!)

Harold laughed and guessed that they hadn't eaten for several days:

"Follow us back to Tostig's camp and we will get you fed and watered."

The party returned back in the order of Harold and Cyan leading, followed by Olaf, who had yet to receive any recognition for saving Harold's life, three housecarls, Rhys leading fifty-five hungry archers and a body of fifty mounted English knights pulling up the rear.

They reached the camp and the smells of food being roasted pervaded the air. Tostig shouted to Harold:

"A great victory, Brother! Let us cut off the hands of these Welsh scum and then drink and feast."

A few Welshmen who understood English muttered and began translating to their nervous fellows. Cyan looked at Harold in horror. Tostig's forces were keen to exact revenge and many had their weapons drawn.

"Stand down I say!" roared Harold. Then, to his brother:

"I have given these men my word that they will be freed and they have been. They have elected to join us and we will now feed them before starting out to find Gruffydd ap Llywelyn."

Tostig had a face like thunder at being humiliated in front of his troops who had watched his complete incompetence as a commander and who had cost the lives of thirty of his men. Harold ordered the cooks to provide meat, bread and beer to the starving Welsh archers, but his knights kept a vigilant watch in case any should have a change of loyalty, as had been amply demonstrated in the dispatching of their captain not half an hour ago.

Olaf joined Rhys in downing a flask of beer as there were many questions he wished to put to the big Welshman. Olaf's English was still a bit Anglo-Norse which was fine for York, but down here much harder to understand and Rhys spoke English with a pronounced sing-song accent.

"Do you think you could train me to use a bow like that," asked Olaf, admiring the amazing 5 feet ten inches of killing power that was slung over the shoulder of the master archer.

"Well, you are a bit on the short side for a long bow but they come in smaller sizes. You see, we start training from the age of fourteen so we can develop our chest muscles. That's why we are all such a strange shape. Now, if you don't mind, I'd like to eat and drink some more of Earl Tostig's reluctant hospitality."

And with that he brought the conversation to a close by cutting a generous slice of venison with his dagger and downing a great draft of ale.

Harold organised what he called a 'killing party' which included Prince Cyan ab Iago, fifty of his best mounted housecarls, the Welsh longbowmen and finally, Olaf Slagbjørn. Harold had a task for Tostig which he didn't want the Welsh bowmen to know about.

"Brother, I want you, once we are gone, to leave a garrison in that castle and destroy Gruffydd's palace. Then I want you to do what you do best; take your Northumbrian levies and scour the surrounding villages and kill any men of fighting age – fourteen or over. Take all livestock and send them back here. I will find and kill Gruffydd and meet you here once I have restored Cyan to power."

"Thank you brother," replied Tostig, "I shall endeavour to do a thorough job and my men are vengeful."

"Finally, I am taking your Norse archer with me. He showed great presence and skill and probably saved my life."

As the sun set over the Irish Sea, the men lit fires against the cold and settled down for some rest. The lights from Harold's fleet at the mouth of the Clwyd twinkled in the distance as did the stars above. Olaf pulled his cloak about him. He wondered how Eric was faring, how Freya was getting on with her little boy in Lillehammer, likewise Tora in Nidaros and Astrid in York. He had had a good day and had saved the life of the most powerful Earl in England. He had also attempted to pull the longbow of Rhys of Prestatyn and failed, much to the amusement of Cyan ab Iago and the humiliation of Olaf.

Despite the zeal in which Tostig set about wreaking carnage on the Welsh villagers, the war was short and soon the blood-letting was ceased by the success of Harold and his killing party. Cyan had sent word that he was keen to parley with Gruffydd, who was in hiding with a small army up in the frozen hills of Snowdonia. Gruffyd's men were cold, hungry and demoralised.

When Harold and Cyan met with the Gruffydd's party, they quickly realised that he was not among their number. Olaf watched at a distance with the Welsh archers as one rider came forward with a blood-soaked sack.

Lifting it by its hair, the rider produced the severed head of their erstwhile leader, Gruffydd ab Llywelyn and handed it to Harold. Thus did Cyan ab Iago briefly take over the rule of Gwynedd and Powys leaving Harold free to return to Wessex and his brother Tostig to return to Northumbria, with such disasterous consequences that would lead to the destruction of the entire Anglo-Saxon dynasty.

*Gruffydd ap Llywelyn 1010 - 1063*

*The first and last King of Wales*

# *Chapter Twenty-six:*
# *Return to York / Tostig's Trap*

With Cyan installed as ruler of the greater part of Wales and a close ally of Harold, the powerful earl was eager to return to court to let the King know of his great victory and thence to his earldom of Wessex.  Tostig returned with his levies to York and with him went Olaf.

Harold had asked Olaf to accompany him to London but was sympathetic to the fact that Olaf had left Astrid behind alone with two eager suitors in the persons of Renweard the soldier and Morcar the brother of the Earl of Mercia.  Harold had his own lover to hurry back to in the person of Edith Swan-neck.

Olaf marched back with Tostig to York where he found Astrid still in the cottage given to them by Edwin. She was tending the garden which was just starting to show signs of Spring flowers appearing. When Olaf called out to her she jumped and her face flushed in guilty awkwardness. Recovering, she rushed to Olaf and threw her arms around his neck.

"Olaf, you've come back safely! I've been so worried about you. I heard the Welsh were cutting off the heads of any English soldiers they caught.  Come and have an ale and tell me all about your adventures."

A fire was burning in the cottage and soon Olaf was recounting the Welsh campaign in all it's gruesome detail.

"So Earl Harold is indebted to you for saving his life? That's incredible! How do you manage to get on the right side of all these powerful people. If it's not the King and Queen of Norway, it's the Jarl of Orkney or the Earl of Wessex, who, they say, is the most powerful man in the land."

Olaf never got to answer as there was a loud knock on the door. It was Renweard who also seemed awkward in welcoming Olaf back.

"Hello, Olaf. Sorry to trouble you but Tostig has asked to see you in the great hall in one hour."

"Oh good," said Olaf, "that gives us a little time to talk about what has been going on here while I have been away then."

"I think I'd better do all the talking for a while," said Astrid.

"Since you went away, just after Twelfth Night I've been left here alone but not alone. I've had the maid to help me but mostly it has been Renweard who has chopped the logs and brought in any game he had managed to shoot. One night, we had been drinking and Renweard told me that Morca wanted to take me as his concubine or mistress, which meant he could shower me with gifts, have his way with me but never have to marry me as I am not from a noble family.

I refused and when Renweard carried the news back to Morca, I started thinking about you, Olaf. Renweard returned saying that Morca was very disappointed but understood. Renweard then confessed that he loved me and wanted to marry me and raise a family. So, out of the three of you, Renweard is the only one prepared to make an honest woman of me. I told him we should wait for your return and talk things over."

Olaf looked at both of them and realised this was his way out.

"Astrid, it's true that, as long as I am tied up with the Godwins, I could never be a husband to you. Have you slept together yet?"

"No, but if he wants to raise a family we shall have to at some point!"

There was a silence, then Astrid snorted and all three burst out laughing.

"Renweard, be a good husband to my dear Astrid. I'm going over to see Tostig.  Astrid clutched Olaf in a big Norse, bosomy hug with tears in her eyes and whispered her thanks. Renweard smiled sheepishly and nodded his thanks. Striding to the door, Olaf felt a great weight lift from his shoulders as he called out:

"I'm just going to negotiate your wedding present as Harold and Tostig owe me."

Entering the Great Hall, two large Danish huscarls rumbled that Olaf was clear to enter.

"Ah, Olaf, come on in, I am in need of your services.  This young lad here is Cospatric. He is of the line of Uhtred of Bamburgh which is his castle by rights and was born there but, when I took him on a pilgrimage to Rome, his castle was seized by his uncle Gospatrick.

Gospatrick, Earl of Cumbria, who was evicted by King Malcolm III of Scotland while we were away and so seized Bamburgh as his own. He has been refusing to pay his taxes and now he has gone too far as two of his henchmen, Gamel and Orm have just attacked my tax-collectors with an armed ambush and killed two of my huscarls. I have a plan and I wish you to be part of it. Let's plot!"

The three of them sat at the long table and Tostig spoke with lowered voice.

"Having killed two of my tax collectors and two of my soldiers, Gospatrick will be expecting a revenge attack from me, not an invitation to parley under a promise of safe conduct. He will think I am offering more favourable taxation and will see this as a sign of weakness. He is too greedy not to take the bait and will come. We will invite them to dine and then have my huscarls hidden behind the tapestries where we will deal with them just as Canute did with Uhtred all those years ago. Do we still have that Welsh archer, Olaf?"

"Rhys of Prestatyn? Yes he came with us and he's being paid by you, as are seven others. The rest went with Harold or went back home."

"Excellent! They will bring a gang of retainers and we will make them wait in the courtyard where the archers will have a perfect shot from up here. Gospatrick, Orm and Ulf will be taken out by my huscarls in the hall. Cospatric, you will ride with Olaf and a dozen of my men to invite them to come here to dine and parley.

Cospatric did not care for this venture and was sure his uncle would try to have him killed. Olaf agreed it was risky, but as Tostig was taking none of the risks, they had little option but to go along with it. Before he left, Olaf asked a favour in return for his services.

He asked for the cottage, lent to him by Edwin of Mercia which technically belonged to Tostig, to be given as a wedding  present to Astrid as a dowry to Renweard. Tostig loved the idea of this:

"Is that the buxom Norse girl that Morca has been drooling over? Excellent, yes absolutely. Anything to annoy that little upstart."

And so it was agreed upon.

The journey to Bamburgh was a two-day ride from York up the North-East Coast of England. For the first time ever, Olaf found himself the trusted housecarl of Tostig, the Earl of Northumbria and in command of a diplomatic mission that was going to break all the rules of conflict, such as they were. His party consisted of Cospatric, who was to do all the talking, Rhys, who was told to do none of the talking, seven Welsh archers, four men at arms and a small Viking who was in overall command.

The reception at Bamburgh was a very cold one indeed. Given the outrage they had perpetrated on Tostig's tax collectors they were expecting a large force of retribution.

The castle was fully prepared for an attack and seige. Gospatrick himself was preparing a ship to escape. When they saw the very small body of men sent against them they laughed with all the arrogance of an enemy showing weakness in the face of an outrage.

Cospatric delivered his message with dignity, sat on his horse, outside in the cold of his own home stolen by his uncle. The offer of parley and special tax dispensations made by Tostig could not be turned down and this spectacular diplomatic appeasement was something that appealed to the greed of Gospatrick.

The reply however, was that a party would be sent with Gamel and Ulf to dine with Tostig in York and sign the papers of an agreement. Olaf whispered to Cospatric that he should insist that his uncle was in the party. Cospatric, being an astute diplomat understood that such a demand would arouse suspicion.

They returned to York without a sword being drawn but with no sign of hospitality being offered whatsoever. On the contrary, jeers and insults were shouted from the fortified walls. Rhys was not happy:

"Bastards! Let me take a few out as they are nicely in range for my boys."

Olaf spoke quietly:

"Our time will come, Rhys, mark their faces well and make sure you take them when they come to York."

"That I'll be sure to do."

They rode back with empty stomachs but in the knowledge that the job had been done and the snare had been set.

On returning, Tostig was elated and made sure that everyone in the party was treated to a splendid feast at his expense. Olaf was given a room in his quarters where he met again with the exquisitely lovely Ealdgyth whom he had met on Christmas Eve after his baptism.

Ealdgyth, as ever, was delighted to see Olaf and was even more unsubtle in her efforts to pump information from Olaf to feed to her brothers Edwin and Morca and more especially to hear what had happened to her husband, Gruffydd ap Llewellyn. Olaf's knowledge of the Welsh campaign and her recent widowhood made him indispensible to her and particularly the approaching trap that Tostig had planned.

It was several months later before a band of some thirty riders were spotted heading towards York from Bamburgh. At the head, with great swagger, were Gamel and Ulf wearing furs and bejewelled swords over their backs. They rode deliberatley with a casual nonchalance as of a party come to collect a debt. Their escort was not wearing armour and did not look as if they had come expecting a fight. Tostig had everything prepared.

Gamel and Ulf were invited into the private dining room of Tostig whilst his retinue were to be fed in the great hall. Olaf, Rhys and the Welsh bowmen were kept in the shadows on the balcony. Behind every tapestry and arras were four bloodthirsty Danish huscarls longing to get the reward promised by Tostig. Tostig had sent his wife Judith away as, being a devout Christian and daughter of Baldwin V of Flanders, she would not like to be witness to such murder. Instead he entertained Ealdgyth to the dinner with Gamel, Ulf and Cospatric. The rich food and wine flowed and, as the guests became more inebriated, Cospatric goaded them to speak unguardedly:

"So why did you feel it was right to kill the Earl's men?"

Gamel laughed towards Ulf:

"They made too many demands on our patience as if they thought they were the important one's in Northumbria."

Red-faced, Tostig stood up, knocking over his chair:

"Now is your time!"

From three different wall hangings came the Danes. A sword pierced Gamel through the back of the neck whilst an axe came down through his shoulder. He was halfway up when two more swords were driven through his body. Ulf had pulled a dagger and stood up with half a thought to try to use Ealdgyth as a hostage.

In that split second a mace had crashed into his skull spilling a mixture of blood and brains onto the table in front of Ealdgyth's plate. He was pierced by a host of enthusiastic Danes, desperate to blood their swords and earn some of the reward Tostig had offered. Ulf's body crumpled to the floor in a mess, opposite Gamel's, whose blonde beard was now stained red.

The huscarls dragged the bodies into the great hall where more Danes had appeared from behind the tapestries. The retinue looked with horror and, having no particular affinity with the two slain thegnes, threw down their weapons and backed away towards the staircase to the courtyard and their horses. There Olaf and the Welsh archers were waiting. Tostig followed with his huscarls and shouted to them to hold their fire. He needed word of this terror to get out. They were denied their horses and told to walk home. Rhys called out to one of the soldiers who looked up:

"Hey! You there boyo. What was that you called me back in Bemburgh?"

The soldier shook his head and raised his hands just as an arrow flew straight at his throat. The others were hustled through the fortified gates and out into the cold night air.

"Now I feel like a proper Dane!" muttered Tostig to Olaf.

Olaf moved back into the great hall but Tostig waved him into the private dining area where a group of large huscarls were removing the hacked bodies of Gamel and Ulf onto a cart in the courtyard below. In the corner of the room Cospatric was trying to calm a clearly shaken Ealdgyth who was in a state of shock and horror at the fact that some of the contents of Ulf's skull had spatterd over her fine velvet dress and his blood was still on her face and neck.

"Oy herregud!" Olaf shouted, reverting to his Norse dialect. "Come on, I'll take you to your maid and get you cleaned up."

Olaf opened the door of the annex where the maid was baby-sitting three young children but was fast asleep.

Ealdgyth, put her finger to her lips and shook her head:

"Don't wake them, I wouldn't want them to see me like this," she whispered. Grabbing a long white nightdress, she took Olaf's hand and moved back into the corridor.

"Do you have a bath Olaf?" Olaf nodded. "then you will have to help me."

Entering Olaf's apartment, she found it tidy and sparse with a log fire heating a cauldren of water. Olaf carefully removed the red, heart-shaped escoffion from her head and her raven-black hair tumbled free, mercifully untouched by the gore. He then proceeded to undo the ribbons and laces and the layers of velvet and silk corsets until Ealgyth's white shoulders were visible.

Olaf poured the hot water into the metal bath and topped it up with cooler water from a pail. He then took a sponge and gently wiped the blood from her face and neck.  Olaf handed her a large towel but she waved it away:

"Don't be so coy Olaf! You've been living with Astrid and I heard a rumour that you slept with the Queen Consort of Norway!"

Ealdgyth's eyes, bloodshot with tears, now twinkled into a mischievous smile.

"Now help me out of this tortuous final garment."

With the release of the ribbons, Ealdgyth's ribcage returned to its natural place and she breathed a sigh of relief. The clothes were now piled on the floor as Olaf helped the ex-Queen of Wales slip into the steaming tub. Olaf began to pick up the rich collection of clothes and undergarments:

"I'll send these out to get them cleaned."

"No you won't!  Throw the lot on the fire. I don't want anything to remind me of tonight's horror.  Let's talk of other things. Why have you left Astrid? You were so close."

"She is to marry Renweard. Tostig has gifted me the cottage and I have given it to Astrid as a wedding present."

"You really are a very lovely, kind-hearted Viking. No wonder Tora wanted to sleep with you. It's not just your looks, which are arresting, you have a gentleness and kindness of soul that women of quality find very attractive."

Ealdgyth stepped out of the tub and the fire threw a light across her body which caused Olaf to catch his breath. She slipped into the white night-gown.

"Did Tora order you?"

"No", said Olaf, "she came into my room unannounced, took what she wanted and left without a word."

Ealdgyth laughed, "That's Vikings for you. I, however, am a Mercian Lady, a Queen and now a widow. I am asking you kindly, will you comfort me tonight, Olaf? I have had a very trying day and I need some solace."

Olaf looked into her dark, oval eyes and noticed that same look he had once seen in Freya back in Dalby village. It said, *I choose you.* It would have been wrong to refuse such a lady.

## *Chapter Twenty-Seven:*
## *Olaf in London*

The year 1064 passed quickly in relative peace and calm. Astrid and Renweard were married by the Archbishop Ealdred of York with Morcar giving Astrid away (reluctantly) and Olaf standing as Best Man for Renweard. It was not a handfasting but a proper Christian wedding with Edwin of Mercia and his sister Ealdgyth lending some aristocratic tone. By early December, Astrid was expecting her first child.

Tostig spent most of his time with Judith at Peterborough or in London and was rarely in Northumbria to notice that, although the greatly raised taxes were now being collected, there was a huge underswell of discontent in the North.

Ealdgyth had become infatuated with Olaf but was careful that their trysts should be a closely guarded secret. The second Advent candle was already lit in York when a Royal courier arrived on a mud-stained mount to bring word to Ealdgyth that King Edward had invited her, with a small entourage, to travel to London as his guest for the coming *Feast of Christemas*. As Tostig was not there, Ealdgyth asked Edwin if she might take two archers and four men-at arms to guard against bandits on the road. Of course, she wanted to bring Olaf and Olaf suggested the reliable Rhys of Prestatyn and four gloomy Northumbrian soldiers. On the long cold journey South, Ealdgyth and Olaf chatted constantly about what possible reason the King would have in summoning them to London at Christmas.

Finally, the smoking dwellings that surrounded the great River Thames came into view and they were admitted into the city of London. The fine Abbey at Westminster was a breath-taking sight and was Edward the Confessor's life-work. They were greeted in the Great Hall at Westminster by the ageing and wrinkly form of the King, along with his young and vibrant wife Edith, daughter of Godwin and sister to Tostig and Harold.

"Ah, Queen Ealdgyth, the legends of your beauty were not exaggerated," said the King in a parchment-dry, throaty whisper. "We cannot have such a beauty in our kingdom without a tall handsome noble by your side."

Olaf shifted uncomfortably.

"The most powerful Earl in the land, Harold, son of Godwin is looking to make a treaty that will bind your Mercian brothers, Edwin and Morcar to unite Wessex, Mercia and Northumbria and appease your late husband's murder in Wales. Such a marriage will bring unity and peace to England. But all of that can wait. It is almost the Feast of Christmas and I need to pray a little. Edith here will show you to your quarters, which I hope you will find comfortable. We received your message and your Norse huscarl will be billeted close by for your protection. Your lady in waiting will be in the annex. The men will be billeted with the Royal Housecarls."

Edith came forward smiling which quickly dropped as a large man wearing furs and jewels came into the King's Presence unannounced and followed the King in an effort to speak with him on his way to prayer. The King was already into the corridor when he sensed someone running and puffing behind him. Outraged, the King turned with bulging eyes as the corpulent man fell to his knees.

"Majesty, I am Gospatrick of Bamburgh and I beg for your help as I seek justice for the murder of two of my men in York."

"Are these the same two who murdered my tax collectors in Northumbria?"

"Majesty, Earl Tostig has raised the taxes to an extortionate amount that we cannot pay."

"The Earl was acting on my orders, how dare you approach me like this? Leave my Presence immediately!"

Two burly housecarls came running into the corridor and lifted the large man to his feet as the elderly King continued on his way to his prayers. At this moment, from the throne room, Olaf caught sight of his face as he was escorted roughly back to the doors.

"Gospatrick!" he gasped to Ealdgyth.

Gospatrick recognised Olaf who had ridden to Bamburgh:

"So, you know who I am do you? I am the son of Uhtred, murdered by Canute in 1016. I am the rightful Earl of Northumberland and you can tell your Earl Tostig that I will kill him personally when he gets here."

The great doors swung open and Gospatrick was evicted outside where a group of his followers were waiting.

Queen Edith was appalled:

"How dare he enter unannounced! How did he get past you? Captain of the Guard, call out the housecarls, I want a quadruple watch on the King. Ealdgyth, may I borrow your Norse lad for a moment?"

Moving out of earshot of Ealdgyth's party, Queen Edith took Olaf into a quiet corner.

"That man is going to upset our Christmas plans I fear unless we do something quickly."

"Your Majesty, if Queen Ealdgyth allows it, I will take out this bloated windbag who is threatening your brother and has committed this outrage against your husband, the King. He has a number of bodyguards with him so I should ask to bring along my trusty Welsh bowman Rhys, who was spared by your brother, Earl Harold on the campaign in Wales. He is loyal."

"There will be silver for you both if you do this for me. Apart from Ealdgyth, no one is to know, on this you must swear."

Olaf and Rhys headed out into the filthy streets of London. It was getting dark but a Royal guard had said Gospatrick's party were heading towards the river embankment where they were meeting at a tavern.

"Well, they shouldn't be hard to find," said Rhys. "Six burly boyos with Cumbrian accents here in London."

They made their way to the river through the squalor and, sure enough, there were two taverns less than half a mile apart. As anticipated, in the second tavern by the fire was the huge silhouette of Gospatrick with his gang of warriors downing draughts of ale and plotting the death of Earl Tostig.

"Seven boyos against just the two of us, it hardly seems fair."

Olaf grinned: "We'll wait this one out, Rhys."

Olaf and Rhys entered the crowded tavern with hoods up, as many in the Inn had, against the cold. They drank ale slowly, unlike Gospatrick's followers who, close to midnight, were inebriated and full of murderous bravura against Earl Tostig.

One went out to relieve himself and never returned. Rhys returned with bloodied knife and a wink to Olaf:

"Well, that just leaves three each!"

The six left the tavern, oblivious of the fact that they were leaving one of their own in a back alley with his throat cut. Olaf and Rhys slipped out behind them in the dark and followed them to the river. Olaf wanted Gospatrick as his own bagged game. Suddenly, the cloud cleared and the party were illumined by an almost full moon, of men staggering around and singing drunken and ribald catches from their home in Cumbria.

"Take two and three," Olaf called out.

Olaf's bow sang in the cold air and caught Gospatrick a mortal wound in his breast. Rhys's great bow went through the huge bodyguard's armour and his swift second arrow felled another thegne. Olaf and Rhys felled a further two before the last survivor cried out for mercy, which was granted. He fled, screaming his gratitude, into the darkness of the London embankment.

It was high-tide, so welcome for Olaf and Rhys as they rolled the heavy, bleeding and lifeless bodies into the fast-moving Thames thereby sweeping away the bloody evidence the Queen was so keen to keep concealed.

"Job well done, my Welsh friend. Come on, let's get back to Westminster and enjoy the whole-hearted gratitude of Queen Edith and, indeed, the whole bloody Godwin family."

Back at Westminster it was now Christmas Eve. Festivities were all pre-planned and the excitement was palpable. Edith had ordered the guards to inform her immediately on the return of Olaf.

The King and his court were celebrating Midnight Mass with the new arrival of the Godwin Earls; Tostig from Northumbria and

Harold, with his beautiful concubine, Edith Swanneck, from Wessex. Olaf was told to sit and wait or join Queen Ealdgyth in the Abbey.  Sweating and bloodied, Olaf chose to go and bathe. Rhys joined his fellows in the Royal barracks and found it very hard not to disclose his sworn oath of secrecy to protect Queen Edith.

And so, the year of 1064 came to a close with the Godwin family very much in control of the country. Ealdgyth, lover of Olaf, was to marry Harold Godwin and unite Wessex with the North. Tostig Godwinson was Earl of Northumbria. The King was ailing and childless with no heir despite his young wife who was sister to Harold and Tostig.  So, what could possibly go wrong for this all-powerful clan?

# *Chapter Twenty-eight:*
# *Olaf in Normandy*

The court at Westminster, though dominated by the Godwin family was still very much under the rule of the King. Whilst Rhys was rewarded with silver, Ealdgyth treated Olaf as she would a nobleman. He was to sit with her at all public events and sleep with her, discretely, as often as possible.

Queen Edith doted on her brother Tostig and was so pleased that Olaf had removed the embarrassment and danger of Gospatrick that she positively encouraged the inclusion of Olaf as Ealdgyth's 'plus one' even after Harold had publicly asked the King if he might take Ealdgyth in marriage. This surprised Olaf but left Ealdgyth unmoved.

Edith Swanneck, however, was deeply upset. About forty years old and ten years older than Ealdgyth, she was still a beautiful woman and had been with Harold for twenty years, married in the old Norse style of 'handfasting', a marriage no longer recognised by the Church. Harold's great scheme was to crown himself King on Edward's death and marry Ealdgyth in a political union to bring the North on-side, bearing in mind she was the sister of Edwin and Morcar. This 'legitimate' wedding would effectively make the six children Edith Swanneck had born Harold, illegitimate and it was clear that Harold wanted a son and heir, born of a wife recognised by the Church. Olaf felt very sorry for Edith who had given Harold her love and devotion for some twenty years of her life.

One morning in early Spring of 1065, Harold summoned Olaf to meet with him. Olaf thought he may have discovered that he and Harold's intended were in fact passionate lovers. The truth was that Harold still loved Edith Swanneck and was only interested in Ealdgyth as a political pawn. No, he had other things to discuss.

"Ah Olaf, come in, come in."

Olaf sat, as beckoned, in Harold's chamber but not before making a deliberate bow to the elegant Lady Edith seated at her embroidery frame.

"Olaf, you saved my life back in Wales so I'm offering you the chance to come down to Bosham with me and accompany me on a very exciting adventure. Being Norse, you'll be a good sailor and as my French is pretty rough you can help if we speak Norse. There are two boys from my family who are being held captive by the Duke of Normandy who is called William the Bastard. The boys were given to Edward as hostages when my father Earl Godwin was sent into exile. They were then snatched by thugs working for the mad, ousted Archbishop of London, Robert of Jumièges and squirreled away to become hostages of William. I need to go there and negotiate their release. One is my youngest brother Wulfnorth and the second is my nephew, Hakon, son of my late brother, Sweyn. If you do this for me, I will make you a thegne and grant you lands with your title. Then we can find you a proper wife!"

Olaf blushed a little and tried not to catch Edith's eye. But Harold took that theme no further.

And so it was that Olaf and a small party of handy-looking housecarls departed from London to the tiny Sussex village of Bosham, near Chichester. There, a boat was waiting and the party boarded, but not before saying a prudent prayer in the little church nearby.

The Channel was choppy and the small boat was thrown about a good deal. Finally, just as the coast of Normandy was sighted, a huge storm blew up and sent their vessel Eastwards towards Flanders. For a while it seemed as if the boat would come apart as it was taking in water at a rapid rate. Just then, a merciful lull in the storm enabled the sailors to steer towards a somewhat rocky coastline.

It was there that their luck ran out and, in unison with a great crack of lightening, the hull crashed into some substantial, submerged rocks. A huge cross-wave caught the vessel and threw it closer to the shore, spilling out several housecarls whose chainmail ensured they would never surface.

A mast cracked and fell just in front of Olaf, who picked up an axe dropped by one of the late housecarls and hacked it free from its moorings. Harold at once realised what Olaf was planning and joined him by clinging on to the severed mast as they were thrown from the boat by another great wave. The move was timely as the boat struck yet another rock and came apart.

Olaf and Harold clung desperately to the mast which was being washed ashore, exactly as Olaf had hoped and, before long, the Earl's long legs had touched the bottom and was able to walk to the shore with Olaf's legs still flailing hopelessly in the sea. Finally, Olaf felt the shingle under his leather shoes and helped run the beam ashore.

Harold was exhausted as the weight of his sword and chain mail had all but pulled him away from the mast but Olaf was able to recover himself armed with only a dagger, a quiver and his lightweight bow.  He stood on guard now in the failing light as a few more of the sailors staggered ashore, coughing and gasping. Several hundred yards away, a body of mounted knights carrying weapons and torches thundered to their proximity and Olaf instinctively threaded an arrow with dripping flights.

There appeared to be just six survivors of the original twenty men as the housecarls had all learned the difficult lesson that Olaf had witnessed at the Battle of Nså concerning the drawbacks of swimming whilst dressed for battle.

The sailors in their leather tunics had made it ashore and now huddled around the Earl with daggers drawn. Twenty-four mounted men-at-arms appeared above on the clumps of grass and sand dunes and approached at a walk with lances raised to form a crescent around Harold's bedraggled group. One knight called out from behind his long pear-shaped shield:

"Are you English invaders?"

"I am Harold Godwinson, Earl of Wessex and I have business with William, Duke of Normandy.

"Ha ha!" guffawed the soldier who proudly showed off his linguistic ability, "you will not find him here. This land belongs to Count Guy of Ponthieu who makes a modest living out of shipwrecked unfortunates like yourself. You are now his prisoner until your ransom is paid. My mother was English and her ransom was never paid so now I must serve him and speak French every day. I'm afraid you must come with us, the Castle of Beaurain is six hours from here and there you will meet your captor, Guy of Ponthieu, who will decide your fate."

After a short walk in the rain, they came to the small barracks and stables where the soldiers were able to keep look-out for any passing traffic in the Channel. Mercifully, there was a covered cart which the soldiers kept expressly for the purpose of transporting prisoners.

Beaurain was hardly a castle, more a fortified Château, but it did have a purpose-built jail where Guy, a short, moustachioed hunchback, could ply his dubious trade. The sailors were told they would not be worth any ransom so had the choice of working as serfs for Guy or being put to the sword. They chose the former.

Olaf was given the same option but Harold intervened on his behalf claiming Olaf to be a thegne and companion of the Earl. It was the best he could do considering Olaf had now saved his life on two occasions. Guy said he would make enquiries about the value of his two captives but, after a few days, his plans were shattered by the arrival of about fifty Norman knights demanding the immediate release of Guy's two captives. Guy's face twisted in despair at the thought of losing his prize but one of the knights threw him a leather pouch of coins which seemed to placate him. Harold and Olaf were then set free to be taken by a different group of armed men to the castle of the Duke of Normandy.

The Normans had brought spare horses with them as well as provisions for the journey of some one hundred and fifty miles. Olaf thought how uncomfortable these tall Norman warhorses were compared to the short, ambling Icelandic mounts he had ridden in Norway. But they were fast and after a rainy journey of fifteen hours, they reached the impressive Castle of Falaise, birthplace and home of William of Normandy.

It was early evening and they were weary and hungry. The duke could not have been more accommodating. The hall in the central keep was smoky from the constant rain down the chimney but it was warm and dry and there was a delicious aroma of cooking. William spoke no English but did understand Norse so that Olaf was able to translate for Harold.

Olaf sized up the duke as being about five foot ten and of very athletic build. He was probably in his late thirties and had a sharp eye, a chiselled jaw and a guttural manor of speech. But he smiled at Harold and said how pleased he was that King Edward had sent his most senior Earl to reaffirm the promise Edward had made to William whilst he was in exile in Normandy. Harold, standing a good six inches taller, neither agreed nor denied that this was the case.

The tension was broken as trays of hot food were brought in and William invited his 'guests' to dine with him and was joined by his wife Matilda whose sister, Judith, was married to Harold's brother, Tostig. Matilda did speak English and happily translated for her husband leaving Olaf free to pile into the food, oblivious of the gazes of Matilda's eldest daughter, Adeliza, aged about eighteen, and trying to catch his eye.

It appeared that William was practically always at war with his neighbours and was planning a raid on Brittany in the coming weeks and should like it if Harold and Olaf would come along to see how effective the Norman knights were. Harold agreed and Olaf nodded. Then Harold brought up the subject of the two Godwin boys being held as hostages.

"My youngest brother Wulfnoth and my nephew Hakon have been kept here for over ten years. I brought considerable wealth with me to negotiate their release but it is either lying at the bottom of the estuary or has washed up into the grubby hands of that odious pirate, Guy of Ponthieu."

William listened as Matilda translated and laughed before replying:

"Ze Duke 'as said zay are well treated and staying in 'is new castle in Caen. 'Ee says you can visit zem before ze army travels down to Mont Saint Michel?"

Harold nodded his thanks to William.

Olaf had just discovered how very fine Normandy cider was and its effects on him meant that he now noticed the smiling attention being bestowed on him by Adeliza. Matilda had noticed and whispered something in her daughter's ear. They both giggled and Adeliza got up and went into the scullery to return a few moments later with a jug and two small goblets. One she placed in front of the Earl and the second in front of Olaf.

She then poured a clear, dark, golden liquid into his goblet before attending to the Earl. Olaf smelt the liquid suspiciously and then took a huge draught, almost emptying the cup.

"Oy herregud!" he cried, having managed to swallow the fierce brandy with watering eyes. Matilda and Adeliza laughed and watched Harold who disappointed by sipping it carefully.

"It eez called *Calvados,* cognac made with apples."

The hilarity was lost on the humourless Duke who invited Harold to join him in another room for a game of chess, which needed no translation. This left Olaf with the ladies and a couple of guards. Matilda stayed with Adeliza, realising her daughter was a little infatuated with the visitor and knowing she must offer her daughter for a noble match in pristine condition.

A steward appeared when Matilda rang a little bell and was instructed to show Olaf to his room. Adeliza stood up and planted a small peck on Olaf's cheek:

*"Bonne nuit, Olaf, fais de beaux rêves."*

Olaf smiled back and followed the steward to his room where some kind servant had lit a fire.

After a not unpleasant few days in the company of the fair Adeliza, Harold appeared and announced that he and some Norman knights were going to ride up to Caen, not far from the Normandy coast, in order to see the two Godwin boys, Wulfnoth and Hakon. Olaf was informed that he was coming too.

They set off in the morning with six knights with shields, helmets and lances, whose pennants fluttered in the summer breeze. It was just over a two-hour ride when they arrived at a brand-new castle in gleaming white stone from the local quarries. They clattered over the wooden drawbridge and into the courtyard to be greeted by several men-at arms who took their horses. A tall thin lad wearing a Saxon-style moustache called out to Harold:

"Brother? Is that you? It's Wulfnoth and here is Hakon."

Hakon came forward looking about sixteen with long blonde hair inherited from his father Sweyn Godwinson. Harold choked:

"Boys? Is it really you? I am so sorry." Tears streamed down his cheeks to his moustache as he held the two lads in a family embrace. Twelve long years they had been held captive and no-one had come for them.

"I'll get you home," said Harold. "But first I have to win over the Duke. He wants me to go on campaign with him in his squabble with Conan II, the new Duke of Brittany."

After a light lunch at the castle, Harold and Olaf bid farewell to the unfortunate hostages and headed towards Mont Saint Michel with the mounted knights in order to meet up with William's army. The journey was about seven hours and, as light was fading, the knights suggested that they stop over at a château owned by the young Hugh d'Avranches whose mother, Emma de Conteville, was the half-sister of Duke William and, therefore, his nephew.

Hugh and Olaf were of a similar age but Hugh was thickly built with a physique that would turn to portliness in later life. When the knights explained who they were, he nodded and smiled saying that William had come through there the other day and told him to expect guests, including the Earl of Wessex.

The table in the hall of his fine castle was all set out for a feast and Hugh proudly introduced his pretty young fiancé, Ermentrude of Claremont who, it was explained, was the daughter of Hugh, Count of Claremont. A knight from William's escort came forward to translate.

His accent was immediately recognisable as the Anglo-French rider from the beach at Ponthieu. He quickly explained to Harold that he was, in fact, in the service of the Duke and was placed as a spy in Guy's small force. That is how William came to hear about Harold's shipwreck so quickly. He told Harold that his name was William Mallet but was now obliged to call himself Guillaume de Malet and was sworn to the Duke under force.

After a good night's revelries, the Earl and Olaf presented themselves in the courtyard for breakfast before making the journey to the massive Abbey de Mont Saint Michel, which they could see from many miles off. William Mallet came with them to help with interpreting.

Approaching the beach, there seemed to be some fighting taking place as Duke William's men were clearly making heavy weather of routing a small contingent of Conan's soldiers. Two foot-soldiers ran forward and threw their arms into the air as they plunged waist-deep into a lethal patch of quicksand. The soldiers screamed for help as the relentless gravity and suction guaranteed their swift demise. Harold and Olaf, almost simultaneously, rose in their stirrups and kicked hard to the rescue of the two terrified foot soldiers. Leaping from their mounts Harold lay flat on the wet sand with Olaf passing him his bow for the, all but doomed, soldiers to catch hold of. Just then, William Mallet arrived and prostrated himself on the wet sucking sand.

He, however, had a lance to offer and Harold was able to extract the terrified soldiers from a hideous death. Harold, Olaf and William Mallet pulled the men to safety to the cheers of the Norman army, watched, with jealous admiration by the Duke of Normandy.

*Mont Saint-Michel*

Duke William tried hard to conceal his anger that his army had failed to suppress the slippery Conan of Brittany and that his forces had not impressed Harold but rather had shown them up for their incompetence and that he, Harold, had emerged smelling of roses. Inwardly, William fumed with jealous rage.

The Duke, after a futile and expensive campaign, and failing to get Conan to commit to battle, decided to cut his losses as supplies were starting to become a problem. He ordered a withdrawal back into the Norman city of Rouen. Harold gave Olaf a wink as if to say *this would never have happened under my command.* But William had still his master plan to play.

Riding into the great Cathedral city with its awesome Norman architecture, William announced that there would be a great mass to celebrate the deliverance and victory of the Norman army and to bestow a gallant knighthood upon the valiant Earl of Wessex for his services in action.

As they rode into Rouen, beautiful maidens threw flowers from their windows as Harold's pride and vanity swelled. Olaf warned of a ruse but Harold was not listening. Harold was invited to a great banquet for Norman nobility in which Olaf was excluded. For the first time since their landing, Olaf was not there to keep an eye on his Earl. Instead, he and William Mallet went into town to enjoy the local taverns and talent. Since the voluptuous Ulli back in Norway, Olaf had not given vent to his desire for common girls. It was not long before William returned with a dusky maiden named Hèloïse to amuse the delighted Olaf.

She was as attracted by his thick blonde hair and beard and his deep blue eyes as he was with her richly dark brunette hair and sultry eyes. William translated for a while before leaving them alone to make pictures with their hands and giggle at each other's lack of comprehension.

Olaf booked a room at the tavern and enjoyed a night of gallic abandonment, attempting to satisfy the almost unquenchable appetite of the unfeasibly shapely Hèloïse. Olaf awoke to the babble in the street below and with itching ankles from flea bites. But of Hèloïse there was no sign save for some long dark hairs on the pillow. Pulling on his clothes, he made his way back to the castle to attend to Harold.

The Earl of Wessex looked slightly worse for wear as, apparently, a great feast had been prepared in Harold's honour whereby he was presented with a fine coat of mail, a beautifully crafted sword from the finest swordsmith in Normandy and, most tellingly, a helmet which William placed upon Harold's head in person. Harold was now a knight of the realm and must therefore swear fealty to William.

Olaf shook his head ruefully:

"This doesn't bode well, my Lord. Is he going to make you swear an oath?"

Harold looked pained at having this spelt out for him by Olaf.

"I have to go along with it if I am to have any chance of getting the boys back to England. Now help me get this mail shirt on then go and tidy yourself up, you look a mess and you've straw in your hair. We are to be at Rouen Cathedral at a quarter to twelve where I am required to join them for a Mass and the oath of fealty on my part to that cunning Norman fox."

Olaf struggled with the great weight of the chainmail shirt and knew it would have cost Duke William a small fortune plus the fine sword. Whatever his plan was, he wasn't doing anything in half measures.

Olaf managed to wash and brush his matted hair. He put on some quite dashing Norman clothes that Matilda had laid out for him in Falaise. He looked at his reflection in his dagger and thought that he would pass Harold's scrutiny for the ceremony.

It seemed like the whole of the Norman clergy and nobility had arrived in Rouen and were all flocking into the great cathedral. The duke's half-brother, Bishop Odo of Bayeux was heading up the service with a host of acolytes, much to the chagrin of the Bishop of Rouen who was acting as suffragan or helper to Odo.

The service was all in Latin so Harold was able to clearly understand all that was going on. On the chancel steps was a great wooden box or reliquary with crosses on each corner and covered with a coloured cloth.

The monks sang the mass until the Credo and there they stopped. The bishop now continued in French and gestured to Harold to approach. At this point the monks began singing the Sanctus and Duke William came forward and took his place on a carved wooden throne.

In his hand he held a sword which he lent over his shoulder like a sceptre of power. A second reliquary was brought out covered with a scarlet cloth. Bishop Odo placed Harold's hands so that they touched both. A further prayer in Latin and then the questions to Harold about his acceptance of William as his overlord and recognising his claim to the throne of England as promised by Edward the Confessor. Harold, half understanding, bridled noticeably at this but nodded and muttered "Oui" through clenched teeth. Bishop Odo then made the sign of the cross and removed the cloths on the two reliquaries proclaiming loudly:

*"Regarde, Sainte Ouen et Sainte Catherine!"*

There was a great intake of breath from the congregation and a great deal of crossing themselves and genuflecting. The monks sang the Dona nobis pacem after the Agnus Dei and the Bishops and acolytes processed out, following a vast golden cross and two golden candlesticks. Harold turned on his heel and stormed out of the Cathedral with a face like thunder with Olaf struggling to keep up with the Earl as he pushed his way through the throng and out into the fresh air. The thousands of candles and the pungent smell of incense combined with the aroma of six hundred unwashed Normans made for a suffocating environment and Harold, in the light of what had recently happened, had just suffered a claustrophobic panic attack.

In the bright sunshine the bells pealed above the great rosary window. Waiting for them on the steps of the vast West door was William Mallet.

"My lord," said William with a courteous nod, "I think now would be a very good time to make your escape via Caen with the two Godwin boys. I can help you there and explain that the Duke has ordered their release. Then I should like to return to England in your service. I have horses ready and I managed to recover some of your treasure washed up at Ponthieu – easily enough to purchase a boat."

"Good man!" said Harold, "let's leave quickly and get out of this nightmare before anyone notices."

They took four good horses, one laden with gold and silver and were just about to depart when a girl came running up the hill clutching flowers.

*"Olaf! Où allez-vous ? S'il vous plaît restez ici avec moi, s'il vous plaît ! ..... »* It was Héloïse.

Olaf smiled, sheepishly:

"Some help here please William!"

William called out to the distraught girl:

*« Olaf doit partir avec son seigneur mais il te remercie pour une merveilleuse soirée... au revoir ! »* (Olaf must depart with his lord now but thanks you for a wonderful evening.... good-bye!)

The four horses clattered away over the cobble stones as the pretty girl threw her flowers to the floor with a petulant *"Merde!"*

They arrived at Caen at eight o'clock in the evening after a seven-hour ride.  William Mallet called out to the guards who opened the gates at once.

"Bon soir, gentlemen. My name is Hubert du Mont-Canisy. My English is not perfect but I am ze seigneur of Deauville and Caen I am instructed to help you wiz your journey 'ome. I 'ave one boy for you to take wiz you. Ze uzzer 'as moved to Bayeux. When you 'ave kept your word to ze Duke 'ee will be returned. I 'ave a ship for you at Deauville which is a gift from Duke William."

Harold's face reddened:

"This is not acceptable! I must have my youngest brother and my nephew returned. They were abducted by Archbishop Robert of Jumièges and brought here by force. He also brought a forged letter from King Edward naming Duke William as his successor and has made me swear an oath of allegiance under duress. I have done this and now my kinsmen must be returned to our family."

Hubert du Mont-Canisy shrugged a gallic shrug with his palms turned upward:

"I am sorry m'sieur, it is out of my 'ands."

And so it was, the following day, that Harold, his nephew Hakon Sweynson, Olaf Slagbjørn and William Mallet set sail for England. The ever-thoughtful Duke had even purchased the freedom of the four surviving sailors from Bosham who were waiting for them at Le Touquet to guide the ship safely home after what had been nothing short of a disastrous episode. Just as in the game of chess they had played in Falaise, William had completely out-witted his opponent. Harold would never see his youngest brother Wulfnoth again.

Two knights with lances and Hubert du Mont-Canisy watched the ship depart North carrying with it not only the future King of England but Guillaume Malet de Graville, whose mother was indeed English and whose elder sister, Aelgifu had married Ælfgar, Earl of Mercia and father of Edwin, Morcar and Ealdgyth.

This was the same Dowager Queen Ealdgyth, widow of Gruffydd ap Llewellyn, whom Harold was proposing as Queen Consort and with whom Olaf had enjoyed nightly excursions. William Mallet, therefore, was her uncle and the Duke's planted agent in England.

## *Chapter Twenty-Nine:*
## *The Northumbrian Revolt 1065*

The ship sailed up the estuary to Southampton and the four travellers disembarked: Harold, Hakon, Olaf, and William. Harold gifted the ship to the sailors, who were grateful to escape with their lives, and sailed back to Bosham to ply their trade.

Moving up to Winchester, Harold met with the King who held Court there. King Edward was with the Queen, Harold's sister Edith, and his brother Tostig, when he presented the results of his ill-fated trip to Normandy: a young nephew called Hakon and an oath to support William's claim to the throne of England. Edward was absolutely furious, as were his delighted courtiers, who never missed an opportunity to launch a political assault at the Godwin family.

Harold stood silently as Edward administered a huge royal public dressing down as to the great danger in which Harold had placed the security of his kingdom. Edward then produced a young lad of about fourteen years.

"Earl Harold of Wessex, do you know who this boy is?"

"Yes, my King, this is the son of Edward the Exile who was deposed by the Danes and returned here in 1057 but who died shortly after his arrival."

Edward continued:

"His only son, Edgar, is now called 'the Ætheling' as he is the next in line to the throne. He is the last remaining male of the direct line of the House of Wessex. His grandfather was Edward Ironside and he has a direct bloodline back to Alfred the Great and thence to the original royal line of Cerdic who founded the royal line of Wessex and ruled from 519 to 534 AD.

He is the only real claimant to the throne of England and I require you, Earl Harold, to swear an oath that you will uphold his legitimate right to the throne of England for which you must act as regent."

Olaf gasped as he recognised the word 'Ætheling' that had been explained to him by the Prior at Lindisfarne. He looked at Harold seeing a man who was about to perjure himself for the second time in just a month. But Harold was in too deep now and his eternal soul was cast aside for the ambition which drove him, like a gambler on a losing streak, sure that his luck must change for the better sometime soon.

Harold took the oath and then explained to the King that he had recently built a beautiful hunting lodge, at huge cost, just by the River Severn which his craftsmen were in the last stages of completing. No expense had been spared and the luxury with which it was furbished was clearly designed and laid out to impress the King and win him back into favour. It came, therefore, as a terrible shock when messengers arrived from Hereford with the awful news that the Welsh, in a mood of bloody retribution, had descended upon Harold's luxury hunting lodge, just as the artisans were finishing their exquisite work, and massacred the entire workforce and thereafter razed the place to the ground. This came as a severe blow upon a bruise for Harold.

Harold released Olaf from his service with a generous purse and a promise of land yet to be bestowed. Olaf headed straight back to London and into the arms of the Dowager Queen, Ealdgyth, who greeted him tearfully.  For the moment, Olaf was safe under the protection of a powerful noble lady and, furthermore, she wished to return back to York to be within the safety net of her brothers Edwin and Morcar.

Queen Edith had been sponsoring a beautiful Abbey in Wiltshire in order to placate the then Pope as to her marriage to Edward which had still to be, and never was, consummated. So, King Edward and his wife Edith, Harold and Edith Swanneck, Tostig and Judith and other members of the Godwin family all travelled down to Salisbury and nearby Wilton for the dedication of the church.

It was at this time of religious devotion that a messenger arrived with the news that the North was in absolute uproar. The locals had massacred the two hundred Danish huscarls and had put to death anyone who was deemed to be associated with Tostig in any way whatsoever. Edwin and Morcar had finally brought their plan together to usurp the Godwins from the North of England and oust the hated Tostig.  Harold was immediately sent North with an army to face down the rebellion.

But from Mercia, Wales and the whole North of England, the army had gathered together into an immense body under arms. Harold met them as far South as Northampton where they were in no mood to parley.

There were bodies hanging from trees and burning villages as the mob went on the rampage against anyone who allied with Tostig. Tostig, they said, was a Southerner with no knowledge of the Viking North whom he had over-taxed, had stolen from the Church and murdered citizens and local nobles under the guise of a flag of truce.

Tostig must go and there would be no negotiation on that point. The local appointment of the people was Morcar, son of Ælfgar, Earl of Mercia and brother of Edwin now Earl of Mercia. Harold wondered how long this plot had been in the hatching and wished he had his shrewd-minded Olaf with him to advise. Harold returned with the demands of the rebel force.

Back in Wiltshire, Edward had summoned an emergency council near Sorviodunum (Sarum) not far from Wilton. There were ugly scenes in which magnates accused Tostig of a tyrannical rule of cruelty and avarice. It got worse when Harold returned from Northampton with the rebels' demands.

Tostig screamed that his brother was not only in league with the rebels but had conspired to cause the rebellion in order to seize Tostig's land in Northumbria. Harold, yet again, swore a sacred oath that he was in no way involved.

On October 27th, 1065, Harold rode to the rebels to avert a civil war. In Oxford, Harold granted the rebels their demands. Morcar was to be made Earl of Northumbria with Tostig removed from his land and title. On November 1st, an outraged Tostig, his wife and family along with many of his loyal thegns, including Cospatric, crossed over to the ever-hospitable Count Baldwin of Flanders, father-in law to Tostig.

The distress of Tostig's mother and sister was as nothing compared to the rage of the King himself. Such was the King's mental anguish that he fell sick as a result and his sickness grew worse from day to day.

Although his lifetime ambition to complete the Abbey at Westminster was all but fulfilled, he was unable to attend the dedication of the magnificent building, so Edith acted in his stead. On January 5th, 1066, the King was surrounded by just four figures:

Edith his wife, Archbishop Stigand, the loyal Robert - a steward, and Harold Godwinson.

The King began making his final and terminal decrees regarding his legacy and final will. His last words were all about keeping his young wife safe. His recorded words were '*I commend this woman and all the kingdom to your protection*' ... a long way short of naming Harold as his successor. On the morning of January 6th, King Edward, known as 'The Confessor', died quietly in his bed.

# *Chapter Thirty:*
## *The King is dead, long live the King!*

Olaf was with Ealdgyth in her apartment in Westminster when there was a gentle knock on the door. It was Queen Edith and her eyes were red with tears.

"Lady Ealdgyth, forgive my interrupting, but I think you should know that the King has died this morning and they are taking his body to Westminster Abbey, the place which occupied so much of his energy during his reign and which was Dedicated only the other day.

There will be a Lying in of State and the funeral will be the day after tomorrow. Because of the Dedication of the Abbey and the Feast of The Epiphany, all the Bishops and Archbishops in the land are in London plus the five Earls, my three brothers and your two, Edwin and Morcar. Only Tostig will be absent. I think my brother Harold will summon the Witan to ask for the Crown and he plans to be crowned as soon as possible.

This means of course that you will have to give up your Viking friend here as you will be Queen Consort until he marries you. He will need an heir too as his children with Edith Swanneck will not be legitimate.  I must go to the Abbey now and attend to the funeral preparations."

Edith departed and closed the door behind her.  Olaf stood and looked at Ealdgyth who smiled sweetly at him:

"Well Olaf, I have some other news. I am not yet certain, but I believe there is a part of you that I shall keep and that Harold will have his heir quite promptly. I think I may be with child."

"Oy herregud!" said Olaf looking to the ceiling.

"Don't worry, Olaf, it will be our little secret. Harold wants to marry as soon as possible after his Coronation so he will believe it is his. Fortunately, Harold is blond too."

"And what about that young lad, Edgar the Ætheling? He is the rightful heir, surely, and Edward made Harold swear to be his guardian and regent."

"Edgar is thirteen, is frightened and has no supporter's while Harold is forty, the most powerful Earl in England and the brother of the Dowager Queen. Who would you rather have as king when facing a Norman invasion? In any event, Harold has connived with Edwin and Morcar to support his claim to the throne using me to seal the deal.

"Ah?" said Olaf.

The following day London was a seething mass of richly dressed magnates, all jostling for position in the new gleaming white Abbey of Westminster, for the royal funeral of Edward the Confessor. Incredibly, immediately afterwards, there was to be the Coronation of the Earl of Wessex as King Harold II.

Harold had wasted no time with the Witan the previous day and, with the exception of a few voices calling for Edgar as the rightful and legitimate heir to the throne, it was a walkover for Harold. Even those who hated the Godwins realised that, with the support of Edwin and Morcar, there really was no-one else in the running.

Archbishop Stigand, who was a strong supporter of Harold's cause, led the funeral service and the coffin of King Edward 'the Confessor' was carried silently up the Abbey nave, under the huge, vaulted ceiling, by eight burly housecarls. Ealdgyth was placed at the front of the Abbey next to Queen Edith and the three Godwin Earl's, Harold, Gyrth and Leofwine and her brothers Edwin, Earl of Mercia and Morcar, most recently Earl of Northumbria.

Olaf managed to squeeze in at the back and could hear the blurred chanting of the huge gathering of clergy. After an eternity, the housecarls lifted the bier, decorated in white lilies and with bell-ringers carrying small bells, processed back down the aisle into the nave, followed by Archbishops Stigand, Wulfstan and Ealdred, then Edith with Harold on her arm and the other members of the English nobility. The procession veered off to Olaf's left and disappeared down the steps of the crypt where the stone masons had prepared a great sarcophagus in which the frail body of the late King would be interred for all eternity.

For one hour the people stood in the crowded Abbey and gazed at the exquisite craftsmanship that had been Edwards life ambition. The muffled bell that had been ringing a single tone was now stopped and soon after replaced by a great peel of bells.

The clergymen, who made up the choir with some boy-trebles, began singing a psalm about the coronation of Solomon and from the great West door came a procession of Archbishops followed by the Earl of Wessex, now changed into fine woven clothes and wearing a purple robe.

The Abbey had changed from funeral to coronation mode with almost seamless ease. From somewhere there had been placed a carved wooden throne up in the Quire and towards this the procession headed.

Archbishop Ealdred of York presided this time and called upon the great throng of people, using the common language, if they would except Harold as their King.  They replied in a great roar:

"Aye, Aye, Aye!"

Then Archbishop Wulfstan handed Harold a golden Orb surmounted by a cross. Archbishop Stigand handed Harold the Virga, a long staff rather than a sceptre, and, finally, Archbishop Ealdred placed the crown of England, complete with *Fleur-de-lys,* upon the head of Harold Godwinson and anointed his forehead with Holy oil. The three archbishops then cried out in unison to the populace:

"Vivat Harold, Rex Anglorum, Vivat Rex!"

To which the great multitude cried out:

"Vivat Rex, vivat Rex!"

Olaf was desperately trying to get a better view of all this but being at the back of the Abbey and as it was starting to get dark, he thought he would slip away and try to get himself a place at the Palace of Westminster for what must surely be a sumptuous feast, not only for Epiphany but for a whole new dynastic succession. He feared for poor Wulfnoth, left behind to face the full wrath of Duke William.

Walking out onto the cobbled street crowded with people, oblivious to the falling snow, he followed their gaze and outstretched, pointing arms. Looking up he caught his breath as, far up in the firmament of stars, there appeared to be one, far brighter than the others and moving purposefully across the sky, like Odin's chariot.  It was a comet, a portend of some sort and did not bode well on the day of Harold's Coronation.

hIC RE SIDET:hAROLD
REX:AN GLORVM:
STIGANT
ARChI EPS

## *Chapter Thirty-One:*
## *Return to York*

The great feast at Westminster Palace was as Olaf had hoped and, with there being so many earls and thegns and even an unfortunate Ætheling, who sat miserably with his mother, having been completely side-lined from his rightful inheritance, Olaf was seated halfway down with lesser thegns. The steward told Olaf that the new King had informed him that Olaf was to be treated as a thegne for his great service to him in both Wales and Normandy for which he would shortly be rewarded.

During the feast Harold made a short speech in which he thanked the assembly for their trust in him and assured them that he would keep the country strong and safe. He then announced that the court needed to prepare to leave for York as his marriage to Ealdgyth would take place in York Minster at twelve o'clock one week from today on January 13th. He said he hoped his beautiful future Queen would soon provide the country with an heir who, being from the House of Godwin and the House of Mercia, would unite the country in peace and prosperity. There was much cheering and the little wink that Ealdgyth flashed to Olaf went unnoticed by all but him. Olaf's heart missed a beat.

The journey North was a three-day affair and Olaf rode with a body of housecarls and a handful of Welsh archers including Rhys of Prestatyn, whose non-stop lilting prattle helped pass the time.

Finally, the walls of the city and the great West façade of the Minster came into view and there was a muffled cheer from under the cloaks of the party, shielding their faces from the biting wind. Olaf felt a tinge of excitement to be back in York and was keen to see Astrid. Morcar was now Earl of Northumbria from the ousted Tostig and it was important to Harold that the people of the North should see the uniting of the two houses.

Olaf peeled off from the King's column who headed directly for the Great Hall and guided his mount across the close to the small doorway of Astrid's cottage. There was a smell of burning logs and something good in the pot. Olaf was cold, tired and hungry and hoped Renweard would not mind him sharing their supper. Olaf knocked using his bow as his hands were gloved. Astrid opened the door and stood back in shock, clutching a baby.

"Olaf! You are back? I have had no word from you. I thought you were probably killed in Wales!"

"No, I am here, alive and well and have been serving Harold of Wessex in Wales, Normandy and London. He's King now and has made me an ealdorman so I have money and a little patch of land."

Astrid put the baby in its cot and thew her arms around Olaf.

"Oh Olaf! I am so glad to see you again. I have had a terrible time."

She began to sob uncontrollably so that Olaf could feel her tears on his cheek.

"Those thugs, Gospatrick's men, they came here not long after little Anders was born. They wanted to kill anyone who had served Tostig and they slaughtered all of his Danish huscarls and then they took the local people including Renweard. They took him out to the wood and hanged him from a tree. He had lived here all his life and hadn't done any harm to anyone. He didn't even serve Tostig, he served Morcar."

Olaf listened to all of this in silence.

"They tried to take me too and the new-born baby but Morcar arrived just in time and they stood down. I was too terrified to go out and poor Renweard just hung there for a week, picked at by the crows. Finally, Morcar sent some of his men to cut him down and we buried him in the grounds of the Minster where we said a requiem mass for his poor soul."

Again, Olaf listened, aghast. He had been fond of Renweard and the hideous fate of being hanged by a baying mob filled Olaf with a great anger. Having served Tostig himself, Olaf thought, there might I be had I stayed behind.

"You are welcome to stay here Olaf if you don't mind a crying baby. This house was gifted to you and you kindly gave it to us. But Renweard is gone now so you may treat this as your home once more."

"That's very kind," said Olaf. If we can keep matters platonic out of respect for Renweard and the fact that I am very in love with Ealdgyth of Mercia, who is to be married to King Harold tomorrow."

"Olaf please tell me you haven't been trifling with Harold's betrothed. Not even you are that mad." Astrid laughed.

Olaf looked the picture of innocence.

"Erm....any chance of some of that stew that smells so good?"

## *Chapter Thirty-Two:*
## *The Wrath of Tostig*

It was late October 1065 when Tostig, accompanying King Edward on a hunting party based out of Sarum, first heard the news of the uproar in Northumbria. One of his Danish huscarls rode in with the devastating news that he was the sole survivor of Tostig's two hundred bodyguards. The thegns of Northumbria had raised a great body of men and had ransacked the palace at York, emptied the treasury of all its taxes and stolen all the weapons from the armoury.

Tostig's household servants were beheaded and his officials hanged. They then marched South to bring their grievances to the King. Edward sent for Harold and ordered him to take an army to supress the rebellion by force. The rebels' forces seemed very organised and came down as far South as Northumberland.

Harold finally met them at Oxford where he heard their demands; that their own man be made Earl and that Tostig be banished for crimes against the people. The whole thing had been carefully planned by Edwin and Morcar, quite possibly with the connivance of Harold. When Harold met the rebels, he agreed to all their demands, including allowing Morcar to become Earl of Northumbria. Had Harold done a deal to get Tostig, a possible rival for the throne, out of the way by promising to marry Ealdgyth? Whatever, the rebellion was now under control. The King was absolutely furious, which may have sped up his demise and Tostig was now the guest of Baldwin V of Flanders, his father-in-law.

Tostig's rage at his own brother's unfathomable treachery made for some ill-advised attempts on the English coastline. Remembering how his father, Earl Godwin had invaded England and forced Edward to restore all his lands, Tostig decided to launch a raid from Flanders on the Isle of Wight. In April, his soldiers landed and plundered everything they could find and then sailed along the South coast raiding and plundering everywhere until they reached the fishing town of Sandwich.

There they seized the towns shipmen and pressed them into service. Harold marched in force down from London to confront his brother, but Tostig put to sea and sailed North to the Humber. It was there that Tostig discovered the strength of the animosity against him.

Edwin and Morcar called out their housecarls and Olaf too was summoned to fight for Morcar. The sailors from Sandwich deserted at the first opportunity as did many of his warriors. Of the original sixty ships that Baldwin had given him, Tostig sailed up to seek refuge in Scotland with only twelve.

While in Flanders, Tostig had visited William of Normandy as his wife Judith and Williams's wife Matilda were sisters. Although William's rage at Harold's betrayal of his sacred oath was palpable, he greeted Tostig as family and invited the unfortunate Wulfnoth to join them.

Tostig had worried that William might have killed his younger brother but he was left unharmed, although still a captive. On the subject of helping Tostig reclaim his land and title, William was uncooperative, he had plans of his own and they were taking shape nicely since the Pope had sent him a banner and his blessing.

Tostig sailed to Denmark and tried to cajole a Danish invasion from his cousin Sweyen. Having just concluded a peace with Harald Hardråda after twelve years of warfare, Sweyen was in no doubt that an invasion of England was way too risky. There remained just one option left.

Tostig arrived at the court of Harald in Nidaros with a small band of housecarls including Cospatric, who had again lost Bamberg fortress after being ousted by Morcar. Tostig met Harald in his great hall, which looked more like a barracks than a palace. He was easily the largest man Tostig had ever seen, with fierce eyes, long deep red hair and a beard partly plaited with studs. With him stood two huge warriors who Harald introduced as his Huscarls Ødger, and Erik. Others in the party who eyed Tostig's men with suspicion were the swarthy master archer, Urbicus Acropolitis, the tall swaggering figure of Eyestein Orre and Harald's teenage son, Magnus, who seemed to have inherited all his father's aggression. Behind them on the dais sat the willowy figure of Queen Tora, nursing a fair baby on her lap with azure blue eyes.

At first Harald was extremely dubious about the venture but, over dinner, Tostig impressed him and he enjoyed the flattery that Tostig heaped upon him. As the mjørd flowed, Tostig knew that Harald's vanity was his Achilles Heel and sure enough, by midnight, he was seeing himself as the next Canute the Great as King of England and Norway.

They would meet up in the Orkneys which Harald now controlled following the death of Thorfinn in 1065. Magnus, with precocious ferocity, had invaded and forced his two sons Paul and Erlend to submit in exchange for sparing the life of their grandfather Finn Arneson, who had, against all expectations, been released by Harald rather than thrown into the snake pit as many had hoped.

Tostig returned to Scotland leaving Cospatric in the Orkneys with young Magnus to liaise. In September 1066, Harald landed in the Orkneys in his great dragon ship 'Ormen' with around three hundred ships, including the ones he had taken from Sweyn. Tora also came with Maria, Elisiv's daughter, betrothed to Eystein, Tora's younger brother. Elisiv had returned to Kiev and Harald wanted a Queen beside him when he was crowned.

Tostig and Harald met up at the mouth of the Tyne with Tostig's very modest fleet being dwarfed by the huge gathering of ships that Harald had prepared in Oslo.

Erik had made enquiries when speaking with Cospatric in the Orkneys saying that his son had gone missing and that enquiries in Bergen stated that he had taken a ship to England. When Erik described him, Cospatric lit up saying that Olaf was very well known in England having served both Tostig and Harold, the present King.

"Well, I just hope I don't find him on the opposite side over there. If Harald finds him, he will be in serious trouble. He thinks Olaf has deserted and he hates deserters."

Meanwhile, King Harold and the Fyrd waited impatiently for William's fleet to land on the South coast as the Summer came and went. The Fyrd were made up mainly of farmers who were obliged to serve as soldiers for a given number of weeks in a year. But it was now September and they needed to get back to their farms to bring in the harvest to see them through the Winter. But still the Normans did not come.

# Chapter Thirty-Three:
## Fulford Gate and Stamford Bridge

With Harold down on the South Coast and Ealdgyth back in London, now quite clearly expecting a baby, Olaf stayed with Astrid in the close and resumed the non-platonic relationship they had enjoyed before Olaf left to go campaigning in Wales. It was a beautiful Summer that seemed to go on forever and the good people of York busied themselves repairing the terrible damage done during the revolt, so that the city was now returned to its semi-fortress state with a new set of wooden gates.

On the South Coast, Harold disbanded his army in the first week of September and ordered his fleet to sail back to London. At this very precise same time, the Norwegian fleet crammed itself up the Humber, disembarked and set up camp at a place called Riccall, about ten miles from York.

As the fleet had been stopping at places like Scarborough to plunder for provisions, Edwin and Morcar sent word out that a Viking invasion was imminent and to gather at York as fast as possible. Olaf's cosy peace was shattered.

It was a glorious September morning when a rider galloped into York to announce that a huge Viking army which included Tostig and the King of Norway were marching up from the Humber River and could be deploying outside York in a matter of hours. Edwin and Morcar had been actively recruiting for the last two weeks and now had a half decent force of about five thousand soldiers.

Olaf knew though that these were not professionals and would have only limited skills against a shield wall that included some monstrously large battle-hardened huscarls the size of Ødger and Eric, brilliant swordsmen such as Eyestein and marksmen from Byzantium led by the finest archer Olaf had ever worked with, Urbicus Acropolites.

Neither Edwin nor Morcar shared these misgivings and the new gates of the city were thrown open for their forces to take up position on a marshy slope by the village of Fulford Gate. Initially it proved to be a good defensive position. The Norwegians arrived, not all of them, as Harald had left nearly a third of his army to guard the ships from any attack. These included the youngsters that Harald did not want to get hurt in the initial battles, Eystein Orre was in charge with Harald's son Magnus and the two sons of Thorfinn, Paul and Erland.

Magnus was incandescent with fury at being told by his father that he would not fight today. Still, they fielded some six thousand men but Harald only deployed around three thousand in the shield wall and kept the remainder concealed behind a slope. The English wall outnumbering the Norse warriors nearly two to one still had great difficulty in pushing them down the slope into the marshy ground.

Finally, the Norse line began to give and the English shield wall pushed, step by step until both lines were at the bottom of the hill. Olaf, sensing that something was wrong, from his vantage point on the high ground then saw Hardrada emerge from his right with a large force of about three thousand of his best. He called out to Edwin that they were about to be surrounded and must pull back.

This they did in good order to the safety of the city leaving the majority down in the boggy marsh with a Norse shield wall to their front, knee deep in mud, and now Hardrada and his fiercest huscarls, hacking them to pieces from behind.

It was a terrible massacre and practically none of the English front line survived as those who did try to run were such easy targets for Urbicus and his Byzantine archers. The battle had lasted a little over an hour and had ended in disaster for Edwin and Morcar, but at least they had survived.

"Olaf! Thank God you spotted that! Another few minutes and we would all have been caught."

"He's an excellent tactician, I've watched him in action in a number of battles and I've never seen him lose, even at Niså where we were outnumbered by nearly three ships to one."

"Well, he greatly outnumbers us now, so I think we'd better surrender before he torches the place," said Edwin.

"I think we need to get a rider down to London post haste to see if Harold can get up here in time to be of help." Morcar proffered.

"Ahem, I've already done that. Some of those sailors who were press-ganged by Tostig had stayed up here scraping a living catching fish. As soon as I heard that a Viking fleet was at Scarborough, I commandeered one of those Flemish boats and told them to get word to Harold in London. All being well, he might just be on his way. We just need to buy some time."

Edwin and Morcar looked at Olaf in wide-eyed astonishment.

It was some two hours later that a large party marched up the hill, the costumes and faces splattered with blood. One large huscarl came forward to demand that the city surrender on pain of it being razed to the ground and every soul inside being put to the sword.

"These are the demands of our King, Harald III of Norway; that in two days you will have collected the large amount of gold and silver that you stole from Tostig and you will deliver this to an agreed point on the Derwent River called Stamford Bridge. We will need one hundred and fifty hostages and the keys to York City. You have until September 25th by midday to prepare this. You may collect your dead unmolested."

Olaf recognised the voice at once and translated for Edwin. It was the voice of Ødger.

"Tell him we accept and you may receive our surrender on the 25th of this month at Stamford Bridge."

Olaf had been speaking English for nearly two years now and was able to disguise his voice by pretending to speak with a strong English accent. Ødger put his head to one-side as if recognising the voice but the character on the gatehouse had a thick blond beard and a weatherworn face looking nothing like the boy who had travelled to Nidaros with him.

The army returned to Riccall with their wounded whilst a small group set up a camp by a narrow bridge on the Derwent called Stamford Bridge.  Ødger found Eric sitting on a tree-stump sharpening his axe.  His face and beard were flecked with blood and he had a gash on his right arm that was still bleeding.

"Let me sort that out," said Ødger tearing at a length of cloth that was hanging on a line specifically for the use of the wounded.

"Just a scratch," growled Erik, "wasn't much of a fight, was it?"

Ødger changed the subject: "I can't say for sure but there's a young Norse fighter on the gatehouse at Yorvik who looks and sounds like he could be Olaf."

"What!" Didn't you ask him?"

"No, my job was to put over the King's terms to the Jarls who have holed up there. When we take the city, we can find him. Just don't let Harald hear about it. He will kill him for certain."

At that moment Eystein Orre appeared with a young English jarl who didn't look like he would be much good in a fight.

"Erik," said Eystein, "I'd like you to meet Cospatric, the ousted Jarl of Bammemburgh.  It seems we have a mutual friend inside the walls of Yorvik...none other than your son, Olaf.  It appears that he, not content to be a sworn huscarl in service to King Harald, has since served with both Tostig and Harold Godwinson and is now fighting on the side of that usurper of Tostig's earldom, Morcar and his brother Edwin of Mercia. Very awkward for us, his friends and family."

Erik spluttered a little until he found his voice: "It appears my son has been the victim of circumstances.  I expect he was captured by pirates and sold in England?"

Cospatric intervened in a mix of Northern English and Norse: "Far from it, he arrived by ship with a buxom lass from Bergen with plenty of money and under the protection of Jarl Thorfinn and, according to Tostig, letters from Queen Tora herself.

They are just rumours of course, but whilst you were all away fighting the Battle of Niså, Tora gave birth to a beautiful baby boy with blonde hair and blue eyes who she named, rather unsubtly, Olaf.

Why would a queen send Olaf away to her cousin in Orkney with gold and letters of protection?  Harald's son Magnus is here and though only sixteen, has all the fierce attributes of his father, red hair, blazing green eyes, height and an absolute *uggligr,* where we get our English word '*ugly*'. I have been to Nidaros with Tostig and have seen Queen Tora and the two-year-old Olaf. There is no chance whatever of Magnus and Olaf being brothers from the same father, that's for sure."

Erik rumbled like a volcano about to erupt and then roared with laughter. When he could speak, he said:

"Of all the huscarls who would have given their right hand to have enjoyed a romp with the beautiful Tora Torbergsdattir and my little Olaf sneaks in there ahead of all of them. She must have led him on as he was only eighteen and she in her late thirties. Poor boy! Now it all makes sense. She wanted a pretty baby, not another monster like Magnus Haraldsson! By Odin I hope the King doesn't know any of this?"

"My sister has a very sweet face and persuaded Harald it was his. I remember well the very night when Olaf did me a favour by separating my betrothed Maria from her elder sister, who I sent to Olaf's room. Tora found her standing outside his door and scalded her, sending her to Tora's own chambers. That's when Tora must have pounced and poor Olaf didn't stand a chance."

This time everyone laughed.

In York, Olaf, blissfully unaware that his story had been the cause of so much mirth in the Norwegian camp, continued to help with the hostages and the ransom. Edwin and Morcar had named the unfortunate hostages and had gathered a great wealth of silver that had been looted from Tostig's taxes during the rebellion.

The sun rose on September 25th, a stunning Autumnal morning and, by eight o'clock, everyone knew it was going to be a very warm day. Olaf was hoping against hope that Harold would arrive in time as he didn't want to think what would happen to him if he were to be taken by Harald's forces, despite his own father being there. Then, the miracle happened. Two riders arrived at the smaller West gate and demanded to be admitted. They presented themselves to Edwin and Morcar as the advance guard of King Harold's forces that had just marched nearly two hundred miles from London, night and day, and would be in York within the hour.

They said there was to be no cheering or noise as Harold wanted complete surprise. Two thirds of the Norse army had decamped and were making the two-hour march to Stamford Bridge. Spies had informed Harold that they had left behind the bulk of their armour as it was a warm day and they certainly did not expect to fight.

Harold's army appeared in a shimmering cloud of dust with horses at the walk and pennants flying. Girls waved from the windows but everyone was quiet. The hostages almost cried with relief and many went into the Minster to pray. Harold's army dismounted to drink and eat what provisions they had. It was nine o'clock and Stamford Bridge was about a forty-five-minute walk, so they had time for a short rest and to prepare their armour.

At Stamford Bridge the Norse army was very relaxed and had brought beer with them and were enjoying the prospect of collecting a large sum in silver and a gaggle of hostages.

Harald and Tostig chatted affably about marching down to London to remove his brother from the throne. In the distance a cloud of dust should have warned them but they assumed it was from the carts laden with silver and the one hundred and fifty hostages. Tostig mentioned in passing:

"Do you happen to know a Norwegian archer named Olaf? He's a very good shot with a bow and saved my brothers life on campaign in Wales and during a shipwreck in Normandy."

Harald's face reddened: "He's here? He was one of my sworn archer-huscarls. He disappeared after Niså. So, he deserted to England, did he?"

"Yes, he arrived here in York about two years ago with money and a letter of introduction from Thorfinn via his cousin Tora, your Queen Consort."

Harald's face contorted with rage as he momentarily contemplated all the implications of Tora sponsoring the flight of an eighteen-year-old nonentity. He was about to scream for Erik when the alarm was raised and the cloud of dust revealed a jingling army in full battle armour and flying the flag of 'The Fighting Man', Harold's battle pennant.

*"Oy herregud! Til vårpen! Til vårpen, må vi kjempe!* (O dear god! To arms! To arms, we must fight!).

*"Shielð veggr!"* (Shield wall!).

Warriors dashed for their weapons, shields and helmets and those across on the York side of the bridge desperately scrambled onto the East bank over the narrow crossing. For a moment it was chaos as the Norwegians tried to form up in position for a shield wall. Harald needed to buy some time to deploy.

"Erik, you must buy us some time. Hold that bridge!"

Erik looked at Harald for a second and from his face, guessed immediately that the cat was out of the bag and that he knew about Olaf. Hence the suicide mission. Having no armour, Erik decided to go Berserker and tore off his tunic.

Grabbing his great war axe, he rushed towards the narrow bridge as a few English soldiers gingerly mounted from the far end. Erik roared abuse at them as they came forward to fight. One after the other they came but at most it was always no more than two on one and Erik carved them down with his great axe until the bodies piled on the bridge.

The cuts and wounds on Erik's naked torso grew with every conflict and now the wound on his arm had opened and was bleeding freely. He was certainly living up to his name 'Slagbjørn' and was thrashing about like a wounded bear.

Still, they came, stabbing and thrusting until Erik could barely wield his great axe which swung a terrifying blow through the helmet of a soldier as the man behind him had just a second to jab a fatal spear into Erik's heart. The great warrior staggered and fell from the mortal wound as the English cheered. Leaping onto the bridge, Ødger rushed to the aid of his friend and continued to fight off any advance from the soldiers on the bridge. Once again, the slaughter and death toll on this narrow bridge beggared belief. The English were slipping on the blood and gore of their fellows and were becoming reluctant to come forward against what they thought was the same immortal warrior that over thirty of their fellows had failed to kill.

At that moment, as Ødger tried to catch his breath in the lull, a long spear was plunged upwards from a floating barrel under the bridge which jabbed him cruelly through his bowels and into his stomach. The two cowardly soldiers below were rewarded with a deluge of blood and faeces.

Instinctively, they jumped into the river to wash away the gore and were drowned in the swift flowing Derwent. The death toll inflicted by Erik and Ødger was estimated at between thirty-five and forty slain.

Finally, the English force rushed across the narrow bridge to find the Norsemen in the final stages of deploying their shield wall. Olaf, standing by the King, had watched in disbelief as Harald ordered his father to throw away his life as a Berserker suicide mission. Olaf's grief gave way to rage as he rushed over the bridge beside the mounted King Harold and his standard bearer.

The shield wall was all but formed as the English army rushed at them in great numbers. There was a crash as the two armies met in a huge collision. Harold and some of his housecarls were mounted and charged their horses into the wall, breaking open a gap to allow some soldiers through the fissure. Behind the shield wall a vast warrior was cleaving down more English bodies. Olaf recognised him at once from his size alone and carrying a great double handed war axe that few men could have wielded. Fighting back the tears, Olaf screamed:

"Harald Sigurdsson! For my father Erik Slagbjørn and my friend Ødger Sköll!"

The arrow flew, just as it had for the bear back in Dalby and, likewise, caught Harald Hardråda in the windpipe. The fiercest and most feared warrior in all Europe, staggered back, dropping his great war axe as a number of English warriors fell upon him ensuring he never arose again. Olaf thought he caught a glimpse of recognition before Hardråda fell.

*You are safe now, Tora,* Olaf thought to himself before moving out of harm's way. He returned to the bridge to discover the bodies of Erik and Ødger had been pushed into the river but both had died a Viking death in battle and with great courage. Both would feast in Valhalla tonight thought Olaf, abandoning his Christian baptism.

Returning to the battle, Olaf caused great agitation to the Norwegian groups of warriors who had broken away from the main wall. With no armour for protection, they were suffering terrible casualties. Harold had now dismounted and called for Olaf to watch his back. With two housecarls he headed to Tostig, still standing where Harald Hardråda's infamous 'Landwaster' flag was flying. Harold's two men brushed aside Tostig's mercenary bodyguards and Olaf pointed his bow at Cospatric shaking his head.

Cospatric dropped his unbloodied sword and walked unarmed towards the English position. Tostig, seeing his feared elder brother, turned and tried to flee. Harold pursued and brought his great sword down through his brother's left shoulder and through his heart. This fratricide brought to an end the disastrous quarrel that destroyed the House of Godwin and prosperous Saxon England for ever.

It was after four o'clock and that should have been the end of this very bloody battle but for the fact that Harald had sent two gallopers to Riccall. Given that it was eight miles to York and a further ten to Riccall on the Ouse River it was a marathon feat of Eystein Orre and the other warriors to cover that distance in armour and be there by four o'clock.

Notwithstanding, some three thousand Norwegians fell upon the flank of Harold's army that so shocked them that they initially fell back. Those who fought, however quickly realised that some of the Viking warriors were actually dropping dead from exhaustion and others could barely raise their shields or their swords. The retribution was swift and many fell, unable to defend themselves. Olaf's swaggering friend Eystein, brother of Tora, was hacked to pieces leading the charge. Urbicus Acropolites took down at least six before he was hit by a well-aimed throwing axe. By six o'clock the general rout was well underway as the survivors desperately fled back to their ships under the merciless pursuit of Harold's army.

Olaf ran with them and prevented the boys, Paul and Erland Thorfinnsson, from being killed, also the badly wounded Magnus Haraldsson, now King of Norway. The estuary from the Ouse to the Humber was awash with blood. Harold, Edwin and Morcar oversaw the prisoners being loaded into boats and stopped the slaughter where they could. After the ships had sailed back down the Humber and out towards the Orkneys, the empty ships remaining numbered some two hundred and seventy.

# The Battle of Stamford Bridge
# 25th September 1066

## *Chapter Thirty-Four:*
## *1066 Senlac Hill – Last Stand*

The tiny flotilla of wounded and battle-shocked warriors returned to the Orkneys through the night. Several died of their terrible wounds on the journey. The remainder landed at sunrise and made their way to Birsay where Tora and Maria were waiting for news. Upon hearing that both her father the King and Eystein Orre, her betrothed, were among the great mass of slain, Maria became hysterical. Tora had the genuine grief for her brother but also relief that the tyrant was dead and her son was King, albeit badly wounded. That night Maria was found dead in her bed either from a heart attack or had she poisoned herself?

Back in York there was some rejoicing but Harold's army was just too exhausted to do anything other than sleep. Olaf returned to Astrid without a scratch on him. Harold was incredulous that his little archer had taken out the great Hardråda himself and heaped praises on him. Olaf just replied:

"He killed my father!"

Both Edwin and Morcar had taken part in the fighting and both had suffered injuries as had many of Harold's fighting men.

Harold himself went back onto the field and identified from the heaps of dead, the body of his brother Tostig. He had him brought back to York on a cart and there, in the great Minster, a Mass was said and the body buried on sacred ground on September 28th. Unknown to Harold, at nine o'clock that very morning, a fleet of

700 ships had arrived at the Bay of Pevensey, on the Sussex coast and had made camp around *Anderitum* - its old Roman fort.

Harold announced that there was to be a great victory feast on the night of the 30th September and the partly restored palace of Tostig was to be the venue before he and his battle-weary army made their way slowly back to London. With just a few days to recover the army was in dire need of a feast to celebrate the smashing of a great Viking Army led by Harald Hardråda, whom everyone had thought invincible. King Harold had placed Olaf on the top table with himself and the Earls to honour him for killing Hardråda. Beside him sat Astrid, beaming in a lovely gown of blue velvet.

Harold himself felt invincible and was quite prepared to take on Duke William, although he felt it was now too late in the year for the Normans to invade. Just as everyone was getting properly drunk, the door was thrown open and a messenger fell through the doorway, spattered in mud and with his hair matted with sweat.

"Sire! Sire!" he called. The great hubbub died down and the messenger ran towards the King.

"Sire I have come from London. We have word from the South coast of Wessex. William of Normandy has landed in the Bay of Pevensey with a great army of professional warriors."

"Dear God! This is a disaster! People, anyone who is not too badly wounded and has a horse get your things together including all armour and weapons. We ride for London in one hour!"

Outside the West Gate of York, a small army of some three thousand housecarl warriors gathered. The foot soldiers (Fyrd) were excused but would make their way South in the morning. Olaf gave Astrid a big hug and mounted up by the King. Edwin and Morcar had excused themselves on account of having received not very substantial wounds and the necessity of having to protect the North from a possible Scottish attack from Malcolm III who was a good friend of Tostig's. Harold was not impressed.

By two o'clock in the morning, still a little drunk and confused, Harold's army of housecarls rode out at the trot for the 200-mile journey to London. All the way South, messengers were sent out to the Shires to send men to London to form a new Fyrd. Harold's march South was at a frenzied, almost brutal pace and, for the horses, the stops were few and short.

William's forces were incredulous that none of the Fyrd were there to impede their landing and, as they unloaded everything from horses to flat-packed castles, a cloaked rider came into the camp and up to William's tent. He spoke French.

"Bonjour Sire!"

"Ah! Bonjour Guillaume. Thank you for your intelligence, it has been extremely useful. Who knew that Tostig would get Hardråda to invade Northumbria and try to steal my crown? Do we know who won? Which Harold or Harald do I need to fight?"

"No, Sire. I have no information on that score. What I do know is that Harold marched North from London over a week ago and, if he survived a battle with Harald, he will still be in York leaving London unprotected. The English fleet is anchored off the Isle of Wight where I told them you would attack."

William replied: "We have just 7,000 men with no immediate possibility to resupply so we must forage off the land and let him come to us."

Others in the tent who included Bishop Odo of Bayeux, Hubert du Mont-Canisy and William fitz-Osbern nodded agreement.

Guillaume continued:

"Sire, my advice to you is we move East towards a port called Hastings as there is little to forage here. At Hastings there is a good road to London when we wish to take the fight into Harold's capital."

Back in London all was haste. Harold's two surviving bothers, excepting poor Wulfnoth, were Gyrth and Leofwine and they rushed from their Earldoms to support their brother in London.

Harold had arrived in London, exhausted after two forced marches and a ferocious battle and was in no mood to read the very challenging letters from William regarding his gross perjury.

It was then a matter of pride for Harold that he refused the more cautious plan put forward by Gyrth and Leofwine. They suggested that Harold rest in London and consolidate his forces whilst they marched against William using the Southern Fyrd and housecarls. On October 12th, therefore, before hearing of support from the Northern earls, Harold set out from London with just 1000 exhausted housecarls. The order was sent out to the shires that everyone should meet, fully armed at a landmark 'hoar tree' on the cross-roads of Caldbec Hill and the Hastings-London Road.

There Harold would plant his 'Fighting Man' banner and make a stand against William to buy time for reinforcements to arrive.

On the evening of October 13th, Harold, Olaf and about one thousand housecarls arrived at the old crab-apple tree on Caldbec Hill. A number of thegnes and several thousand fyrd-men from Kent and Sussex, strangely armed with farmyard weapons, had already arrived. They had also brought many vats of beer and cider as if they were expecting a party. Olaf glanced at Harold who understood his misgivings.

Having seen the Norman army at work, this gang of yokels was not going to stop them. But, as the hours passed, more and more

English turned up to fight including, mercifully, some one thousand more housecarls properly equipped for a shield wall. Olaf had been deeply concerned that Harold's army had no archers at all when through the darkness came a figure he recognised. A high lilting voice called out:

"Well, we couldn't let you have all the fun now, could we? There's a rumour going round in London that you killed Hardråda with that toy bow and arrow you carry."

Olaf laughed: "Rhys! You made it. I thought I was going to be the only archer in Harold's army. I was at Stamford Bridge. We only had axe-throwers but they did manage to take out a Byzantine called Urbicus. He was the finest archer I've ever fought with."

"Ah, boyo you haven't seen me in action then, have you?"

"Of course I have. How many archers did you bring with you?"

"We are twelve longbows in all, how many do the Normans have?"

"About a thousand, according to the scouts."

"Ah, well there's a thing, I don't think we've got a thousand arrows!"

All through the night the numbers of Harold's army continued to swell as men started to arrive from Wiltshire and Wessex. There was even a large party of Danes who had settled in England and fancied a brawl. All night long the fyrd-men drank and caroused with no thought of getting any sleep. At first light Harold sent for Olaf to go with him and his brother Gyrth on a little reconnaissance of the Norman camp which had moved to the base of the hill during the night.

All three were at once taken aback by the sheer size of the Norman army, but especially something they had not been expecting. The Norman knights had managed to bring horses with them on their ships. The chainmail armour of the knights glinted in the morning sunlight as the horses pawed the ground impatiently.

William's army was not yet formed up and Harold might have been tempted to charge down the steep slope but for the fact of the cavalry. Harold turned and rode back to his camp with Olaf and Gyrth following.

The call to form up went out across the line. The fyrd-men grouped together according to their shires and hundreds. The men of Kent, Wessex, Wiltshire, Devon and Cornwall with men from London in the centre around the standard of Wyvern. The line was of housecarls interspersed with fyrd units with the Danes taking the left flank.

As the Normans formed up unmolested, a peculiar thing occurred. A horseman with a lute on his back and a sword in his hand rode up the hill. Olaf recognised him as Taillefer, an eccentric jongleur and minstrel at William's court in Rouen. Olaf didn't know if he was acting mad or was really insane but now he knew. A hundred yards short of the English line he began throwing his sword into the air and taunting the English and singing snatches from the Chanson de Roland.

"Do you fancy a shot Rhys? Asked Olaf, he's just at the limit of my range and he's wearing armour."

"Well, he's very annoying, that's for sure."

Rhys pulled the great warbow and the arrow whistled off to its astonished recipient striking him straight through the chain-mail and into his chest.  The sword, still in the air came down pummel-

first striking the horse between the ears. The steed whinnied then turned and galloped back down the hill into the Norman infantry, dragging the screaming Taillefer by a stirrup.

"Being a Welshman, I hate to shoot a singer but he *was* very annoying."

There was a great cheer from the line. First blood.

Finally, the Norman army was deployed and formed up and very impressive it looked too. Something like three thousand cavalry, a thousand archers and four thousand infantry. Furthermore, William had a Papal Banner to fly to underline the righteousness of his cause.

As the minstrel lay dying on the grass, William gave the order to advance up the steep slope. He had divided his army into three phalanxes each with its own commander, the largest of which was commanded by William himself. Each had an equal proportion of archers, infantry and cavalry. The archers came forward to within the hundred-yard range and began firing into the shield wall. What the English had not encountered before was the French crossbow.

The shield could protect from the archers but the bolts could split a shield in half. Olaf decided the archers should aim specifically for the cross-bowmen who wore only a padded jacket for protection. In less than ten minutes Olaf and Rhys's boys had killed thirty of these. The remaining archers had been only marginally effective and now needed to withdraw to collect more crossbow bolts.

Now all three phalanxes moved forward through the withdrawing archers and the first hand to hand fighting began. The Normans carried long kite-shaped shields and mostly fought with swords. They wore heavy mail over their tunics.

The slopes became steeper as they neared the top of the hill and the infantry found themselves blowing hard with sweat trickling into their eyes from under their helmets. Olaf and the Welshmen saved their arrows as they would be far more effective firing into the retreating enemy.

They used the time to forage for Norman arrows that had missed their target. There were many. The shield wall exploded into a volley of javelins, throwing axes and rocks tied to sticks. With the gravity of the slope many staggered backward only to be pushed forward by those behind. The English line stretched across the top of the hill for some 600 feet and the warriors were packed in tightly twelve deep.

The crash as the Normans hit the shield wall was a muted one as they were unable to run and, even though the fighting raged for an hour, as they tried time and again to punch a gap in the English line, the wall held solid. A horn sounded the withdrawal and a pitifully small number of arrows flew from the position of the 'Fighting Man' into the backs of the retreating infantry.

"We could do with a few more archers!" shouted Rhys but the truth was that there were around sixty dead Normans on the slope due to arrows whilst Olaf and the twelve archers were all unscathed.

Once the infantry was out of range, the mounted knights, the pride of the Norman army, prepared to sweep the English off the slope with a devastating cavalry charge. Moving forward at the walk, then at the trot, the horses were eager to charge. Finally, they broke into what was a sort of canter up the slope, impeded by the numerous bodies scattered along the ridge.

Having never encountered an Anglo-Saxon shield wall before, or the fearsome two-handed war-axe wielded by many housecarls, the knights were in for a shock. Unable to get any real impetus up the slope, they jabbed at the wall with their lances until in places it parted to allow the housecarls and these terrifying weapons to do their work. Man, and horse fell to these axes and many riders withdrew, appalled at the carnage being dispensed by the housecarls.

At length the order to advance was given and the shield wall moved forward step by step pushing back or killing Norman soldiers. The wall was ordered to hold fast and Harold sent a message to Gyrth to go on the offensive.

A great cheer went up as several thousand of Gyrth's contingent charged down the hill. The whole of William's army fell back as the charge gathered impetus, reaching the point where the archers stood and doing great slaughter so that Olaf, watching from the hilltop looked across at Harold and waited for the order for an all-out attack against what appeared to be a defeated enemy. Leofwine had now joined his brother in the fray as many Norman knights rode through the ranks of their own infantry and archers. A rumour went through the ranks that William was dead and, at this juncture, the battle was all but won.

From the rear, Bishop Odo was desperately trying to regroup and lead a counter-attack armed with a mace. William rode into the centre brandishing his helmet for all to see his face. Gyrth spotted his moment and rushed at William, hurling his spear at the moving rider but failing to hit his target. The spear however, struck the beautiful stallion he was riding, a gift from Alfonse of Spain and William's pride and joy.

Unhorsed and enraged, William rushed at Gyrth, mace in hand as Leofwine ran to the aid of his brother. William fell upon Gyrth as he tried to draw his sword and bludgeoned him to pieces. Leofwine, concentrating on saving his brother, was run through by the lance of a galloping William fitz-Osbern. Within minutes, the House of Godwin had lost two Earls.

The effect this had on the morale of both sides was almost instantaneous and game changing. Harold watched, with horror, his two brothers being cut down and immediately halted any notion of a general advance. The thousand or more English left several hundred yards down the hill were in the open as William remounted and with fitz-Osbern and Odo led a mounted charge into the English foot-soldiers, many of whom tried desperately and unsuccessfully to get back to the line. Very few did.

The Battle of Hastings 14th October 1066

The battle was paused for both sides to regroup and the English line withdrew back to the ridge where they remained rooted to the spot. When it resumed it became a gruelling stalemate with the Normans unable to penetrate the wall but with sections of the wall unable to resist chasing the fleeing enemy and being caught in the open.

As the day wore on, the tide began to slowly turn, the English line became thinner and thinner. This meant that some cavalry could gain the flat ground at the top of Caldbec Hill and would have the advantage over infantry. Harold was praying for nightfall. If he could make that he could expect reinforcements before morning as he was beginning to be desperately short of men even though the wall was still holding.

At this point William knew he had to win now or lose the battle. He threw everything into one last desperate attempt to break the housecarl line.

A section of archers crept up the hill using bodies for cover on the English right as all the other archers, about five hundred of them moved to the centre. They were in open order to allow the Norman knights to ride through them to attack the line. As the hail of arrows dropped from the sky the English raised their shields to protect themselves from a rain of death. At this point the concealed archers, who were very close, fired directly flat at their targets panicking the shield wall as so many were falling.

The final deathblow was dealt to the English army by the fact that by now the Norman cavalry had gained the top of the ridge on Harold's right. As the Norman arrows ran out, the knights charged along the flat summit breaking the whole right flank.

The wall began to disintegrate, and it became every man for himself with Olaf and an exhausted band of housecarls forming a defensive ring around the 'Fighting Man' banner with Harold in the centre, clearly rattled that his army was falling apart.

*Another hour and it would be dark, we must hold them*, he thought.

At this point a random, stray arrow came whistling toward the circle around the banner. Olaf snatched up a shield but Harold was carrying his double-handed broadsword and a chance in a million blow struck the English King in the face, breaking his eye-socket. Harold fell back as blood gushed from the wound.

Seeing what had occurred, a killing party led by William himself smashed into the circle and fell upon the wounded King, hacking at him with their swords. Olaf tried a desperate shot which nearly came off. The arrow would have flown straight and true but for a nudge from Rhys:

"Come on Boyo, it's time to find a little cover in those woods. I've lost five of my lads dead and we think it's time to go."

The arrow flew higher than aimed but still managed to glance off the helmet of William, the nose-piece giving him a bloody, possibly broken nose. William looked up from the body of Harold which his knights were still desecrating and saw Olaf. With blazing eyes and blood streaming down his chin he screamed in French. Olaf got the gist of it, that he was a marked man.

Rhys pulled Olaf along with him into the woods behind where many wounded and dying had escaped. Then they came upon a sizeable body of warriors from Gloucestershire who had recently arrived to learn that the King had been killed and the housecarl wall was melting away. They had decided to set an ambush in the woods. In the closing light it seemed incredible that the Normans would still look to pursue the defeated English through the forest undergrowth.

But that is exactly what they did. Hacking down stragglers, they came upon an orderly line of English foot soldiers.

At first, they halted to try and see the size of the opposition but when Olaf, Rhys and five of the surviving archers shot several knights out of the saddle, they charged forward, unable to see the great gulley *Malfosse* (evil ditch) before them. Too late, horse and rider crashed into this ditch as others crashed on top of them, crushing them underneath and were massacred by the men from Gloucestershire.

"Come on Rhys, it really is time to go now. Let's get back to London and see if this Edgar the Ætheling is up to the job of saving England."

It was nightfall and Duke William decided to sleep in a tent on the battlefield with all the dead and dying to prove the field was really his. Guillaume de Malet entered the torchlit tent carrying the body of Harold Godwinson wrapped in a cloak.

"Sire, his mother has asked for his body in exchange for his weight in gold.  Edith Swanneck herself has identified the body; it is indeed Godwinson."

"Non, Guillaume, he stays here. I want no martyrs. I will bury him here by Senlac, the lake of blood. Did you find the body of that Norse archer he brought with him to Normandy?"

"No, Sire, I believe he got away into the woods where there was a terrible ambush, we lost many knights. The name of the archer is Olaf Slagbjørn."

The area around William's nose was dark red with dried blood and the bridge had gone a dark purple.

"My nose is broken, he nearly killed me. I want him dead. He is now the most wanted man in England. Find him!"

"You were lucky Sire, I heard he shot Hardråda in the throat."

"Find him Guillaume! Leave me now, I will sleep. Goodnight"

"Goodnight, Sire."

**To be continued...... 'Outlaw' Book 2 by this author**